and

"A swoon-worthy novel . . . Steamy chemistry and secrets unravel." —*Woman's World*

"Grey's unconventional meet-cute, compelling series backbone, and authentic characters move an interesting plot forward. . . . An engaging series start." —*Kirkus Reviews*

"Grey's prose is strong and her characters are fun." —*Publishers Weekly*

"Grey launches her First Comes Love series with a perfectly matched pair of protagonists, a vividly etched supporting cast, and plenty of potent sexual chemistry and breathtaking sensuality." —*Booklist*

"Each new Amelia Grey tale is a diamond. . . . A master storyteller." —*Affaire de Coeur*

"Devilishly charming . . . A touching tale of love." —*Library Journal*

"Sensual . . . witty and clever . . . Another great story of forbidden love." —*Fresh Fiction*

"Grey neatly matched up a sharp-witted heroine with an irresistible sexy hero and lets the romantic sparks fly." —*Booklist*

BY AMELIA GREY

The Heirs' Club of Scoundrels Series

The Duke in My Bed

The Earl Claims a Bride

Wedding Night with the Earl

The Rakes of St. James Series

Last Night with the Duke

To the Duke, with Love

It's All About the Duke

First Comes Love Series

The Earl Next Door

Gone with the Rogue

How to Train Your Earl

Say I Do Series

Yours Truly, The Duke

Sincerely, The Duke

Love, The Duke

Anthologies

The Heirs' Club of Scoundrels

Kissing Under the Mistletoe

LOVE, THE DUKE

AMELIA GREY

St. Martin's Paperbacks

First published in the United States by St. Martin's Paperbacks, an imprint of St. Martin's Publishing Group.

LOVE, THE DUKE

For information, address St. Martin's Publishing Group, 120 Broadway, New York, NY 10271.

www.stmartins.com

ISBN: 978-1-250-85045-4

Our books may be purchased in bulk for promotional, educational, or business use. Please contact your local bookseller or the Macmillan Corporate and Premium Sales Department at 1-800-221-7945, ext. 5442, or by email at MacmillanSpecialMarkets@macmillan.com.

Printed in the United States of America

St. Martin's Paperbacks edition / April 2025

10 9 8 7 6 5 4 3 2 1

CHAPTER 1

MAN'S PRACTICAL GUIDE TO APPREHENDING A THIEF
SIR BENTLY ASHTON ULLINGSWICK

Never refuse sincere help.

Following two cold and dreary days of an interminable carriage ride, all Drake Cheston Kingsley, Duke of Hurstbourne, wanted was to sit by a blazing fire with a brandy to take the chill off his bones. He always looked forward to a stay at the private hunting club with his two friends. Though he seldom spent time with them anymore.

Fortunately, for them, he thought as he took in the other two dukes sitting with him in front of the fire, each swore he'd found the love of his life, and they were usually reluctant to be away from home for more than a few days. Hurst understood. Somewhat.

He didn't begrudge them their happiness, but he, still a bachelor, missed the days when pleasure was wilder and more plentiful. Marriage had reined in those carefree days, given the men's responsibilities both as dukes and husbands. Rick and Wyatt now seemed to talk more about what it had been like to settle down. Regardless, he was looking forward to their time together.

However, this night, a disturbance to his much-anticipated week began before he'd taken his second sip of brandy.

The butler of the establishment approached the trio saying a messenger had arrived and would speak to no one other than Hurst. Strange since he didn't know a soul who lived anywhere near the club. Curiosity caused Hurst to give a brief nod for the butler to show the man into the richly paneled drawing room of the lodge.

"We haven't been here long enough for our boots to warm," Rick complained, not trying to hide his annoyance at the interruption.

"True, but I am interested in whatever missive the courier has for me."

"Perhaps we could have finished our first drink before you agreed to see the man," Rick scoffed before taking a sip of his brandy.

Wyatt lifted his glass in salute to the grudging comment.

They were all fatigued from traveling the entire way in bad weather, so Hurst ignored his friends' quarrelsome remarks as he caught sight of a young, clean-shaven man walking toward the trio clutching a leather packet to his chest as if he guarded the king's crown.

"Begging your pardon, Your Grace, may I approach?" His question ended with an audible gulp. "I have a letter and was told to give it to no one but the Duke of Hurstbourne."

Shaking off his road weariness and irritation at the intrusion, Hurst placed his drink on the table by his chair, rose, and stood with his back to the crackling fire. "How the devil did you find me?"

"It wasn't easy, Your Grace."

"I would hope not." The reason for choosing such an exclusive place to hunt, and paying handsomely for it, was to make sure no other guests would be allowed for the week. The dukes didn't want to be bothered by anyone seeking their attention.

Wary, the messenger seemed to consider his next words carefully before saying, "I offer apologies, Your Grace. I expended great effort to catch up to your carriage before you arrived but failed."

"When a man is on a hunt, he isn't usually the one being hunted," Rick mumbled.

Wyatt smiled into his brandy.

"Your butler reluctantly agreed to tell me your destination when I insisted what I had was urgent."

Hurst motioned for the man to come closer. "Give it here then."

After fumbling with the leather strips binding the closed packet, the young man finally produced a letter in his trembling hand. "I-I was told to wait for your reply and return with it immediately."

Hurst's curiosity increased along with a sudden sting of tension. A quick glance assured him the seal wasn't one he recognized, so it couldn't be from anyone in his family, his solicitors, or managers. What could be the reason for such haste to find him? He broke the wax but didn't unfold the letter when he noticed the courier continued to stand stiff-necked before him.

"Wait over there." Hurst nodded toward the door.

"Yes, Your Grace." He tucked the folder under his arm again, reached into his coat pocket, and pulled out a quill, a jar of ink, and several sheets of folded foolscap. Keeping his gaze on Hurst as if he expected to be stopped at any second from continuing, he slowly bent and placed the writing implements on the small table beside Hurst's glass.

Hurst stared at the man in disbelief. Glancing at his

friends, he saw they also appeared astounded by how prepared the courier was.

Clearing his throat, the man explained, "When I was told your destination, I knew I needed to be ready in case you were in a field or forest when I caught up to you. I wanted to make sure you would be able to respond."

He certainly did. Perhaps whatever was written in the letter was more urgent than Hurst first assumed. The man walked over to the door and Hurst retook his seat between his friends.

"After all that," Wyatt remarked, "you must read the message aloud."

"What are you saying?" Hurst huffed a laugh. "Are you telling me to read my personal correspondence to you before I peruse it myself?"

"You must," Rick added to Wyatt's bold statement, and pointedly looked at the quill and ink while stifling a grin. "If you don't, the suspense of it will finish us off. The chap followed you for two days in a sleeting storm to deliver that. By the looks of him you would think someone had fetched him from the Thames."

In truth, Hurst had few, if any, secrets from his two broad-shouldered friends who wore their privilege as well as they wore their clothing, which was damned well. He'd known them since their last year at Eton. All three were restless and reckless, but only Hurst had already learned to manage and harness both impulses. He'd had to. Over the years he'd kept the two from attempting one daring and risky escapade after the other. Until their marriages, of course. That had finally settled them down.

Wyatt and Rick were shrewd enough to know they needed a sensible friend. And Hurst was. Most of the time. He'd had to be sensible when he was growing up.

His father never was. But, with his father long passed, Hurst did his best not to think about those days anymore.

He rolled his shoulders to ease stiffness from the carriage ride and brushed his blond hair away from his forehead, a long-held habit he'd had no success breaking. Without guilt, he muttered a couple of oaths under his breath, opened the letter, and read aloud, "Dear Your Grace, we haven't spoken in years, but I hope you will remember me."

Hurst glanced down at the signature. His heartbeat thumped up a notch. Yes, he remembered Winston Stowe.

> Having been stricken with an illness that has left me weak and unable to fight off the fatigue of it, I feel my days growing shorter. I've had time to contemplate life. When you made the vow to help me in any way, I knew it was only an emotional promise given the moment I rescued your life. I'm not insisting you repay your debt, but only asking that you consider marrying my sister. Ophelia has a good heart and an even better soul. I know you could easily love her and be a good husband.
>
> I will always be thankful for our years of close friendship.
>
> With much respect and admiration, I am always gratefully yours,
>
> Winston Stowe.

A stitch of concern tightened the back of Hurst's neck as he stared at the page. *Marry?* That was an incredibly serious matter. Hurst remembered Winston had a sister, but she was still young enough to be in the nursery when Hurst last saw him. Even if she'd been older, girls wouldn't have been allowed to tromp around in the icy snow or boggy woods the way Winston and he had when they were together.

Wyatt casually leaned forward and rested an elbow on his knee. "I don't recognize the name."

"No reason for you to," Hurst answered, his eyes scanning the words again as he tried to assimilate what he was feeling about Winston's unusual request.

"Who is he?" Rick asked.

"A childhood friend who lived on the estate next to where I lived at the time. We were like brothers and often explored the woods, ponds, and marshes together." Hurst recalled fondly the tawny-haired boy with rounded cheeks and a friendly smile. "I don't think I've seen or heard from him in several years."

"More importantly," Wyatt remarked dryly, "did he save your life?"

"Yes. And then he taught me how to swim." Hurst stared at the serious expressions on their faces and realized he didn't want to relive that memory from his past any more than he wanted to think about the years with his father. Bad memories made a person feel bad, and Hurst was at the private lodge to hunt, drink, play cards, and enjoy himself.

He folded the letter and laid it on the table before picking up his drink and downing a hefty swallow.

"I'll also add," Hurst continued, "he was always a gentleman about saving my life and never mentioned it again."

"Until now," Rick responded. "No matter how veiled it was, it's presumptuous of him to ask you to marry his sister."

"Presumptuous or desperate?" Wyatt asked. "And really, what has the man to lose by asking? He's not the first person to want you to marry his sister, or daughter, or cousin. Nor will he be the last. With you being the only eligible duke in all of England, when the Season starts you will be sought by families of all the belles in London. You can be sure that right now every young lady and her parents are plotting to take you off the marriage mart and straight to the altar to say, *'I do.'*"

It was true. Hurst grunted. Ever since he became a duke, fathers, brothers, uncles, and strangers had been approaching him with promises of lucrative dowries in exchange for offering their daughters' hand in marriage. At parties, dinners, and balls, mothers unashamedly praised their daughters' admirable qualities. He'd always listened to what they had to say but had no interest in any of them. Whenever he met the lady he was to spend the rest of his life with, he'd know it. He was sure. It wasn't any kind of mental powers he had, but a feeling inside him.

He couldn't say with 100 percent certainty but felt sure he could live with any of the bevy of young ladies looking for a husband. They were all beautiful in their own way. The issue had always been that he didn't just want a lady he could live with. He wanted the one lady he couldn't live without, and he had to believe he would know her when he saw her.

However, Hurst couldn't forget the concerning fact that he was getting older and had no heir for the title.

He rubbed his chin thoughtfully and pushed aside that thought. The blaze from the fire and the potency of the brandy heated him. "I suppose what concerns me most is that he says he's ill and the urgency of having his messenger wait for an answer."

"With fever probably," Rick replied. "Perhaps the same type of intermittent fever that comes over me time and again without warning."

"Whatever the case . . ."

Wyatt leaned forward again and gave first Rick and then Hurst a questioning expression. Hurst had a feeling he knew what his friend was going to ask, and he didn't have an answer.

"What do you suppose he meant by she *'has a good heart and an even better soul'*?" Wyatt's unwavering gaze stared straight into Hurst's green eyes.

That comment had lingered on Hurst's mind too.

When he remained quiet, Wyatt offered, "Perhaps she's not as comely and fashionable as most young ladies of the ton, so he's touting her other attributes."

"Possibly frail?" Rick's thick, golden-brown brows rose before he added, "Though maybe he only meant she wasn't willful or easy to provoke, and to assure you of her calm nature and unblemished virtue."

"Or could it be that his words meant nothing other than she has few options?"

Hurst's jaw tightened, but he remained quiet and took another gulp of brandy while he listened to the suggestions about what Winston's words had meant. Every idea was possible and reasonable, but true? He had no way of knowing.

"Her lineage?" Wyatt asked.

A disgruntled laugh rose from Hurst's chest. "Solid. Stowe's grandfather was a younger son of the former Earl of Canterfield. Stowe's father was a vicar, and I'm quite sure he is too."

Suddenly it was so quiet among the three of them that Hurst heard every spit and crackle of the fire. His friends looked uncertainly at each other before Wyatt stuttered a cough. Rick shifted from one side of his chair to the other and then back again.

"What's with you two? It's a common occurrence

for younger sons of titles to become a vicar," he argued, if only to pacify himself. "You both know I seriously thought about becoming one myself when the duke suggested I should be a clergyman to plump my allowance."

If the title of the family didn't buy the sons a commission in the military or set them up to become rectors or vicars like Stowe's, they usually disintegrated into lonely, old, and woefully indebted wastrels as Hurst's father had. When only a young boy, and often with no money to see there was enough food in the house, Hurst promised himself he'd never allow that to happen to him as he grew older. He would have gladly been a vicar or captain in the army if the title hadn't unexpectedly become his when his uncle and cousin perished.

However, Hurst wasn't going down that memory path tonight either.

Brushing unwanted thoughts of the past away, he considered what Winston asked. It was a shock. It would be madness to agree to marry someone he'd never met. More than that, it felt wrong.

"Forgetting that for now," Wyatt said while motioning for their glasses to be refilled, "is what your friend said true? Did you promise to help him in any way?"

"Yes, but I'd forgotten until now. I couldn't have been more than nine or ten, but I'm certain I meant it at the time."

Hurst pressed his head against the back of the chair and found himself staring up into the face of a wild boar that had been mounted over the fireplace. He suddenly felt just as snared. He had made the promise to Winston, no matter their ages, yet he found himself saying, "I don't want to promise to wed someone I've never met. I know marrying ladies you didn't know worked well for the two of you, but I don't want my bride to be a stranger."

"Damnation, Hurst. We knew them," Wyatt grumbled, and nodded to Rick for confirmation.

"For a short time, yes," Rick replied with an easy air of amusement, pulling at the corners of his mouth.

"A very short time," Hurst mumbled, rubbing the inside corners of his eyes with thumb and forefinger. "Days, not weeks. You both had complicated reasons for needing to wed quickly. I don't have anything to spur me other than a slight prick of my conscience for an oath made years ago to someone who meant a lot to me at the time. If I married his sister, I would probably meet a lady the next day and fall deeply and madly in love with her and not be able to do a damned thing about it." He placed his glass on the table with a thunk. "Yet, I did swear to do anything he might ask of me."

"When you were a boy," Rick clarified, as he reached over to nab the letter from the table. "Let me see this. I don't believe your honor is in question here." He folded out the paper and stared at it. "It says he is only asking you to *consider* marriage. The man's not actually calling in the debt."

Wyatt took the missive from Rick and had his turn reading it for himself.

"He is right about this. It reads that Stowe is giving you freedom to choose. This means you are well within your rights to decline honorably and never think of this again."

Hurst felt tension behind his eyes. That sounded just like something the boy he remembered would do: let him off the hook. "Let me see that again." Hurst pulled the parchment from Rick's grasp.

Perhaps they were right. But like all decisions, this one shouldn't be made quickly. Staying calm and thinking things through led to making better choices.

He glanced from one friend to the other. Their words

had sound merit. The truth was, he wanted to marry. He needed to marry to protect the title. His family was currently without male heirs except for him. Which was why the title had fallen to Hurst when his great-uncle and cousin died in an explosion while inspecting one of their silver mines. Hurst needed to get about the business of choosing a bride and fathering a son. But he couldn't put aside the feeling there was a lady out there for him. He just hadn't met her yet.

"If we all agree Winston is only asking you to consider offering for his sister's hand, then let's consider it. Ten-year-old boys save each other's lives all the time."

"And at fifteen, twenty, and sometimes twenty-five," Hurst said with the quirk of a smile.

Wyatt chuckled and nodded. "Rick must have been at least twenty when he decided to climb the trellis and enter Miss Avery's bedchamber for a tumble under the covers with her."

"He was too deep into his cups to remember anything about that night," Hurst reminded them both.

"I might have been thoroughly jug bitten, but I do recall it was at her behest that I join her," he argued as if trying to absolve himself. "At the time, it seemed worth attempting the risky venture."

"Luckily, I caught up with you in time to stop you," Hurst added. "The only reason a father would allow a trellis on a wall that led directly to his daughter's bedchamber would be so he could catch an unsuspecting gentleman in a parson's mousetrap."

"And always preferably a duke like you," Wyatt added.

Rick offered a crooked smile. "I've always been grateful you saved me from that fate worse than death but would never assume I owed you a debt because of it. It's simply what friends do for each other."

"We can't count the times you've saved us from doing something beyond our reasonable expectations to master," Wyatt agreed. "As when we raced our curricles down Rotten Row in the dark of night. Any one of us could have overturned."

"Or run up upon a slowly moving carriage." Hurst remembered those days.

Rick sipped his fresh drink. "We never would have even remembered you swore an oath to us."

Hurst considered all the two said. Renewed concern nipped at him. He tried to shrug it off.

"After we finish the hunt, go see him," Wyatt suggested. "Check on his health and perhaps meet Miss Stowe."

That suggestion had merit, and he did want to see Winston, but it wasn't something he could do right away. "You know from here I've promised to go north to see Aunt Sophie. She's already planned for me to attend several house parties with her. You know I can't let her down after all she's done for me."

"The parties are for you to meet young ladies in hopes of making a match, are they not? And for her to meet older gentlemen, I presume."

Hurst chuckled. "Either way, I can't disappoint her."

"In the meantime," Wyatt said. "What are you going to tell your childhood friend? You can't leave him agonizing about what your decision will be while you attend to other things. He went to great lengths and sent a loyal servant to find you. He deserves a quick answer."

Hurst looked at the messenger standing patiently by the door. Taking the stopper out of the ink jar, he dipped the quill into it and spoke the words aloud as he wrote them on the paper the man provided.

Dear Winston,

It was good to hear from you after so long a time. I am concerned to know of your illness, but feel your strong, youthful constitution will withstand the troublesome illness and you will be hardy by spring. I will plan a visit to see you soon."

Hurst hesitated, sighed, then nodded before continuing.

It is with deep regret that I must decline your request to marry your sister.

Love, The Duke.

"'Love'?" both friends questioned skeptically at the same time and with the same degree of consternation.

Hurst discarded the quill and said, "I acknowledged I loved Winston as a brother at one time. What do you think I should have written?"

"Why not, 'Yours truly, the Duke'?" Wyatt asked.

"Or, 'Sincerely, the Duke'?" Rick suggested.

Hurst deliberated over both suggestions, before saying, "The endearment stands."

CHAPTER 2

MAN'S PRACTICAL GUIDE TO APPREHENDING A THIEF
SIR BENTLY ASHTON ULLINGSWICK

Disguise yourself so you won't be recognized.

Something wasn't as it should be, and Hurst didn't like surprises.

More than slightly interested, he leaned back into the chair behind his desk at his London townhome and regarded with one sardonically raised brow the woman who had entered the book room of his home.

He was immediately taken with her, and it had nothing to do with her face; she presented herself as a man, but instinctively Hurst knew the person who had insisted upon seeing him about an urgent matter this night was female. No matter how superb her disguise.

The black summer wool coat had been generously padded to cover slim shoulders. A moderately starched neckcloth, elegantly knotted, contrasted beautifully against a red quilted waistcoat seamed with shiny brass buttons. She wore dark trousers that he was certain had been made to fit her tall, slender frame and not hastily altered for her. Well-heeled and highly polished riding boots added to her striking figure and poise. Even the masculine-shaped wig, dark as a raven's back, that concealed her hair was handsomely styled and becoming.

Yet, expert tailoring, and a dusting of face powder over a slight brush of kohl intended to mimic a shadow of beard, couldn't obscure the natural pink tint of her lips or hide the deep stirring beauty of delicate-looking, parchment-pale skin. Her arched brows had been darkened to match the wig, but that didn't matter. Her shapely, rosebud mouth simply couldn't belong to a man.

Someone had gone to great lengths wanting to dupe him. But who was she, and why was she there?

Hurst slowly rose from the chair as his butler left the room, closing the door behind him. He'd known of women dressing as a male to gain entrance into a gentlemen's club or private gambling party for a variety of different reasons, including only to satisfy their curiosity about such establishments. Never had he heard of one doing so to enter the sanctity of a man's home. That took nerves of iron, and he was rather impressed by her gumption.

Keeping his gaze squarely on his guest's vibrant blue eyes, Hurst asked in a questioning tone, "What can I do for you, Mr.—what was your name again?"

She didn't immediately respond, appearing indecisive. He had the feeling she struggled with how to best proceed now that she was standing in front of him. Cautiously, she glanced around the room, as if to ascertain there was no one else lurking about. With sharp inquisitiveness, she gave the brown damask draperies, overly crowded bookshelves, and aged painting of his great-grandfather that hung over the fireplace a quick perusal before facing Hurst again.

Now that she was here, whatever it was she wanted, she was suddenly reluctant to voice it. He was in no hurry. He'd give her all the time she needed.

After a long breath and with an air of resolution,

she seemed to make a decision, then settle herself. Her shoulders loosened, and she took a few confident steps toward him before pausing. In a serene voice, she said, "Warcliff is the name I gave to your butler, but that doesn't matter now, Your Grace. You see, I am not a man."

Having expected her to deny the obvious, he was surprised and quite intrigued by her immediate response of honesty as well as her daring. One thing was sure: If a man was inclined to disguise himself for any reason, Hurst was quite sure he'd never do so as a woman. He wasn't one to care much for intrigue or drama, but her approach and his reaction to her was too remarkable not to let this play out.

"Go on," he encouraged, without equivocating as he moved around to the side of his desk.

"I'm Ophelia Stowe."

Shock jolted through Hurst and shuddered every bone in his body. He forced himself not to physically react too strongly to her astounding revelation. She was the sister Winston had asked him to marry weeks ago. What the devil was she doing in his home? Dressed as a man. And hadn't his childhood friend said she had a gentle soul? That certainly didn't fit with the boldness of the lady standing before him now.

"I'm glad you agreed to see me, and sorry I had to use such an elaborate masquerade," she offered, taking another step farther into the room.

"Wait." He held up both hands to stop her forward movement while he digested who she was. If she still had hopes he'd marry her, this wasn't the way to go about looking into that possibility. "First, I didn't agree to see you. I agreed to see a man. Second, why would you think you required such detailed means to hide who you are in order to talk to me?"

"I need to speak with you privately, and this was the only way I could think to assure my anonymity." She blinked rapidly a few times. "I wasn't sure you would agree to meet me."

Did she consider him an ogre? "Why wouldn't I see you?" he asked, his commanding voice clipped.

Her shoulders stiffened once again. "Perhaps you have forgotten, sir, but you rebuffed my dear brother's appeal without so much as a how do you do and wouldn't even consider the possibility of marrying me. Not that I would have agreed to it anyway either. You didn't even keep your word and come visit him as you promised in your short response. I think it improbable that a duke such as yourself would make the time to see a lowly vicar's sister."

What kind of poppycock was she saying? No one in Winston's family was of lowly birth.

Maybe she did think of him as an ogre. And maybe he was. It took a lot to raise ire in Hurst, but Miss Stowe's forthright manner was on a fast racehorse track to do so, whether she knew it or not.

When he returned to London, estate and business matters stood in the way of traveling to see Winston.

The problems were urgent at the time, and frankly still troublesome. Hurst had come home from his aunt's house to find that his largest and most fertile farmlands had been flooded and frozen most of the winter and early spring rains caused a destructive mold on the already-boggy area. Valuable crops couldn't be planted for fear the blight on the acreage would spread to neighboring properties and farther. Wanting to be knowledgeable concerning all the issues, Hurst worked alongside his managers, tenants, and specialists to find treatments that would eradicate the mold so the land would be fertile again. Even now they waited to see if the diseased parcels would recover and flourish once again.

Hurst couldn't expect a sheltered young lady to understand the intricacies of such difficulties, and he'd be damned before he'd offer an explanation to counter her unveiled accusation against his honor.

He set a determined stare on her lovely face, and then folding his arms across his chest he strengthened his stance to match hers. He'd also returned from his aunt's, and the round of parties she took him to, believing he needed to stop thinking that he should wait until he found the right lady for him before he married. He wasn't getting any younger and needed an heir. But now, looking at Miss Stowe and feeling the growing interest in her, he knew he ought to wait for the right young lady and not settle until he had.

"There is a huge difference between agreeing to marry someone sight unseen and meeting with them, Miss Stowe. Furthermore, I have every intention of visiting Winston."

Her expression sagged as she glanced at the recently tended fire for a second or two before responding with, "That's impossible now. I'm sorry to say my brother passed away shortly after he sent the letter to you."

The sting of guilt pricked Hurst as sharply as the tip of a footpad's dagger. "My sympathies. I really wanted to see him again," he said as honestly and gently as he could. "I believed he would be strong enough to weather his illness. I'm sorry."

She hesitated and took an unsteady breath before saying, "Thank you. That is some comfort, but I'm here because Winston still needs your help."

"Of course, I'll do whatever I can." It was damned unsettling to talk to a lady who wore the clothing and the look of a man. Especially a quite lovely lady who had very real reasons to pull on his heartstrings and his desires, but he was managing. "We can discuss it tomorrow when you return with proper attire and chaperone so neither of us will be shunned from Society or forced into marriage because of your prank."

"Ah," she said after inhaling a deep breath. "You've already made your thoughts on marriage to me quite clear."

"I want to marry, Miss Stowe, but not that way. Rest assured I was only thinking of your reputation. Not my own. I'll have Gilbert call for my carriage, so I'll be assured you get back to wherever you're staying without anyone ever knowing you were here." Hurst made his way to walk past her. "You can wait in—"

In a surprise move, she took hold of the crook of his arm and stopped him.

Flames leaping from the blazing fire couldn't have heated him more than the unexpected contact. At her touch, a quiver of sensual awareness pounded through his stomach and settled low. His fascination with her was real and exasperating.

Both glanced down at her hand firmly holding his elbow before their eyes met again. There was a gentle strength in her determined grasp, but more intriguing was an undefinable emotion he felt surging between them as they stood close together. For a moment the room was so quiet he would have sworn to anyone he heard both their hearts beating. For a moment he had the oddest feeling she was the lady for him. That was an odd thought he dismissed quickly.

Slowly, she relaxed her grip one finger at a time as if

she wasn't sure she wanted to let go of him at all. And for one wild second he wasn't sure he wanted her to. There was such a warmth of loveliness about her that it was easy to forget she had tricked her way into his house.

"Please, wait and hear what I have to say." Her voice was beseeching, though her gaze never wavered from his determined stare. "I've been planning this for a long time."

That was apparent by her well-fitted costume. "Planning what?" He pulled on the sleeve of his coat and shook his head, wanting to fend off the purely masculine feelings swirling inside him. "No, don't tell me. I don't know what kind of trouble you are in, Miss Stowe, but I think you came to the wrong man."

"I hope that's not true. I wanted to come to London right away, but I couldn't risk leaving the village before the proper mourning time was over."

His gaze flickered over her face again. Unable, for the time being, to shake off his inconceivable attraction to her, he nodded understanding but insisted, "Whatever you have to say can wait until tomorrow."

She blinked as if she might have truly realized the gravity of her actions for a moment, but then her shoulders rolled back. Her chin lifted again. "There's good reason I've gone to such trouble to see you alone," she said resolutely.

Hurst stiffened at the tug of her honest plea, but it did nothing to alleviate his worry about her getting safely home before someone else saw her dressed as she was. "No reason could be good enough."

"You can't know that until you hear me out." Her dark velvety lashes fluttered in sudden indignation. "It won't hurt to at least listen to what I have to say since I am already here," she argued. "I daresay most men would be thrilled a woman had crept into their home cloaked by masquerade."

He muttered a near soundless oath. "Woman, perhaps yes, Miss Stowe. You are a lady."

He moved to head for the door. Again, her arm snaked out, but she caught herself and snatched back her hand, clasping it to her chest. The defensive action and the shifting emotions crossing her face was enough to stop him.

No doubt, he did owe it to Winston to keep his sister from being banished from Society, or worse. Nonetheless, that's not what gave him pause to reconsider and listen to what she had to say.

"Please," she said. It was the faint sound of desperation mixed with a feminine vulnerability in her voice that pulled on his heartstrings once again. He couldn't turn away from her or his interest in why she had sought him with such desperation.

Staring into her eyes, he moved his face close to hers and realized straightaway that was a mistake. He wasn't prepared to be intoxicated by her fresh womanly scent or the hushed sounds of her anxious breathing. They teased his senses with primal thoughts, throwing him out of kilter for a few seconds before he shook them off and snorted with derision at the reality of what was happening. He couldn't figure out why he was so sensitive to every move she made.

Hurst relented and grudgingly said, "I will give you the courtesy of hearing what the devil brought you here while we wait for my carriage to arrive." He strode over to the door, called for Gilbert to have it brought around in front, and then walked back and stood before her again.

She may not understand the ramifications of what she had done, but he did. “Tell me why you are here, Miss Stowe, and make it quick.”

Standing her ground and suddenly looking more hopeful, she murmured, “Thank you.” There was a skip in her breath before she stated confidently, “The day after Winston passed, I discovered the door to the room that holds the sacraments of the church where Winston had been vicar slightly ajar. It is always locked. At first glance nothing seemed out of place, but a closer inspection revealed the box that held the Chatham’s chalice wasn’t properly locked and the priceless relic was gone.”

“And?” he asked, impatient for her to move on with the story.

“Someone must have taken the keys to the room and the box from Winston while he was so ill and stolen the chalice.”

“That seems presumptuous, Miss Stowe. Surely it has simply been misplaced. Or sent out to be cleaned or repaired. The chalice may well be on a shelf, waiting for someone to pick it up.”

“No, it is gone. I have handled all nonspiritual matters for Winston the past couple of years. It wouldn’t have been removed from the box without permission from me.”

A skeptical grunt slipped past Hurst’s lips.

Undaunted, she added, “Maman and I searched every nook and cranny in the church and the vicarage.”

“The devil you say. You couldn’t have possibly.”

Her shoulders tightened again. “We did, and perhaps you should watch the words you choose to *say*, Your Grace.”

Hurst didn’t take well to the slight reprimand for his

language. He understood that she was upset and highly passionate about this, but he had limits too.

"Considering your attire, you are lucky I haven't said worse words that aren't appropriate for your hearing."

Undaunted, she dropped her arms loosely by her sides and assumed an air of authority. "We read through Winston's personal diaries, sermons, and everything he possessed." She stopped, twitched, and then continued. "It was difficult to do, of course, but necessary."

That was understandable.

"We left nothing unturned, no piece of furniture unmoved, and everything that could be looked at was."

He was beginning to believe her about that.

"Anyway, we combed through the recent registries, visitors' logs, and prayer books. Not a hint of anything revealed what might have happened to the chalice. We knew when the new vicar arrived, he would inventory the treasury and livings of the rectory for the elderly bishop. The priceless chalice would be missing. We had no doubts Winston would be accused of the theft as they were his responsibility. His impeccable name and legacy would be tarnished forever. That thought, along with my mother bearing the shame of the townspeople thinking her son was a thief, has been crushing to both of us."

It was clear by her expression and the way she held her hands together tightly in front of her that both those possibilities were devastating to her. "Then if it can't be found, I will make restitution for the theft." This, he realized, would be a way to repay his debt to his friend and keep the parish happy as well.

Surprise, mixed with apprehension, swept her features and she swallowed hard. "That's very generous of you but not what I want."

Hurst furrowed his brow again. “Then what do you want from me?”

“I want you to help me find the chalice and return it to the church before anyone knows it is missing.”

CHAPTER 3

MAN'S PRACTICAL GUIDE TO APPREHENDING A THIEF
SIR BENTLY ASHTON ULLINGSWICK

Determine if something has been stolen.

Was she fooling him? Hurst straightened fully, drawing in a deep breath, and refocusing on her face. "I don't understand, Miss Stowe. It's been at least two months. Hasn't the new vicar already taken inventory?"

She continued her indomitable focus directly on his face. "If I could continue?"

He didn't know what to do other than nod and wait to hear the rest of the story.

"The first new vicar arrived one day and took to his sickbed the next. After a couple of weeks, his illness worsened, and he decided to return to his former home. He never managed to do a proper accounting of the livings. When a different vicar arrived, he was most peculiar."

Hurst rubbed the tension settling in the back of his neck. "What do you mean?"

"He is either a hypochondriac or superstitious. I don't know which, but something."

"A vicar?" That sounded incredible, but she looked as serious as a winter storm.

"An anxiety or perhaps melancholy of some disorder has him believing something is causing the vicars to get sick. First my brother, then Vicar Samuelson. Truth to tell, there was the absurdly short tenure of a Vicar Haroldsmiths that very few people are even aware of and now Vicar Morgan, who spends most of his time at a nearby inn refusing to move into the rectory yet, insisting it be cleansed, aired, and cleansed again. Consequently, he hasn't inventoried the livings either. Now the parish is growing unhappier with him by the day and there's talk of seeking yet another vicar. I must find the chalice before anyone knows it's gone."

Hurst scoffed again and held up his hands as if in surrender. "Miss Stowe. I still don't see how I can help."

"That's because you won't allow me to finish."

"Then do it quickly and without so many vicars."

She inhaled an audible breath. "I questioned the servants, and from one of the maids gleaned evidence that led me to believe the chalice was indeed stolen and brought to London. Now, with the mourning passed, I can finally begin my search to recover the chalice and save Winston from being wrongly accused of being a thief."

He met her declaration with cynicism. "Is that all?"

The staunch set of her shapely lips told him she wasn't happy with his answer. She trained those beautiful, bright eyes on him as if affronted because *he'd* said something wrong.

Her chin lifted again, and her features suddenly seemed filled with all the fortitude of a snow-covered mountain. The seriousness of her expression intrigued him once more. *Damnation.* It was unsettling that she fascinated him to the point he was now wondering how she would look with her face washed clean and dressed as a lady.

What was he to do with her? "Regardless," he said. "What do you think I can do about it?"

"Help me find the thief. When we do, we'll find the chalice. The maid who saw him didn't get a good look as he donned his hat but thought he had a weak nose and chin."

Hurst felt his eyebrows pinch and rise, but somehow, he managed to hold his retort.

"I'm sure the thief was a titled man," she hurried on. "Possibly a duke or maybe an earl because of the crest on the carriage door."

"What?" This was madness. "You probably think I stole the blasted thing."

Her lashes rose and she glanced at his bookshelves with rising interest while saying, "I'm not discounting anyone. Perhaps you should remove your jacket and let's have a look at you."

"There is nothing weak about me, chin or otherwise," Hurst grumbled at her cheeky comment. "You know I wasn't at the church because I never went to see Winston."

"Yes. True. You didn't."

She had the impertinence to peruse his bookshelves again. Her pluckiness had no boundaries.

With his gaze fastened tightly on hers, he candidly remarked, "A duke has no need for a church chalice, Miss Stowe."

"It's more than an ordinary sacrament piece and seldom used for that reason," she explained. "There are collectors who hunt for such precious items. This one was saved from Cromwell's theft and destruction of churches and monasteries. It's priceless for its historical value alone."

"Churches have been known to claim to have something that was saved from the Crusades or Cromwell's wretched raids." Hurst shook his head. She seemed sincere, but did she truly not know that there were claims not just in England but all over the world that small pieces of wood, tiny swatches of cloth, and even toe bones were said to be relics from biblical and other historical times? Not every claim could be legitimate.

"It's probably not true," he suggested. "There weren't many items saved."

"You are wrong, sir," she said indignantly. "Chatham's chalice has been well documented through the years by bishops, kings, and probably dukes as well."

Resisting the urge to stay quiet, he answered, "I would venture to say that most owners of religious artifacts say that."

"A sacred church relic isn't something a clergyman would have lied about then or now."

Hurst started to say more but decided there was no use arguing that point further. Her mind was set on the history of the chalice. Exasperation had him gritting his teeth as he asked, "Whatever the case may be, do you think me a seer who can find lost things?"

"Of course not," she huffed unevenly. "But you are the only titled man I know."

"You don't know me."

Her expression softened and for a moment Hurst felt he might have wounded her in some way.

"I feel as though I do," she answered, taking a step back from him. "Winston always talked about you as if you were his best friend or brother he never had. He told me of the many days he spent roaming the woods and riding horses throughout the hillsides with you before your aunt took you away. He talked of them so often they must have been the happiest of his life. I know he loved you."

Once again Hurst felt the piercing burden of guilt. "That was a long time ago, Miss Stowe."

"But Winston never had any close friends. Perhaps that's why he always talked about you."

He and Winston had enjoyed a good friendship, but they grew up and went their separate ways. Hurst's life moved on when he went away to school and made different friends. Their lives took different directions.

"According to what the maid said," Miss Stowe continued, seeming satisfied he wasn't going further into the past, "there is a titled man in London who has a shelf in his book room where he keeps artifacts. I am hoping you will agree to search the book rooms of peers for me and—"

"Wait. Wait just a—blasted minute," he grumbled, unable to restrain his grievance about her suggestion. She was unbelievable. "What nonsense are you spouting? You want me to go searching for this revered chalice in the homes of peers? I've never heard such an ill-conceived contemplation."

"Perhaps it is outrageous," she maintained earnestly.

"It is beyond outrageous," he answered sternly. "It's wrong."

She seemed to reconsider before replying, "I'm not seeing it that way."

"There is no other way to see it," he insisted. "Besides, you don't know how to go about looking for a thief. Neither do I, and I don't believe you realize the number of clandestine maneuvers it would take to accomplish what you want to do."

"Excuse me, sir." Her eyes flashed with sparkles of conflict even though she seemed to be in complete control. "My brother saw to it I was well-read and studied in all subjects of learning just as he had been."

She hesitated, then gave him the most impish smile he

had ever seen. His stomach did a slow roll that tightened his lower body.

"I have read a book on how to catch a thief," she announced proudly.

Hurst didn't think he could be more surprised had the young lady who was dressed as a man pulled a pipe from her pocket, put it to her enticing lips, and started puffing. But he was. Surely, he hadn't heard her correctly.

"A book?" He could only stare at her for a moment. "You've read a book?"

"Man's Practical Guide to Apprehending a Thief."

A chuckle whispered from his throat. "Right. It says 'man' and you are a lady. And you think that will help you find a thief? Throw that thing away before you get yourself in trouble."

"I will not. I paid good money for it and it's been useful."

"How?"

"Well," she hedged. "I'm not quite sure yet because I haven't started trying to catch the thief."

"You don't have a chance in Hades, Miss Stowe."

She seemed to be trying to burn him with her eyes she stared at him so hard. "I will clear Winston's name with or without you. Your help will make it easier. And quicker. I don't have much time given the vicar situation, but the clock is ticking."

Surprisingly, she looked sane and sounded sincere. She was strong, defiant, and blessed with a beauty that couldn't be hidden by her disguise. There was no doubt she was passionate about this, but it was unachievable in his estimation. Hurst gave another short snort of laughter.

"How do you plan to do that with no assistance from me, Miss Stowe? Do you plan to use some secretive measures you learned from a *book* or the extreme tactic you used tonight to sneak into every titled man's home in Mayfair?"

A flicker of unease flashed across her eyes. She glanced away from him and stared into the lowering fire for a moment again before saying, "I'm not sure of it all yet. Because my brother considered you such a fine man and dear friend, I have been hoping for your assistance. No matter. I will find a way. Time is short, but I am determined to succeed."

Her shining eyes were steady. She was serious. She actually thought she could find this thief in a place as big as London.

This idea was foolish, but Hurst found himself asking, "Why not just hire a runner from Bow Street to find this chalice for you?"

"You sound as if you think I have unlimited funds to do with as I please as you do, sir. The trustee for my inheritance and Maman's holds on to every penny as if it were our last. He wouldn't even release enough money for me to buy *Debrett's Peerage and Baronetage* of English peerages. He said it was too expensive and, as a lady, not something I needed. I couldn't tell him why I wanted it. If I could get my hands on that book, I could look at the crests for the coat of arms and possibly narrow my search to the one that was on the thief's carriage door. Besides, how could a runner get into such homes of earls, dukes, and viscounts?"

"Probably easier than you, Miss Stowe." He purposefully mumbled the words with a breath of frustration, knowing he could have handled this better if he weren't so attracted to her.

"But not you?" she responded pointedly. "With your title, you can be invited into their homes *and* into their book rooms. While you were there, no one would think it odd for you to look over the bookshelves to see if there was one filled with artifacts, and maybe a chalice."

"And then what would I do, Miss Stowe?" he asked, his voice growing louder at what he considered absurd reasoning. "If I saw the chalice you are referring to, would I just grab it and run like a thief myself? I don't think you know what you are asking."

A wave of surprised innocence flashed in her eyes. "Did you raise your voice to me?"

"What?" Did he? "No. A little. Maybe. What you want me to do is preposterous."

"Is that any reason to show anger in your tone?"

"Anger? No. Frustration." He shifted his stance as regret gathered in his chest. He didn't want to scare her. For some insane reason he was drawn to her and wanted to protect her from this ridiculous idea. "I didn't mean anything by it. Sometimes I might raise my voice a little when I'm irritated with unreasonable people."

"My brother never elevated his voice to me no matter the subject we were discussing or how angry he was with me."

"I'm not your brother, Miss Stowe," he said quietly. "My upbringing was different from Winston's. Every time my father came home from being out all night and I discovered he had gambled away all his allowance again, I was upset. Time and again we were left with nothing to eat in the house but old bread and cheese and in danger of having no place to lay our heads until payment of his allowance came around again. So yes, sometimes we raised our voices to each other, and I need no reprimand from you about it."

"Oh, I see," she said softly, seeming reluctant to meet

his eyes, but clearly understanding why he argued differently. "Yes, I suppose all families are different."

Hurst struggled, suppressing the need to say more about her outlandish idea, and wishing like hell he hadn't revealed so much as a nugget of his past to her. That wasn't something he usually revealed to anyone no matter how angry he got, and why he had to her he wasn't sure. It wasn't something she needed to know. He didn't talk about his father to anyone, and he had no idea why he had blurted anything about his unsavory past.

He shoved thoughts of the days with his father out of his mind and concentrated on the lady in front of him.

"There's no one else I can go to, except—"

She looked deeply into his eyes and Hurst felt as if he heard the breath swoosh out of her lungs. He felt a strong pull toward her once again. The passion inside her was almost palpable. She spoke with such fervor and courage that he wanted to help her but couldn't possibly consider what she asked. To make matters worse, he hadn't been able to shake his attraction to her.

Miss Stowe hesitated and Hurst could tell that a sudden thought had come to her. That she studied over it so carefully worried him. "Except what?" he asked, pushing down the sense that he wasn't going to like whatever it was that just entered her mind.

"I suppose I could try other peers. It's possible one of them might be more agreeable than you even if they didn't know Winston."

Her brows furrowed slightly as if she were truly considering that idea. Her mettle was extraordinary.

"That would be useless," he answered tersely. "If I thought you might seriously consider contacting someone else about this madcap scheme of yours, especially in the same manner in which you came to me, I would alert your trustee to put a stop to this madness."

"How dare you be so unkind."

"For your protection against such a scheme I would do it. I owe it to your brother."

"You owed it to him to come see him," she responded quickly.

"But I didn't," he snapped back.

Her hands jerked to her waist, flaring the coat away from her body and emphasizing the gentle roundness of her hips. "Just because you don't want to help me is no reason others of the peerage can't judge my circumstances for themselves. I came to you because I thought you might have a soft spot in your heart and want to help your old friend."

Hurst had enough of her placing guilt on him. Deserved or not. He advanced on her. "What I will do for you, Miss Stowe, is agree not to tell your maman, guardian, trustee, or anyone else about this impromptu meeting, your reason for it, or how you presented yourself as a man. I suggest you don't tell anyone about it either."

She remained quiet, but her gaze held fast to his. That worried him. "Who else knows about your quest?"

"No one. I pinned all hope on you and your long-held friendship with Winston. You are the only one I've trusted with my plan to search book rooms. You don't seem to comprehend the urgency of how short my time is to find this vessel before the livings are inventoried."

Hurst felt her words deep in his chest. He was the *only one she trusted.* A good way to stir a man's need to protect and defend the weaker sex was to hear her say she trusted him. Was that the truth or had she said that on purpose to appeal to his masculine instincts?

He searched her face for false feelings and found none.

Why, he had no idea, but the truth of it was he wanted to help her. But he couldn't let that sway him or encourage her on this wild and unattainable quest of hers. It was nothing short of madness.

That truth didn't keep all his earlier impatience from melting away at the disappointment he could see she felt. Hurst swallowed down the surging impulse to relent and agree to aid her in some way. What the devil could he do? Buying her Debrett's book, hiring a couple of runners from Bow Street to investigate the theft, or anything else he could think of seemed no better plan than the flimsy one she had devised in that beautiful head of hers. All of them would be almost impossible for anyone to accomplish with success. It would be best for him not to encourage her in any way concerning this impractical scheme.

"Wanting to help your brother is admirable, but ill-fated for multiple reasons," he said with all honesty. "When you are ready to accept this, I will pay for the loss of the chalice and ask that Winston be absolved from any involvement in the theft. That is all I can do for you."

A flicker of despair passed over her features. "The sacrament is too valuable to be replaced so easily, Your Grace, even without its history. It is hammered gold with small rubies surrounding the middle. In monetary terms the silk bag to store it in might be worth more than the chalice. It's embroidered in stunning South Sea pearls and the drawstrings are made of spun gold and silver. It's not only that, I don't want the memory of my brother's name to be ruined or even touched with scandal for all time. I also can't bear the thought the relic will be hidden away in some greedy old man's book room, its history forgotten about, and all it will do is gather dust and silverfish to nibble on the bag."

Hurst had never heard an impassioned voice so soft or seen eyes so beautifully saddened. Her plight went straight to his heart, making him feel like the worst kind of rake for casting her feelings aside.

She inhaled deeply and seemed to accept defeat admirably well, but then as she turned away, he caught sight of her expression as it shifted, and he, as sure as he knew his own name, realized that she had no intention of letting this go.

Exasperated, he turned and pulled the bell cord for Gilbert. When he turned back, she was gone.

CHAPTER 4

MAN'S PRACTICAL GUIDE TO APPREHENDING A THIEF
SIR BENTLY ASHTON ULLINGSWICK

Don't get caught looking for clues.

Ophelia Stowe wasn't brave. Only determined.

Like most of the eligible young ladies basking under the large glimmering chandeliers at the elegant bustling affair, including the two standing with her, she was looking for a man. The difference was, they were looking for a husband. Ophelia was looking for a thief.

Admiring gentlemen for romantic purposes wasn't the reason she was in London. Which, admittedly, was odd for a lady. Especially one who had been invited to a soiree at this magnificent home. She supposed at near twenty-one some might consider she was destined to become a dried weed on the shelf. That possibility didn't cause her a twitter of concern. She figured she'd marry one day. But not now. There were other things to do first. That didn't mean she didn't understand most ladies' desire to wed. Snaring a suitable husband in her first Season was what a proper young lady was brought up to do. And by all accounts Ophelia was proper—or had been until she'd arrived in London a few days ago and then dressed as a gentleman to present herself to a duke.

However clever the plan was, it hadn't gone well.

Shaking off that remembrance, Ophelia glanced away from her chattering new friends, caught sight of her mother, and smiled. Roberta Fawnsworth Stowe stood quietly with a small, stylish group of ladies and a gentleman while the hum of music, conversation, and laughter mixed with the movements of the room.

Having made her debut in Polite Society more than twenty years ago and staying in touch with solid members of the ton since made it easy for Roberta to fit back into London's social events with ease. Wearing her half mourning gown of black silk banded by white ribbons at the high waist and lace cuffs, Roberta was a striking lady of medium height, and a natural beauty even with a little gray showing in her honey-colored hair. She was perhaps too thin and pale at present, but there was a kindness and loveliness about her that seemed to draw people.

Once she let it be known she and her daughter, Ophelia, were in Town and accepting callers, invitations to parties, balls, and dinners started flowing in. Her mother's easy acceptance couldn't have worked better for Ophelia's new plan.

With no forthcoming aid from the stubborn Duke of Hurstbourne to investigate book rooms, Ophelia was left to search for the thief on her own. Knowing the best way to gain entrance into the homes of titled gentlemen was to be invited. And the best way to accomplish that was to make friends, which led to accepting Miss Georgina Bristol's mother's gracious invitation to meet all the young ladies making their debut. That had opened the door for Roberta's and Ophelia's attendance tonight and to other parties that had been scheduled for the Season.

Glad to see her maman seemed to be handling the evening well, Ophelia smiled again. Her mother's countenance remained peaceful as usual. That was asking a lot of her given the circumstances of what she knew her daughter would be doing tonight.

After Ophelia's attempt to gain the duke's help failed, despite her repeated appeals, she had no choice but to elicit her mother's aid in her scheme. Maman had no problem with her daughter entering Society and the social Season but took to her sickbed over Ophelia's desire to search for the chalice in book rooms of the titled men's homes where they would be welcomed as guests. Roberta was adamantly against that. At first.

Granted, her maman had some valid arguments for thinking neither the bishop nor anyone else would think Winston had a hand in the disappearance of the sacrament. Ophelia had clicked them off in her mind many times: *Everyone in the parish knew Winston was dedicated to the church and had never shown any leanings toward wanting earthly treasures. What would Winston do with the priceless vessel if he had stolen it? What would he do with the money if he had sold it?*

Ophelia answered them all with *What if they did think he was responsible?* He would forever be labeled a thief. There was also the possibility the bishop, church elders, or others might think that Winston's illness of fevers had affected his mind with some sort of disillusionment and that had made him steal from the church.

After many conversations and plenty of persuasive discussions, Roberta had acquiesced to what her daughter must do to save Winston's legacy. Ophelia's only goal was to find the chalice and return it to the sacraments room before her brother was accused of stealing it.

"What do you think, Ophelia?"

Startled out of her thoughts, Ophelia struggled to quickly clear her mind of her troubles and focus her attention back on the conversation at hand. She smiled and said, "Pardon me, Miss Bristol, but the music is so loud and the room so crowded it feels as if everyone is talking into my ear at the same time. I didn't hear what you said."

The brown-eyed beauty who had been given a priority of attention from gentlemen during the evening gave Ophelia an understanding expression and leaned in toward her. "Please call me Georgina. We are friends now. And it's Lord Gagingcliffe we're talking about. Do you think he is much too old for me to consider making a match with him?"

"Oh, I suppose not really," she answered honestly, trying to remember the man she met earlier in the evening. "I don't think age matters so much unless it involves many years. It's how you feel about him and whether he appeals to you in a romantic way. Didn't you say he was dashing and divinely handsome?"

"No, no. You are thinking about Mr. Wilbur Sawyer." She placed her closed fan over her heart. "I could swoon every time I see him, but he hasn't a title so my parents are reluctant to entertain him. Lord Gagingcliffe is only modestly handsome, older, and the man Papa has great hope for a match between us. He is a baron, so I would be a lady." She sighed wistfully. "Yet, I don't think I could possibly agree to marry him."

Obviously, there were too many men interested in the beautiful Miss Georgina Bristol for Ophelia to keep up with their names.

"I felt the same way when I was introduced to the man my father wants me to marry," Miss Katherine Walker offered, along with a proud sniff and a glance around the ballroom. "Not a blink of affection or attraction passed between us the entire time we spoke to each other." She looked at Ophelia and sighed. "Do call me Katherine. As Georgina said, we're all friends now."

"Yes, of course," Ophelia agreed.

"You consider the man. You would be a viscountess if you married him," Georgina reminded Katherine, flickering the hand-painted fan under her sharp chin.

"An unhappy one," Katherine countered quickly. "And I want to marry a man who makes my breaths flutter and knees go weak every time I look at him."

"I know exactly what you mean." Georgina sighed. "That's the way I felt when I looked into the dreamy eyes of the Duke of Hurstbourne when presented to him at the grand ball last night. I'm sure he saw stars in my eyes."

"I felt the same way when I was introduced to him," Katherine added, seeming surprised Georgina had a similar reaction. "But my mama says he's never looked seriously at any lady and to set my bonnet for a man who is interested so that I won't lose the opportunity for matrimony my first Season."

Apparently, the duke appealed to all the young ladies—including Ophelia.

"I agree with Georgina that a viscount must be given more than passing consideration," Ophelia added to the conversation. "No matter his age. Maybe the two of you were not discussing the kind of things that would lead to delightful or intelligent conversing that would better suit you. Did you ask what he enjoys when he's not seeing to his estate duties?" she asked, finding a way to gain more information on the viscount. "Perhaps he collects beautiful snuffboxes, old paintings, or artifacts of a certain type, and the like. Did he happen to say?"

"Yes," Katherine answered, rolling her light-blue eyes. "As a matter of fact, he often mentioned his fondness of horses, horses, and more horses. Stallions, geldings, mares, thoroughbreds, fillies, and other such names. It amazes me that it's perfectly acceptable for a man to talk about a large muscular animal with a lady, but political and money matters are too complicated and too delicate for us to hear about."

The three laughed, and Ophelia made a mental note to put the viscount at the bottom of her list of peers she needed to investigate further. Chances were good he was not into historical relics if his main focus was always on what was in his stables.

Their discussion continued, but somehow even with their banter, swells of lively music dancing around them, hums of drumming chatter, and booms of masculine laughter swirling about, thoughts of the much-sought-after duke crowded back into Ophelia's mind.

After their discussion in his book room, she'd be happy to never speak to him again, but that wasn't likely to happen. She could very well see him tonight since they were in the home of one of his good friends. With the Season in full swing, she could find herself evading him at many of the parties that were planned.

That aside, she wondered if he would recognize her at all if their paths crossed. She looked far different wearing a ball gown and her own honey-blond hair. It had taken her a long time to decide to present herself as a man to gain entrance into his house and speak to him about helping her. If not for her maid's brother working for a tailor and agreeing to lend his hand to make the clothing, she'd never have accomplished it.

She was grateful the duke hadn't laughed at her disguise. In fact, the way he scrutinized her so carefully with sharp interest had indicated he appreciated her efforts. But certainly not her plan. That had turned his temper hot as a poker left too long in the fire. She hadn't minded the show of temper so much. It was an interesting change from her family's perpetual unruffled countenances that had kept her home quiet.

The duke's manner wasn't what she was used to. Her brother and father were never so expressive for any reason. They always seemed to be in a continual state of calm. Their countenances seldom gave away their feelings. They'd been taught to remain serene no matter whom they were talking to or what the discussion. That was expected of a clergyman and his wife. And children too. Ophelia was to never appear exasperated, annoyed, filled with alarming disbelief, or any other such emotion when they disagreed with her or anyone else. They were to always be at the same emotional level of composure. Not so for the duke. He had freely shown her all he was feeling. And she feared she'd shown him a little of her repressed emotions too.

Long sighing gasps from Georgina and Katherine brought Ophelia's attention back to the present.

"What's wrong?" she asked, glancing from one friend to the other as they stared at something behind her.

Georgina placed her fan over her lips. "The Duke of Hurstbourne just entered the room."

Katherine leaned in and whispered, "And he's glancing around. No, wait." Her expressive eyes rounded and brightened excitedly. "I think he's looking at me."

"Don't be ridiculous," Georgina scolded. "You are too short for him to see enough of you to tell whether he'd be interested in you. He couldn't possibly see you in this crowd or any other. I, on the other hand, am tall enough."

As Ophelia listened to the two of them, she was wondering what had happened to Georgina's thoughts of the handsome Mr. Wilbur Sawyer.

"You cannot sway me with that comment, Georgina," Katherine snapped back at her. "I know that if I can see him, he can see me."

"Who told you that? I am tall enough and quite certain it's me who has caught his eye. He seemed quite taken with me last evening." She lifted her chin and chest and smiled.

Ophelia's gaze followed her new friends'. Her heartbeat seemed to flutter. Oh, yes. The Duke of Hurstbourne was looking in their direction. And it was no wonder they each thought he was considering them. To Ophelia, it appeared as if he was looking straight at her too! With such strong intensity a chill shivered up her back, but strangely not in a fearful way. She felt as if he was trying to draw her toward him, but surely he wouldn't recognize her. Her disguise had been excellent.

The duke stood just inside the doorway leading into the small ballroom of the private residence. Not only was her heart tossing around strange feelings, her breath caught in her throat, and her stomach clenched in an unexpected fluttery kind of way as it had when she saw him a couple of nights ago in his home.

It didn't seem to matter whether she was close to the duke as she'd been in his book room or across a crowded, noisy ballroom; he was an imposing man—tall, powerfully built through chest and shoulders, and magnificent in how he carried himself with such an easy air of self-confidence. She couldn't force herself to turn away from him at his home or now at this party.

His blond hair fell in a wispy wave across his forehead to just below his ears and an inch or two past his nape. Elegantly attired in a black evening coat and trousers with his shirt, neckcloth, and waistcoat an understated white, he was quite easily the most fine-looking man she'd ever seen. He stood with all the self-assured swagger she'd expect from a man of the elite and privileged ton.

She remembered his wide masculine lips, narrow nose, square chin, and clean-shaven face. Quite sure she would never forget it. With pale hair and the most heavenly shade of green eyes she'd ever seen, he had a rakish appeal that sent her heartbeat into an abnormally fast rhythm.

But whatever the reasons for the stirrings inside her whenever she saw the duke, she shouldn't be experiencing them. Ophelia wasn't accustomed to being attracted to a man. It made her feel flushed and out of sorts with her usual sensible self.

At such a dire disadvantage, a vicar's daughter trying to see a duke, it had taken all she could do to compose herself in his presence when she'd first walked into his book room.

She hadn't expected him to be so dashing and appealing that her heart raced at catching sight of him. Not only that, thinking the duke so attractive felt like a violation to her brother's memory. It was clear the man never felt the depth of friendship that Winston had for him. Her unsuccessful meeting with the duke at his house meant twice now His Grace had refused to help her brother when asked to do so.

It would rain gold from the heavens before she'd give him the opportunity for a third. But she couldn't worry about him anymore. She expected to hear from her mother's friend in Wickenhamden any day now the bishop had appointed a new vicar. That thought always caused a sinking feeling in her stomach.

Suddenly the duke was cutting a path through the guests with ease as he threaded through the crowded ballroom, seeming to know exactly whom to stop and speak to, whom to laugh with, which man to place his palm on a coat shoulder and give an encouraging pat on the back, and which young lady to give an extra smile. And looking genuine while doing it all.

For a second, it flashed through Ophelia's mind that he could have been hers. But he had said no to her brother. Surprised and miffed by the pang of disappointment that came from nowhere, she turned away. She had to remember that he wanted no part of her family's teetering ruin if she couldn't find the chalice before the theft was discovered. His help would have been so valuable. He would be a welcome visitor in most every house in the ton. He could have made her quest easier and quicker.

But unable to stop herself, she looked back at the duke again, a dashing figure of a man if there ever was one. That's when she knew, raining gold from the skies or not, she still closeted hope in her heart that he would help her find the thief.

Confident and glad for the distance between them, she silently prayed there was no chance he could have recognized her, and he was indeed staring at Miss Georgina Bristol.

Ophelia excused herself from the ladies and walked over to her mother. They moved away from the group she was with. "Maman, everyone's concentration seems to be on the Duke of Hurstbourne."

Roberta looked over her daughter's shoulder with interest. "My, yes," she said softly. "It is him. I haven't seen him since he was a young lad, but I would recognize him anywhere. He hasn't changed at all. He was handsome as a child and even more so now he's a young man."

Daring another glance in the duke's direction, it appeared he was being introduced to a petite young lady who incessantly waved a delicate fan across her face.

The man who Ophelia assumed was the lady's father was smiling from ear to ear—obviously at the attention she was receiving from the duke.

One good thing had come from her managing to have that private conversation with the duke in his home. It gave her more courage to do what had to be done.

"Did you forget how he treated Winston, Maman? The duke's answer to his letter was nothing more than a brush-off, and he never came to see him or write to inquire of his health."

"Pshaw," she answered, brushing the comment aside. "You can't hold that against him. Dukes are busy with important people to see and many business matters to attend to, as are most gentlemen. Drake, I mean the duke, was always so polite, and at times appeared to be older than his years. But he loved to engage in more than a bit of tomfoolery too." Roberta sighed. "If only he'd been interested when Winston had asked him to marry you."

Ophelia frowned. She wished her mother had never found that copy of the letter her brother wrote to the duke and shown it to her when they were going through Winston's correspondence after he passed.

However, she couldn't worry about that. She had other, more important things on her mind than remembering the letters exchanged between the duke and her brother.

"Maybe it would help if I spoke my disappointment to him."

Ophelia tended her bruised self-confidence with, "Maman, please don't consider doing that. I'm glad I escaped commitment to him. As my husband, he would have never agreed for me to search book rooms, and I would have been duty-bound to obey him. I'm glad Winston never told me what he was doing, so I didn't have to disappoint him by insisting he not contact the duke."

Roberta stared in the direction of the duke again. "Still, it might have been nice to have a duke in the family." Her mother gave her a bit of a teasing smile. "I, for one, appreciate Winston's effort to try to find you a husband. It was so like your brother to want to see that you were taken care of."

A thickening tightened in Ophelia's throat. "He always did." She swallowed down the sadness that suddenly wanted to overwhelm her and looked out over the crowded room, seeing merriment in every face hearing the lively music. "You and I have each other and will be fine without the duke, Maman. After we have successfully handled this problem, I'll secure a job as a governess and, between the two of us, we'll have an adequate income to lease a small house where I find employment so we can visit often. Right now, I think this is a good time for me to slip out of the ballroom unnoticed."

Roberta nodded and settled her gaze back on her daughter. "I worry about your plan, dear. And you know it's not just that I see all your upbringing flying out the window, though that is disheartening."

"Don't worry." She reached over and gave her mother a quick buss on the cheek and a deep-breathed smile, hoping to ease the tension she saw creeping around her mother's eyes and her own unease about her plan. "I know what to do, remember. If a servant sees me, I'll say I managed to get turned around and I'm lost. If the master of the house catches me in his book room, I'll tell the truth: It's my first time in London, and I've never been in a house so large. I couldn't stop looking at all the grandeur."

Roberta let out a breathy sigh with a smile. "Are you sure there is no way other than placing yourself through the possibility of defending your actions?"

"Maman," Ophelia said, sounding a little more frustrated than she intended. "I need to go. Promise me you won't worry."

Her watery blue eyes glistened. "I can't do that, my darling girl."

Ophelia took hold of her mother's hand and lightly squeezed. "All right then. Worry with a smile on your face while you continue to renew your friendships, and don't forget to casually ask every one of them if they know anyone who collects artifacts. I'll return shortly."

Trying not to appear as if she was in a hurry, Ophelia left her mother's side and walked gingerly toward the vestibule, nodding and greeting the people she passed along the way. She wasn't normally the type to be afraid, but she'd be a fool not to be a little apprehensive. That would help her to be cautious. If anyone suspected she was searching book rooms for a stolen item, she and her mother would be tossed out of Society before they could blink.

From a book she'd read on how to catch a thief she remembered that book rooms were usually laid out to the left of the entrance and at the back of the house. Since this home was larger than any other home she'd ever been in, that bit of information was useful. Furthermore, she also learned large homes had advantages, plenty of places to hide if ever necessary.

The corridor was dimly lit, but she strolled down the length of it with her arms and hands hanging calmly by her sides when what she wanted to do was tighten her fingers into a nervous fist. She must act as if she knew exactly where she was going so no one in this section of the house would have reason to question her.

At a junction in the corridors, sounds of voices and silverware clinking came from one direction, but it was quiet as a mouse down the other. After a few more moments of hesitation, she shored up her courage and headed away from the noise, carefully peeking into each room as she passed.

Halfway down the next corridor she stopped, thinking she'd heard someone behind her, but when she looked, the passageway was clear. The sounds of tinkling glassware couldn't be heard either. All was quiet.

Truth to tell, she had little evidence to go on in her search, but she couldn't let that stop her. Fortunately for her, because of unforeseen reasons, Mrs. Turner, the maid who had seen the suspected thief, had traveled to London with them. The odd vicar suddenly decided to turn off all who worked at the vicarage and hire new employees. He wouldn't say why, but Ophelia assumed it had something to do with the sickness that had him so skittish. Feeling bad the staff were dismissed without real cause, she and her maman hired the three of them, even though their household funds were already stretched tight.

Mrs. Turner was positive the suspect had talked at length with Winston a week before his illness escalated so quickly and that he had taken the man into the storage room, presumably to look at the chalice. She had overheard the man telling Winston about religious artifacts he'd collected and kept on a shelf in his book room. The same way some people were obsessed with collecting rare books or paintings, Ophelia supposed. Because they could.

Mrs. Turner never got a good look at his face, but she was certain the man returned a day or two before Winston passed. That day as the man was leaving, she heard him call up to his driver, "*To my home in London!*" as he entered the carriage.

At the end of the corridor on the left, Ophelia found the master of the house's book room in the approximate place the *thief* book has suggested it should be. Stepping inside the spacious area with its distinguished, masculine appeal and rows of shelving made her stomach feel hollow and jumpy about what she had to do. Her courage cooled. It didn't feel right to look over someone's possessions without their knowledge. But what else was she to do? Her aim was to not disturb anything but to accomplish what she came to do and leave without anyone knowing she'd been there.

She sucked in a deep breath, and in a quick sweeping glance, she took note of the beautifully carved wood casings and cornice boards throughout, an expensively made desk, dark-blue velvet draperies, and plush, overly stuffed leather wing chairs. But mostly, she looked at what had to be thousands of books covering three walls. She couldn't imagine the purpose in having a countless number. No one could ever read that many even if they lived to a very old age.

A low-burning fire had warmed the room to a toasty temperature and lamps were lit. From the guide on catching a thief, she knew both were usually a signal that meant someone was due to come back soon. She should hurry.

She went immediately to the bookshelves hoping to find the one she had been told about. Her eyes scanned each shelf nippily and easily from top to bottom. Nothing but books arrayed these shelves. Tall books, little books, skinny ones, and short fat ones. Some with gold trim and fancy writing, others black with plain lettering. More than a few of the bound volumes looked brand-new and never opened, while others seemed old and worn. But to her appeal, they all seemed to have that call to adventure that seemed to say to Ophelia, *Open me and see what's inside.*

Disappointed she didn't find a shelf filled with relics on her first search, she looked more carefully at tables sitting around the room. All had pieces of what looked to be fine porcelains, silver bowls, vases, figurines, or other things on them. In one area there were tablets of marble carved with various Greek gods on them. She walked over and started examining the exquisite items more carefully and noticed a small silver goblet and picked it up for a closer look.

It appeared old and quite valuable, with the exquisite patterning of a tavern scene on the cup. Someone who collected pieces like this might have a fetish for religious objects too. She needed to look closer at the—

"Excuse me, miss," came a challenging masculine voice from the doorway. "You must be lost."

Sweet merciful heavens, Ophelia thought as a breathless wave of frightening surprise washed over her, and she froze.

She had known that there was a good possibility she would be caught on her very first attempt at doing something so blatantly wrong. And somehow that seemed unfair because of her reasonings for doing the deed. And not only that, but the familiarity of the man's voice tingled pleasurably through her as she recognized who it was that had discovered her.

But the wonder was, would the duke remember hers?

CHAPTER 5

MAN'S PRACTICAL GUIDE TO APPREHENDING A THIEF
SIR BENTLY ASHTON ULLINGSWICK

Stalk the suspect carefully without him knowing.

Hurst had seen her across the distance of the lively ballroom floor almost as soon as he'd stepped up to the entrance. She had a familiarity that drew his interest more than he could adequately define, although he was sure he'd never met her before. He would have remembered.

As he studied her from the doorway, he couldn't quell the thought that he must have been introduced to her. But where? When? Recently, for certain. There was something about her that stirred him as she stood under a chandelier with other ladies; he was sure they'd met at a party last night. Her shoulders were straight but not stiff. Her chin was high but not haughty. A tier of lush golden curls swept up attractively into a fashionable chignon and shimmered enticingly under the dancing candlelight, giving her an angelic look that attracted him immensely.

The feeling was more than just one of awareness or that sensation of being swept off his feet. It was as if somehow deep in his soul he knew she was the lady he'd been waiting for. Which was absurd since he had no idea who she was. Too, it was irrational, and he was as rational as a person could be. He'd always had to be. His father made certain of that. Furthermore, she could be married. Betrothed. Or a figment of his imagination. Maybe he'd just had too much brandy before coming to the ball.

Did he believe in love at first sight? Maybe. He certainly knew there could be instant attraction between two people. No doubt every lady could tell when a man noticed her with interest just as every man knew when a woman had interest in him.

He really didn't know what to think about how she was making him feel. It was inexplicable. For quite some time, Hurst had felt he'd know the lady he wanted to spend the rest of his life with when he met her, but not before they'd said a word to each other. That was further than he was willing to go. Nevertheless, the longer he stood in the doorway, the more intrigued he allowed his feelings to become. He wanted to get closer to her and find out if she was indeed the one.

When he'd stepped into the ballroom and started toward her, he was besieged by men wanting to say hello or introduce him to their daughters or someone else. With as much refinement as he could muster given his mission, he managed to say a few words with each person and gently shake off first one and then other guests. But as someone peeled away, another took his place. He lost sight of her for a time as he continued through the crowd of people vying for his attention. When he drew near to where she'd been, she'd started walking away. Alone.

There was nothing to do but follow her. Back to the vestibule, down a darkened corridor, and around a corner. After another turn, she disappeared into what Hurst knew was Wyatt's book room.

Hurst paused. Why was she going in there? Was she meeting someone? A man? In secret? He didn't want to think about that being the case. Not yet. He hadn't settled that strange feeling inside that said she was meant to be his. And, he wasn't certain he should be encouraging it by following her. But forgetting about wanting to know who she was didn't feel right either. Soundlessly, he eased farther down the corridor, making sure his shoes made silent treads.

At the open doorway, he quietly leaned his hip against the framing and slowly peered around into the interior of the room. She was at the far end with her back to him. No one was with her. The simple high-waisted design of her blue gown with capped sleeves falling softly off her shoulders was fetching. Her nape was slender and alluring with small tendrils of golden spun hair gracing her nape.

Pushing away from the door, he said, "Excuse me, miss. You must be lost."

He was sure she had heard him. She went still. Seconds ticked by and she didn't turn around. Maybe she was meeting someone after all and his voice wasn't the one she was expecting. She obviously needed time to collect herself, and he was all right with that. Ladies should always be cautious.

She hesitated so long he was beginning to think she wasn't going to answer him but then turned and focused directly on his face. In that brief instant, he knew immediately who she was. His heart pounded. There was another gut-wrenching moment when he felt she *was* the lady he'd been waiting for. That couldn't possibly be. He'd already turned her down. Sight unseen.

"I'm not lost, Your Grace."

At the sound of her gentle voice, he took a few steps farther into the room. His gaze tightened in on her fathomless blue eyes, pert nose, and pink rosebud lips. There was no doubt she and the lady who came to his house dressed as a man were one and the same, though she looked entirely different tonight, dressed properly and stunning as Miss Ophelia Stowe.

It wasn't a wonder she'd seemed so familiar with how she carried herself when he first caught a glimpse of her. But what about the other feelings he'd experienced deep in his chest and gut? That she wasn't just another beautiful belle to spend a little enjoyable time with, but she was the *one* for him.

No. She couldn't possibly be. Not someone who would sneak into his home clothed as a man, ask him to pry around in people's homes in search of a relic, and now seemed to be pilfering through his best friend's home. That was troublesome. So no, she wasn't the lady *he'd* been waiting for.

"You have no reason to be in here, Miss Stowe."

"So, you do recognize me. I wondered if you would."

Oh, yes. Her soft lilting voice and vivid blue eyes would be difficult for anyone to forget. "What's that in your hand?" he asked tersely.

She looked at the small silver goblet and then placed it on the table beside her. "Nothing I'm interested in, but I do have cause to be here, Your Grace. I was invited to this party."

Frowning, he hoped he'd talked her out of this nonsense when she was at his home. Her proposal to search all the book rooms of the elite of the ton was absolute madness.

"Specifically," he said, remaining between her and the doorway, letting her know she wouldn't get past him if she suddenly tried to leave. "What exactly are you doing in this room?"

"Why do you ask?" she answered crisply, but remained calm as a tepid, windless July day.

"I want to know. Apparently, you forgot something in your haste to snare a criminal—a chaperone to protect you against a man like me."

Hesitancy marred her forehead, as if she took him at his word. "You do not frighten me, Your Grace."

"I should." He cocked his head back.

Her gaze stayed intensely on his as a not-so-innocent and highly attractive blush spread across her petal-soft cheeks.

Was she too stubborn to admit the truth or was she trying to think of an answer he might accept? He didn't like the idea of either one. "You are, aren't you?"

"What?"

"Up to mischief," he responded. "I distinctly told you not to carry out such a far-fetched plan as to search houses."

"I am under no vows or orders to obey you."

"Do you really think a member of the ton would be so brazen as to steal a religious artifact from a church?"

"I don't know. You have no cause to question me about what I am doing in here. Since you are so full of queries and wanting answers, why don't you tell me why you came to this room?" she managed to ask with a good bit of glowering confidence. "Perhaps I should think you are up to mischief."

He squared his shoulders. "I was following you."

"Me?" That seemed to take her aback for a moment or two. She raked a hand up her long white glove and innocently asked, "Why?"

"To see where you were going," he admitted so casually she had to know he had no guilt for doing so.

"Do you often do such questionable things, sir? Follow ladies?"

She took a cautious step back. For show, he was sure.

There was no fear of him in her expression. She was undoubtably clever and far too brave for her own good. Not to mention more incredibly daring than he'd previously thought her to be.

"No, Miss Stowe. I'm certain I never have until tonight, but I'm glad I did."

"That makes it sound as if you are the one who is up to no good, Your Grace. Following a lady down a dark corridor and cornering her in a room is unseemly."

He gave her a knowing smile, impressed she could hold her own so well under his questioning. In truth, he would have never expected it of a vicar's daughter. They were supposed to be sweet, humble, and shy. And while her fortitude captivated him, it also irritated the devil out of him.

"I think prying in a private area of Wyatt's house, and in a room where ladies seldom enter if not invited, wins the battle of who is the bad person here, Miss Stowe."

"I beg your pardon, sir." Her tone dripped with indignation. "I am not prying. I am merely looking around at all the lovely pieces he has on display—I assume for one's enjoyment. That is not bad."

"You had to be rifling through his things. You were holding one of his cups." He regarded her with another intense gaze. Her gumption was boundless. He pointed to the table where she placed the silver piece she'd been holding.

"Rifling? Prying? What nerve you have. You are not choosing your words carefully, Your Grace. I am merely looking at this fine collection of porcelains, silver, and what looks to be marbles from the Parthenon. Perhaps the Duke of Wyatthaven went on an expedition to Greece with Lord Elgin and picked up a few of the ancient marbles for himself." She nodded toward the area that displayed the precious tablets and then glanced quickly around the shelves again.

"Say what you will about Lord Elgin, he probably deserves your ill thoughts, but watch what you say when you are talking about Wyatthaven." Hurst had kept his voice low but quietly steamed inside at her nerve.

"I am only talking about what is easily exhibited to be seen. There are three fortunes in books in this room alone. Perhaps the Duke of Wyatthaven collects other things as well. Paintings or perhaps religious vessels."

"You think Wyatt stole the chalice you are searching for?" Hurst was astonished that she would say such a thing out loud about a duke. And to another duke. She had gone too far.

"Obviously, I don't know who stole it, so I have to consider everyone," she responded in an annoyed tone.

"Well, I know who didn't." He fixed her with a cold stare as he walked closer to her but stopped a respectable distance away, still between her and the door. "Wyatt has been my good friend close to twenty years. He doesn't have what you are looking for."

"Not that I can see," she admitted evenly. "Your book room wasn't filled with priceless treasures such as these."

"That's because the previous Dukes of Hurstbourne never bought any."

The more she said, the more heated he became. "You are a vicar's daughter," he reminded her. "I knew your father, brother, and mother. You must have been raised better than to plunder someone's home for something that may or may not be lost. I can't believe you would stoop to doing this."

Obviously knowing what he was implying, her chin lifted, her body stiffened, and she glared at his implication. "I am also a vicar's sister," she answered just as controlled as he'd spoken. "Who, by the way, needs help because someone stole a precious item under his watch. I will find it and return it for him even if I must spend the rest of my life in prison after I do."

"Chances are you'll be there before you find it if you continue this madcap path you are on. They won't take kindly to that, Miss Stowe, and neither do I. Furthermore, how will you help your brother from deep within a prison?"

"I don't expect to go," she answered as quickly as he'd spoken, looking anxious and adamant. "At least I am doing something, and right now it is the only thing I know to do in the short amount of time I have."

"What would you have done if someone other than me had followed you in here?"

"Exactly what you accused me of." A hasty puff of air passed her lips as she continued to stare crossly at him. "Much as it would bother me to do so, I would pretend to be lost. Disoriented. Perhaps even faint in hopes of gaining sympathy."

"Faint?"

A brief smile touched her lips, and he felt as if his stomach flipped over.

He frowned, even though he found her comment immensely amusing and wanted to belt out a good laugh. "You don't have a weak bone in your spine, and you know it."

He didn't like admitting it, but there was a charm about her that pleased him. He wondered if she had any idea she could have him under her spell if she tried to entice him instead of irritating him at every turn.

"I suppose that fainting was a bit far-fetched," she admitted without a pinch of arrogance in her tone.

Indeed, he thought, finding her so much more attractive than he'd wanted to. He could be enamored with her, but it simply wasn't possible she was the lady he'd been waiting for.

"In any case, I don't intend to share all my plans with you," she went on after another brief smile. "However, I will say my best excuse is it's my first time in London and I've never seen such luxurious homes. I inadvertently wandered away from the ballroom. But with the splendid beauty, I couldn't help myself. Even the ceilings are worthy of attention with their design of wood casings, fretwork, and paintings. I enjoy reading and bear no shame for wanting to see the book room with its smells of aged books, pipe tobacco, lamp oil, and burned wood."

She looked so innocent and expressively convincing as she spoke, a crack of a smile touched his lips as well. If she weren't in essence accusing his best friend of theft, she'd be delightful.

"You are a spitfire, Miss Stowe."

She gave a slight shrug of her shoulders and glanced around the room again. "No, but I do wonder if the duke might collect other things. The pieces he has in here are truly extraordinary."

It was as if this beautiful, intriguing young lady was deliberately trying to anger him and get the better of him. If so, she wasn't far from reaching her goal.

"We will settle this once and for all right now, Miss Stowe." Hurst moved to stand almost toe-to-toe with her and immediately realized that was a mistake. He caught the enticing scent of her sweet womanly perfume. It teased his senses and tempted him to forget what he was going to say and, instead, gather her into his arms, snuggle her to him, and tease the warmth of her neck with kisses. Hurst blinked that image away and pushed such thoughts to the back of his mind.

Denying the pull of her attraction and leaning in closer, he said, "Wyatt doesn't collect anything but winnings when he plays in matches for his sporting club. Most of these artifacts were amassed by his grandfather." Though tense, he lowered his voice. "I'm going to tell you what I know your brother would say if he were still with us: Searching homes must stop."

She remained strong against his closeness, but he knew it wasn't easy for her when he saw her swallow hard before replying, "I'm not one to back down from something simply because it is difficult, Your Grace. If you'll remember, you refused to help me."

"You are damned right; I did. For your own good."

Her arched brows shot up, but there was no way he was going to apologize for his language. And she might hear worse before their conversation was over.

"You are searching Wyatt's home. A man who has never wanted anything in his life but to win his wife's love. Which he finally did. He had a hospital built for military men wounded fighting Napoleon's army and he fully supports it with an inheritance he received and his winnings from the Brass Deck, his sporting club. The last thing he'd have his eyes set on would be a religious artifact that would be important to believing people."

Settling her shoulders a little lower was her only concession to the point she might have been wrong. "We will leave it that we are on opposite sides of the subject concerning the missing chalice and what I should do about finding it. I think we should peacefully go our separate ways. You don't bother me, and I won't bother you. I will agree what I seek is not in this house."

But she did bother him in ways he tried not to think about. Hurst couldn't agree they peacefully go separate paths. Somehow, she was connected to him in a manner that had nothing to do with Winston or the chalice.

"I am a realistic man. What you are attempting is not only dangerous, but it's like looking for your hairpin in a stack of hay. I don't want to see you in any kind of jeopardy for this perilous behavior. Whoever stole the chalice from the church has probably sold it to someone in the dark underground world of London by now and it's on its way to a wealthy collector in India or the Americas."

He watched her suck in a deep silent breath. Her brow wrinkled in disbelief before it softened and morphed into concern. The truth of what he'd said wasn't something she'd wanted to hear. It bothered him that his pronouncement had hurt, disappointed, or at least worried her, but it was true and had to be said.

"I won't believe that." Her voice was soft, somber, and inflected with sad truth. "I was told the man had made reference he desired it for his own collection."

The way she reacted to his words caused Hurst to relax. He needed to do something to let her know he wasn't the ogre she'd thought him to be. Not all the time anyway. Causing her pain wasn't what he wanted to do. He hadn't wanted to crush her spirit, but what she was doing could easily get her into more trouble than he could get her out of if she were caught. Whether or not he should, he felt responsible for her.

"Your disguise last week was cleverly put together. I would have never guessed you had blond hair." He kept his voice low, persuasive. "It was astute of you to wear a dark wig and darken your brows too."

She responded to his softer tone by easing the tightness of her shoulders. "I had excellent help from my maid and her brother, who is an apprentice at a tailor's shop."

"My bet is that he will own the shop one day. His workmanship is superb."

Miss Stowe's eyes brightened. "I thought so too. I'll be sure to tell him about the compliment, but I won't tell him who it came from."

He gave her a slight nod. "But there is something—" He reached over and brushed his thumb across her eyebrow and then swept down and did the same at the edge of her chin.

Swiping his hand away, she stepped back. Scowling, she demanded, "What are you doing?"

He gave her a playful smile as he admired her strength. "You didn't get all the kohl off your face when you washed. I was merely assisting in its removal."

She gasped and quickly wiped the places he had touched with her fingertips, exclaiming, "That can't be true. I've washed many times since then. You, sir, are no gentleman!"

"Why would any of my friends or peers want a religious relic? Do we look that angelic?" He gave her another smile. "I've honed my devilish charm ever since I left school. Don't tell me that I've failed, Miss Stowe."

"I assure you, you have not," she agreed, wiping the corner of her mouth. "You have been more of a rake than a hero since the moment I walked into your book room."

"I'll take that as a compliment, and you best remember that most men are."

"Thankfully, you're the only rake I've ever met."

Hurst chuckled at her answer. "That is doubtful but good to hear you think so." When he put aside what she was trying to do to unsuspecting people, he found her delightfully enticing to be with. "Does your mother know what you are up to?"

"Most of it," she hedged. "Not all."

"Does she approve?"

"Of course not. The entirety of everything that has happened hit her hard and she is ill over it, sometimes sending her to a sickbed for a few days."

"Yet, she allows you to do this?"

"She accepts that there is nothing more we can do but try to prevent what we know will happen if it becomes known to the bishop and parish the chalice is missing." Ophelia paused and swallowed hard. "I don't have much time. If word gets out, Maman is fearful the neighbors will come to see her asking if it was Winston. The elders or bishop could start knocking on our door, wanting to search us, wondering if we were a party to the crime."

"That sounds irrational, Miss Stowe."

"I don't have to be rational, Your Grace. I need to be successful. There are other concerns. Donations would go down without the renowned sacrament. Maman fears neighbors may start sneaking into the back garden and harass her with questions she has no answers for. They could start following her in the village. She continues to worry more and more for something she has no control over."

That was easy to believe. He knew from experience when he was growing up that there was nothing some neighbors loved more than trying to solve something they'd considered a mystery.

"I've been gone a long time and need to get back to Maman."

With good reason, he thought. Miss Stowe was strong, seductive, and he hadn't seen an ounce of fear in her. Keeping his voice husky but not dangerous, he said, "I think I should escort you to the ballroom to make sure you don't get into more trouble along the way."

"Walking into a room with you would damage my

reputation as much as it would to be caught in here alone with you. I have no desire for scandal of any kind, Your Grace, and assume you are not seeking to be stranded on the edge of a parson's mousetrap with me."

"Such an arrangement doesn't appeal to me." But strange as it was, given the mischief-making she was attempting to do, she appealed to him. More than any other lady ever had. And more and more he thought he knew why. "I don't want to see your reputation have a glimmer of blemish. For any reason. We agree on that. However, it's not only permissible for a man to make sure a young lady finds her way safely back to the party, but his duty."

"Duty?" Her shoulders lifted and her expression turned from apprehensive to disbelieving. "That is an unwelcome word coming from you, Your Grace. For not wanting to meet me before you refused to marry me, for never coming to visit Winston even though he loved you as a brother, for not seeing the importance of finding the chalice to save his reputation, and for my mother's shame should her son be branded a thief, consider any obligation you might have for me fulfilled."

"That is a long list of recriminations for me to live down, Miss Stowe."

"Impossible, I'd say, and I probably left something out." She pinioned him with her blue gaze. "My brother was a man of honor who devoted his life to his calling. I will do everything within my power to see he is not blamed for something I know he did not do. I'm sorry you didn't get to see how he grew from the boy you once knew to the fine man he was."

Miss Stowe left no stone unturned. He had only one answer. "I pray one day you will accept my apologies that I didn't get to do that."

"I might well, if I thought your prayer sincere, Your

Grace. From some of your language and temperament, I'm not sure you've been well-versed in the ways of the church."

A soft rumble of laughter passed his lips. "I've known piety a Sunday or two and, as a lad, shared some of them with your brother."

She managed a bit of a smile. "I am willing to risk my life to keep Winston's legacy intact. If you can't help me with the difficult things I need to do, I certainly don't need you for something as simple as finding my way back to the ballroom."

CHAPTER 6

MAN'S PRACTICAL GUIDE TO APPREHENDING A THIEF
SIR BENTLY ASHTON ULLINGSWICK

Never get caught between purpose and property.

Sighing her frustration, Ophelia placed her sketching pencil on the dining room table and stretched out her fingers and shoulders from hunching over the drawings. It had taken longer than she'd expected to turn Mrs. Turner's remembrances into a semblance of a family crest. What she thought might take only an hour had turned into several. She glanced at the pile of sheets she'd discarded in an attempt to come up with the usable ones she had. In their disarray it looked like hundreds, but she was sure it wasn't that many.

Ophelia didn't have the finest of drawing skills, but she'd managed to draft four possible crests from details the maid was able to provide about the suit of armor, the birds, and the swirls that anchored each side like brackets. The problem was there were many different types of armor from different centuries and, as Mrs. Turner had said, many different birds looked alike too.

It wasn't the maid's fault she couldn't remember more about the titled man or the crest that was on his carriage door. To her, all titled men looked the same, all birds had wings and beaks, and all armor looked alike. Ophelia had to agree that at no more than a glance, the top of a pike could resemble the top of a stalk of wheat. But what else could she do right now but try to create a likeness of the crest?

She took a bracing breath, stood up, and looked at the shy, petite woman with a mobcap covering her hair and a bit of her thinning light-brown eyebrows too. The maid started to rise.

"No, Mrs. Turner. Stay where you are. I need you a little longer. Now that we've finished, I'm going to lay all four drawings in front of you so you can see them all at once. Close your eyes and relax. Focus. Remember what you saw that day and then look at the drawings. When you are sure, let me know which sketch most represents the one you recall seeing on the carriage door."

"I'm not sure which one does," she answered, rubbing her hands together slowly.

"There's no reason for you to hurry," Ophelia said patiently, though she was feeling far from it. "Just try."

Mrs. Turner's small eyes widened. "Like I told you, miss. They are all good to me."

Ophelia tried to keep her smile from appearing as weary as she felt. "But they are all distinctive in small ways. Just take your time and study them in detail. I'm going to walk over to the window so I won't disturb you by standing over your shoulder. It will give you time to concentrate."

Mrs. Turner gave her an unsure nod. "I'll do my best."

Ophelia massaged the back of her neck as she made her way over to look out at the budding kitchen garden.

It was by chance she had the idea to sketch what the maid saw so they could both visualize it better. Once Mrs. Turner made her decision, all Ophelia had to do was get her hands on a volume of *Debrett's Peerage and Baronetage* to find the full coat of arms that best matched the crest. That should give her the family name of the man who'd entered the church to view the chalice and then later, she believed, returned to steal it. Once that was accomplished, she'd find a way to get into his house and show the Duke of Hurstbourne she hadn't needed his help after all. In fact, she relished the thought of telling him.

How dare he insist she stop just because it was dangerous, difficult—and perhaps wrong—to search someone's home without their knowledge. It wasn't like she'd wanted to take anything that didn't rightly belong to the church. Ophelia couldn't give up her search no matter how much the deeply intriguing duke had urged her to do so, or how consuming the task became. That's why she was in London. Every day brought her closer to the possibility someone would discover the chalice was missing.

It was true she'd never learned to maintain the piety level of composure that her father, mother, and brother had insisted was required of a man of the cloth *and* his family, but she had learned to temper her emotions and stay calm whenever she was with them. Most of the time. Certainly not when she was with the exasperating Duke of Hurstbourne. He had a way of bringing every one of her tamped-down emotions roaring to life. Good, bad, and decidedly feminine ones, which oddly she'd found invigorating.

Recalling that caused her to remember his charming smile as he'd made conversation with the young lady in the ballroom who kept fanning her face. Later he looked dashing in his evening attire when he folded his strong arms over his broad chest, emphasizing his splendid body as he protested her hint that the Duke of Wyatthaven might have an interest in religious relics. That had unquestionably displeased him. She didn't mind. At least she knew exactly how he felt. She liked that he was loyal to his friends.

Along with all her feelings, she was dismayed too. Even more so because thoughts of the duke were always creeping into her mind at the oddest times. When she was trying to read or sleep. While she was drinking her warm, deliciously sweetened chocolate. Even now when she wanted to concentrate on something so important as finding the chalice, that man had become a hazard to her peace of mind.

Because of him, Ophelia had been gone so long from the ballroom last night, her mother was close to fainting when she returned. Roberta had worked herself into a dither fearing Ophelia had been caught and detained by a member of the household. They had left the party right away. Which was fine with Ophelia. She had no desire to stay and participate in the trappings of the marriage mart, but she had taken time to say goodbye to Georgina and Katherine while her mother waited for their wraps. The young ladies had been good to accept her so quickly into their lives.

Ophelia heard Mrs. Turner's chair push away from the table and turned around.

"This is the one, miss," the maid said with a broad smile and her finger pressed on top of one of the drawings. "This bird is most like the one I saw for sure. The bird, and pikeman's armor looks the same too."

"All right, good." Ophelia looked at the one she pointed to, and her spirits lifted. It was the one Mrs. Turner seemed most comfortable with when she was describing the bird, breastplate, and helmet. "You've been a tremendous help."

"Excuse me, miss."

Ophelia turned to see the footman standing in the doorway of the dining room. "Yes, Mr. Mallord?"

He stepped farther into the room. "I thought I might see if you planned to use your carriage this afternoon. I could go ask the driver to have it ready for you so you wouldn't have to wait."

"Thank you, Mr. Mallord. That's considerate of you, but I won't be needing it. Maman is too tired from the party we attended last evening to do anything today." Ophelia looked at Mrs. Turner. "And thank you too. You've been so helpful. I'll let you both know if I need anything else."

The footman looked down at the drawings and then up at Ophelia and smiled before walking away.

Ophelia picked up the pencil and drew a star in the corner of the sketch the maid chose. Not that she was likely to forget, but it seemed the prudent thing to do. She stacked the four sheets of thick parchment together, thinking she should keep every one for now. Even perhaps have Mrs. Turner have another look at them again in a few hours. For now, the best place for them would be a drawer in the secretary.

She collected all the sketching materials and made her way to the drawing room, eager to show the crests and share the good news with her mother when she came belowstairs. In the meantime, Ophelia would look around for something to keep the sketches in.

The small leased house was well equipped with almost anything they needed. She hoped to find an empty packet or portfolio, or perhaps a large folder, where she could keep the sheets safely together. It would be too exhausting to replicate them.

To her disappointment, every drawer in the desk was empty. Ophelia then started looking in the chests, cabinets, and side tables placed around the perimeter. The last chest to be inspected had been placed in front of a window between two chairs on the back wall. It wasn't a tall or wide cabinet, so she bent down, opened the double doors, and spread them wide. Peering inside, she quickly saw it was as bare as all the others, but something seemed a little peculiar about it. The rear panel appeared buckled. She wondered if perhaps time or water had warped it. Her curiosity piqued, she took out the shelving and looked carefully, realizing it had a false back that hadn't been properly secured. How clever. She had heard of such things but had never actually seen one.

She pondered if someone had accidentally left anything in the hiding place. Perhaps it was still there. The possibility made her smile and heightened her interest.

Lifting the hem of her skirt, she knelt on both knees in front of it and reached inside. She couldn't quite touch the back panel but was too engrossed to give up, so she stuck her head inside and wiggled one shoulder and then the other a little at a time into the chest until she could reach the panel. She hammered at the corners with the bottom of her fist and one of the top corners popped loose.

Delighted she was making progress, she pushed, pulled, and tugged at the board trying to remove it. Obviously, there was a trick to doing it the proper way, and she was determined to find it. With the heel of her hand, she banged it dead center, and the panel popped loose, almost falling on top of her head. It was a secret compartment, but it was as empty as all the others.

"Miss Stowe," she heard Mrs. Turner squeal from behind her. "I don't know what you're doing, but I should be doing that for you."

"No. I am fine," she answered from inside the cabinet, doing her best to pop the backing on the same way it had come off. "I don't need your help. Carry on with whatever you were doing."

"I wanted to tell you the Duke of Hurstbourne is here and asked if you wanted to receive him, but he followed me in here."

Clunk!

Merciful heavens!

Ophelia knocked her head on the inside top of the chest and conked an elbow on the side in a hurry to try to get out.

In the name of all the saints living and dead, what was the duke doing at her house? And of all times! Her head was stuck in the cabinet and her derriere was sticking out of it.

What nerve the man had to come into her drawing room without an invitation. All her decorous upbringing was for naught in the face of her predicament. A sense of dismay swamped her. How could she ever live down how she presented herself right now?

There was no uncomplicated way out. She started trying to back out on her knees but in her haste couldn't get both shoulders out of the chest at the same time. Going in was definitely easier.

But then Ophelia sensed the duke kneeling beside her. She felt his warmth at what she assumed was his knee grazing against her upper thigh before resting on the floor so close to her. From his movements, the air stirred with the smell of his woodsy shaving soap scent and she trembled when hearing his low husky chuckle.

"What kind of pickle have you gotten yourself into, Miss Stowe?" he asked lightly.

"Nothing that I can't get out of, Your Grace," she answered defensively, hoping her voice didn't reveal just how flustered she was. "If you would be so kind as to excuse yourself from the room." Then, unable to help herself, she managed to reach behind her and swat him, feeling her hand connected somewhere on his face.

The duke grunted. "Hold still and I will help you." He reached into the chest and cupped the back of her head at the very moment she lifted it and heard his knuckles crack against the edge of the opening. She heard another sound from him.

The duke muttered an impatient oath. Obviously, he wasn't thrilled she hadn't acquiesced to his demand. "You can't do this on your own, Miss Stowe. Relax, and I will get you out."

"No, I need you to go away," she responded in a confident but muffled voice, refusing to give in to his offer of help and only wanting him to leave so she could find a way out of her predicament.

"I can't do that. You're moving but not getting anywhere," he argued exasperatedly.

"Sweet mercy, Your Grace, I know that," she whispered, unable to believe what was happening, but then she felt his palms press on the back of her shoulders. His fingers came around the tops of her arms and gently squeezed. She felt his strength, his command of her situation, and realized how vulnerable she was to him. Not because she was captured by the chest, but the way his touch gave her delicious feelings inside.

Weary, and somehow comforted too, she had no choice but to give in to his help. She wormed from side to side as he pushed down on first one shoulder with his gentle strength and then the other, helping to work her out of the chest.

"Don't rush, Miss Stowe," he said in a soothing tone that made her know his lips were just above her ear. "Take your time or you will be black-and-blue with bruises."

There was something reassuring about what he was doing, the way he was handling her with tenderness, and how softly he was speaking so that she felt compelled to obey and offer no further opposition. The trembling inside her subsided.

Just when she thought she had cleared the offending cabinet, the crown of her hair caught in the center hinge that held the double doors together at the top and she was once again snared.

Ophelia stretched up to untangle her hair at the same time the duke reached to help. It was their fingers that caught and wove together. A tantalizing shiver of more tingles washed up and down her spine. His warm breath fanned closer to her temple.

"Should I get Mrs. Stowe to help?" Mrs. Turner asked excitedly from behind them.

"No," they said in unison.

The duke leaned farther over her nape, causing his muscle-hard chest to press against her back. She was aware of his every breath as he whispered softly, "Let me help you."

Let me help you.

Those were the words she'd longed to hear him say from her first thoughts of seeking him out. For a fleeting moment it was as if her dream had come true. The duke was going to help her find the chalice so Winston's legacy wouldn't be damaged. For a moment she soaked in his words and relished the prospect of his help.

But rational thoughts invaded, her fantasy faded quickly, and she stifled a groan. That wasn't what he meant. He only wanted to free her hair—not her brother from the threat of being labeled a thief. Her pride was in shambles, and her head sore. Her elbow was hurting.

She once again surrendered and accepted the only help he was offering.

Inhaling deeply as her fingers fell away from his, she lowered her arms and remained still as possible. It wasn't easy. His touch was tender and welcomed as seemingly strand by strand he took his time.

"Your hair feels like silk, Miss Stowe."

"That's very kind of you, but I hope this will be over soon."

He chuckled so softly she wasn't even sure it was one. But at last, she felt the final tug and she was freed to face him without a pinpoint of pain as she straightened.

With them still on their knees in front of each other, a sense of anticipation erupted inside her. She lifted her head and met his amazing green eyes. They were filled with lively sparkles of interest as he stared into hers. His penetrating gaze made her heartbeat pound harder in her ears and something delicious tingle inside her.

That now familiar fluttering started in her chest as it so often did when she looked at him or simply thought of him. Heat flared into her cheeks as awakening feelings of desire sprouted and blossomed like a rose unfurling its petals. She remembered the calming words, the quiet power of his hand and gentleness of his fingers. She wanted to feel that again.

He leaned toward her, moving his face closer and closer to hers. It felt as if she were taking every breath he took as his lips descended toward hers. The thought he was going to kiss her flashed across her mind as swift as a lightning strike.

What should she do?

She was attracted to this man. Desirous feelings of excitement were bursting all over her. The problem was she wasn't worldly enough to know how to act upon them or what to do about all she was experiencing. This wasn't one of the things that had been a part of her extensive education.

Ophelia had always expected her first stirrings of that ethereal feeling of passion for a man would be for a modestly clothed, doe-eyed, gently spoken man much like her father and brother.

But she'd never thought about the possibility of being attracted to the most irritating, brash, and handsome man in all of England. Probably the world too. And a duke at that. She loved the feelings she was having and wanted more of them. There was no doubt she was thinking about the real possibility of him kissing her right now. On her lips. Not the forehead as her father had always done.

"Miss Stowe," the duke whispered, with his lips so close to hers she felt his breath sweep across her cheek and flutter against her eyes. "If you lean any closer to me you are going to topple us both. If you want a kiss that much, all you have to do is ask, and I will be happy to honor your request."

Merciful angels! Quickly, she settled back on her legs. Was it possible that what he said was true? Was she the one who had been moving toward him?

Probably. He'd caught her in a defenseless moment and seen her in an inconceivable state. His rescuing had made her think about warm embraces, sweet kisses, and soft touches. The sight of him made her think about being cuddled against his chest. The intensity in his expression made her wonder if he might be sensing some of the same feelings that affected her.

"I fear I might be a little dizzy from being trapped in that small space," she answered. She mentally shook herself and looked away from the duke, fighting to regain the abiding calm she used to be able to accomplish with ease and take pride in doing so.

"Then don't fight me anymore, Miss Stowe. Let me help you stand and get back your balance."

His smile was so tender she agreed without complaint. The duke gently took ahold of her elbow, the one she'd banged, but she forced herself not to wince as he helped her to stand.

Through everything she was feeling, she would maintain some pretense of gentility and remain seemingly unflustered as her brother, father, and mother had always expected of her no matter how difficult, unpleasant, or embarrassing the circumstances may be. "*Decorum is more important than anything*," her father used to say. And of course he was right.

So, after inhaling a deep breath, she straightened her dress and smoothed her hair, and then drew back her hand and slapped him.

CHAPTER 7

MAN'S PRACTICAL GUIDE TO APPREHENDING A THIEF
SIR BENTLY ASHTON ULLINGSWICK

If you don't come across a clue the first time, keep looking.

The duke's head snapped back, and shock seemed to rumble through him. He hadn't seen that coming. Neither had she. If anyone had ever asked, she would have denied being capable of such an act as to strike another person. No matter the offense. Usually, she trusted her instincts, but she wasn't sure they had served her well this time. Certainly, her family wouldn't have approved.

He rubbed his lower cheek as he worked his jaw and grimaced. "What in the devil was that for?" he demanded.

Finding her breath, she took a step away from him. "Coming into my drawing room without being invited. You should have waited. And then you didn't leave when I asked you to." She didn't want to think about the strange feeling she had that he might want to kiss her a few moments ago. Or the surprising feeling that she would have let him. That was preposterous and might have had a little something to do with the slap too. She really didn't know and wasn't going to reveal that to the duke.

"But I helped get you out of there." His tone rose in volume as he argued, clearly irritated as he pointed toward the chest.

"You should have left the room immediately and saved me the embarrassment of you being a witness to me in a very compromising position that no lady should have to endure."

His brow wrinkled and mouth tightened as if he couldn't believe what he was hearing. "I wouldn't leave without helping you or anyone else out of a situation like that. There is no such thing as embarrassment when someone is stranded. You get help from wherever it comes from. And the usual response people give is a polite thank-you!"

"I wasn't in distress until I heard you were behind me," she defended just as firmly as he had spoken.

"And a good thing I was, no matter what you say to counter it," he responded in a louder tone and as irritated as her own.

"From the night we met you have been hard on me about everything I do. According to you I've done nothing right."

"That's because most of the things you do usually land you in a heap of trouble."

"I would have eventually gotten myself out," she insisted indignantly. "And then received you properly."

"And more banged up than you are now."

"But with my pride unbruised."

Ophelia realized she was favoring her elbow, and he must have noticed. Reasonable thinking helped her to see they were at an impasse about who was the most wronged and outraged. Her, for showing her rear end, or him, for being slapped. She supposed she was responsible for both. No need to admit it to him. It was hard enough admitting it to herself.

But perhaps she should try to save her respectability before sending him on his way. "I've never slapped anyone before."

His frown relaxed. "And I've never been struck by a lady."

She cleared her throat as she clasped her hands together in front of her, still trying to recoup her aplomb. "I'm not happy you put me in a position that I had to. I don't even know what you are doing here. Following me again, I presume."

"What?" His back stiffened, as he pushed his coattails aside, shifted his stance, and sucked in another startled breath. "Following you?"

"You admitted to doing so last night," she accused, with all the self-righteousness she had been taught to use when necessary.

"That was different," he snapped, more annoyance creeping into his features. "You were snooping in someone's home."

"For a good reason." Ophelia deepened her glare at him, thinking there was no difference from what he was doing.

"No," he insisted. "It's not. I don't know how you can think that."

"It doesn't matter. You caught me unaware both times."

He nodded slowly. "You are quite unbelievable, Miss Stowe, and I don't like you implying I make a habit of following women."

"I don't believe I was going quite that far in my accusations."

"It's a good thing you aren't and a good thing I caught up with you when I did. Both times you were in the act of doing something you shouldn't have been doing and I helped you out with a bundle of problems. Someone needs to keep an eye on you to make sure you stay out of trouble."

His words hit a nerve like a painful tooth. "I didn't

need your aid either time. You should have tried helping me with what I asked of you, not slipping up on me."

"What you want to do is wrong," he insisted again.

Ophelia unclasped her hands, and they formed fists of vexation as her arms fell to her sides. "And your invasion into my privacy today will probably take me years to recover from."

The duke blinked rapidly. The corners of his riveting eyes crinkled oddly as he studied her. "Years? Did you say years to recover?"

"Yes." Ophelia watched his brows lift higher. His lips almost pursed, slightly quivered, and moved from side to side. It took a moment before she realized he was trying to keep from smiling. No, it was more than that. He wanted to laugh. At her. And when she was in a huff!

Implausible as it seemed, it was taking all he could do not to show his amusement concerning her comment—which *was* overstated, she knew, but she *was* overheated. He was trying so hard and making such weird movements with his lips it made her want to smile too. The next thing she knew, she started trying not to reveal her pleasure.

The entire fiasco was her doing. She should be the first to give in and reverse the uncomfortable direction they had been heading. Showing no rancor, she slowly let go a smile and whispered laugh. So did he, and it was so beautiful she felt as if the whole room had started glowing when she saw his white teeth. He looked incredible. A comfortable, happy chuckle sounded softly under his breath as he shook his head. Ophelia liked the attractive way the ends of his hair moved with the motion.

Her stomach developed that quick fluttery feeling as his gaze seemed to skim over her. She was giving him the once-over again too. There was an aura of authority and distinction about him that she was drawn to. Both times she'd been with him before and now. He was far too magnificent for her not to indulge in the chance to admire him and want to know more about him.

And just that easily, her unpleasant adventure, her embarrassment, and her annoyance were over. Much as she wished it weren't so, she found him charming and wanted to enjoy being with him like this rather than fighting to maintain her levelheaded assurance and attitude. Despite her apprehension about him, she was curious about him.

"What were you doing burying yourself inside that cabinet?"

She locked eyes with him again. Casually she murmured, "Looking for something."

"Well, it better have been the most expensive pearl in all of England. You might have spent the rest of the afternoon trying to get yourself out."

Ophelia liked the way the duke's gaze gently moved up and down her face with an enjoyable expression on his. She wanted to see more of this irresistible side of him. Before, it seemed he was always lecturing her, or tense and upset with what she was doing or saying. It made her feel good, maybe even carefree, to exchange a bit of levity and merriment with him. She hadn't felt so lighthearted in a long time.

The shocking thing was that his upset attitude toward her hadn't really bothered her that much. She was keen on his forthright manner in letting her know exactly how he felt. Unlike her father and brother, with the duke she knew exactly where she stood. With just a look he could inform, inquire, demand, or question her. He could also cause delicious tendrils of desire to swirl through her.

The duke nodded toward the chest. "Perhaps I could have a look in there for you and see if I can find the pearl."

Teasing her again showed he wasn't holding a grudge

about the slap. She appreciated that. "Nothing so important. It was a simple empty portfolio I was looking for." She reached and shut the doors with a sound click. "The cabinet is empty and now I'm going to see that it is moved to the attic where it belongs so that I don't ever have to see it again."

The duke rubbed his chin and hid the corner of his mouth with his thumb.

Was he up to something she didn't know about? "Why are you smiling at me again?"

"You didn't get all your hair smoothed down. It's sticking up right here." With a smooth and effortless motion, he reached up and lightly brushed his fingertips through her hair along the crown of her head. An exciting shiver raced over her. Her breaths became short and shallow again while his fingertips trickled softly down her cheek and tickled her skin with delicious prickles of enticement. A loose strand of hair fell to the other side of her face and thankfully distracted her from the duke's attempt to mesmerize her with his touch.

What was she doing, allowing him to touch her in such a way? She quickly sidestepped, fixed him with a perturbed stare, and said, "I'm not falling for that stunt again as I did when you said I had kohl ash on my cheek."

His smile softened more, and he gave her a knowing nod. "It was your eyebrow."

Tingles of attraction shivered over her. "You are insufferable and a menace to my normal good nature."

His gaze settled on hers once again. "You are a bother to me too, Miss Stowe, though I'm not yet sure what I'm going to do about it."

Ophelia felt as if her heart was pulsating in her ears. Suddenly she wished she were once again disguised in a coat, a neckcloth, and trousers. Wearing a man's clothing had emboldened her. Her stride had taken on a formidable length wearing the knee boots her maid had secured. Not only that, but the heels added height to her frame, which added confidence to her behavior. Not that it made a difference to the duke. A lady's dress offered no such trappings. When looking at him that night in his book room, she'd felt entirely different from the way she felt now. The duke made her feel things she wasn't supposed to be feeling until she married. Or so she thought.

Managing to swallow a huff of annoyance with herself for the unexpected thoughts about the duke, she said, "You have made it very clear what you are going to do about me bothering you, Your Grace. You have refused my pleas for help time and again. Now, just tell me why you are here to see me and be on your way."

He gave her a long considering stare. "Actually, I didn't come to see you. I came to pay condolences to your mother."

"Oh." That calmed Ophelia down a notch.

"I remember her well from my childhood. I'd like her to know how sorry I am." He paused as his features took on a more serious slant for a moment. He glanced over at a white cloth package tied with a yellow ribbon sitting on the table between the two settees. "I brought her some confections. Do you mind if I wait and speak to her?"

"No, of course not. That was kind of you. Maman will appreciate you making the time. She considers dukes very busy."

He folded his arms over his chest and gave her a musing smile. "I wasn't a duke when she scolded me for talking Winston into going so deep into the bogs with me one day that we got lost and ended up staying out well past daylight."

Ophelia rubbed her elbow again. "It probably worried her when he didn't come home by dark."

"It did. I thought she'd be angry and start reprimanding him, but all she did was hug him close and tell him not to do it again." A faraway gleam appeared in his eyes as he nodded. "And I'm sure Winston felt it was nice to have someone love him enough to worry about him."

His words and expression made her wonder more about his past. She remembered something Winston had said about the duke. With his mother passing when he was young and his father away most of the time for reasons Winston didn't know, the duke had a lonely childhood living between various relatives and his father. As she looked at him now, that seemed hard to believe. A man who would become a duke one day was passed around from family to family. She was aware that not all parents were as loving and close as hers and her heart squeezed.

As she looked at the duke, she recalled what'd he said about arguments between him and his father the first time they'd met. Then, as now, she'd thought of asking him more about his past and his relationship, but suddenly it was as if he sensed she was going to. His expression relaxed and he took a step back. It was as if he'd said too much and didn't want to talk further about it. And it really wasn't the right time. Instead, he walked over to where his gift for her mother was sitting and picked up the sketches of the crests, quickly sifting through them.

Looking at her, he asked, "What are these?"

She felt her back tighten. "Drawings I made earlier today."

"Family coat of arms?"

"Yes. I'm happy to hear I sketched them finely enough for you to know what they are."

"You have a true and steady hand with a pencil, Miss Stowe." He glanced at them again. "These are perfectly good. I meant, why did you draw them?"

She saw no reason not to tell him. He wasn't going to help her anyway. "I drew them from what Mrs. Turner remembers of the crest on the thief's carriage door."

"Suspected thief," he corrected in a noncondemning tone as he walked back over to her. "Even after our talk last night, you aren't going to give up your search, are you?"

"Give me those." Ophelia reached for the parchment, but he pulled them back. "They were not meant for you to see, sir."

He made no move to relinquish her treasures but started thumbing through them again. "I've never had a reason to be well-versed in the crests of current titled families, but this one looks familiar. It's not accurate, but it could possibly be the family of Lord Gainstay or Viscount Mullensgrove." He glanced up at her doubtfully. "The other three look very much the same, but the birds are different. All birds of prey, I think. The armor is well-done."

That was encouraging. "It's good to know Mrs. Turner came up with a modicum of accuracy. This gives me a real crest to look for and not just something made up from her imagination. Thank you for telling me. I suppose you realize that you have helped me even though you had no intention of doing so."

"No, Miss Stowe, this does not help you. I can vouch for the character of Gainstay and Mullensgrove. They are not interested in a chalice from the church."

She tweaked her shoulders in defense at his immediate rejection of his help and that the men might be considered. "How can you be so sure?"

He tapped the papers against the palm of his hand. "There are things a gentleman might be privy to that he does not reveal to a lady. Take my word for it that both have the utmost integrity and solid character that does not bear looking into for thievery or any other criminal activities. I daresay Mullensgrove hasn't even been in a church since he was a boy, if then."

"Even men with character can fall from grace," she remarked, needing the crests to get her the results she desperately wanted.

"I've done it myself a time or two," he answered quickly.

Her brows rose in interest.

"We are not going there, Miss Stowe. The simple fact is that if I thought either man was capable of such an act, you wouldn't have to go after them; I'd do it." He extended the sketches to her. "You can mark them off your list. And while you are at it you can remove the Duke of Stonerick as I assume you have the Duke of Wyatthaven. I've known both men since our school days. I've been in their homes almost as often as I've been in my own. I assure you what you search for is not there."

"Well . . ." She hesitated, looking at him with mistrust in her eyes. "Perhaps I'll just put them all at the bottom of the list," she said, leaving him with a reminder she wasn't going to give up, no matter how hard it was to reconcile her disappointment with the eagerness inside her to keep trying, no matter that all the odds were stacked against her. Now more than ever she needed the duke's help, and he still refused.

She took the drawings from him, walked over to the secretary, and opened a drawer and placed them inside. Her mother could see them after the duke left. While her back was turned, he had picked up the church registry she had also left lying on the table. The saints of mercy must have fled watching over her.

Why hadn't she thought of putting that book away when she finished with it earlier? Because it would have never crossed her mind that the duke might visit her. She wasn't surprised about him being so curious about what was lying around her drawing room. He didn't want to help but yet he wanted to know everything she was doing.

"What is this?" she asked, stalking toward him. "Do you plan to peruse all my private things while you are here?"

"Not all," he said absently, clearly more interested in what he was perusing than her disdain for what he was doing. "These were in plain sight for anyone to see. I am not searching your home without your knowledge. You are standing right beside me."

"Why are you so interested in what I have collected to aid me? You don't want to help me, so this is none of your concern."

He looked at her as if he couldn't imagine why she'd asked the question. "I'm trying to keep you out of trouble."

"I need no help for that."

Ignoring her firmly stated comment, he asked, "What is this log of dates and names?"

"If you must know. It's a registry of the people who visited the church during the time of my brother's illness."

His questioning gaze held to hers. "Do you consider all these people suspects?"

"Not all, but some could be possibilities, I assume." Her stomach suddenly felt as if it were squirming, and she hesitated. She might as well admit it and not dribble the information out a little at a time. "I brought it—I borrowed it from the church to bring with me in case there was a familiar name I came across while I'm here."

"I don't believe this." He gave her a wry look. "Am I hearing you correctly that you are now taking things from the church?"

"What?" she asked, instantly incensed. "Don't be ridiculous. I haven't stolen it."

His eyebrows rose, and then he smiled. Another beautiful smile that set her heart racing and her mind to wondering again why she would be attracted to him.

"Perhaps men aren't the only ones who fall from grace."

Her hands snapped to her waist. "I will give it back when I return the chalice."

"And perhaps someone borrowed the chalice the way you just happened to borrow this book."

Ophelia gritted her teeth and said, "You are . . ."

He walked to stand in front of her. "What, Miss Stowe? What am I? Merely curious? Rational? Protective of you?"

"Irritating," she answered when only words she didn't want to use came to her mind. *Attractive, engaging, tempting.*

While continuing in his chuckle, he looked down at the book again. Suddenly his chuckle faded away. His smile turned to a frown.

She didn't know if she should feel excited or worried about what he saw. "What is it?"

He met her gaze. "William Halaway's name is here. It looks like his signature too."

"Oh," she murmured softly, moving closer so she could study the page he was seeing. "Are you saying someone you know visited Winston's church during his illness?"

The duke seemed to be looking really hard at the page. "I don't know that," he muttered.

"If his name is written there, he did." Her eyes started searching for his signature. "There would be no other reason for it. Is he titled?"

"No, no, but he has a relative who is."

"That's interesting," she commented as the rhythm of her heartbeat increased at the possibility of finding out more about this man named Halaway and, more importantly, what he was doing at the church. "Perhaps he was with the titled man and signed the registry for both of them. Who is the relative?"

"Me."

Startled, her gaze met his. The duke's kin?

"He's my cousin by marriage."

"Oh," she whispered as an uncommon excitement rose in her. If she was lucky, this would get the duke more involved in her search without her having to even consider asking for his help again. "This is quite interesting, Your Grace."

"Don't start finding him guilty of the theft, Miss Stowe. My family crest looks nothing like what your maid saw, and he wouldn't be in a carriage with the crest on it anyway."

"You can't say that with certainty." She pursed her lips for a moment or two before adding, "He could have been with a titled friend of yours. Lord Mullensgrove or Lord Gainstay? Or even the Duke of Stonerick."

"I told you those names should come off your list. He doesn't know any of them well enough to be invited into their carriages."

"Are you sure?"

"Positive," he grumbled lowly. "I don't know why his

name is on here. I don't keep up with him that closely, but I will find out."

She laid her hand on his wrist and didn't realize it until she saw him look down. Quickly removing it, she cleared her throat and said, "What will you do if the news points a finger at your cousin being involved?"

The duke frowned thoughtfully. "I don't expect that. I've known the man most of my life. He is not into collecting anything other than a full bottle of brandy and enough blunt for a game or two of cards every night."

"Maybe Mr. Halaway needs money to keep his bottle full and money on the table."

The duke stifled an amused grin. "I keep his allowance adequate. You need not worry about how plump his pockets are or anyone else in my family. They are all well cared for. I will question him thoroughly about the reason his name is in the book."

The possibilities for an answer to what happened leaped into her mind. "Let me go with you when you query him."

Laughter sparkled in his eyes as his gaze met hers. A flicker of emotion she couldn't identify seemed to pass between them. It was good. She was certain he felt it too, for his gaze swept up and down her face slowly as if he was taking the feeling in and trying to ascertain what it was too.

"Have you gone daft?" he teased, after the moment between the two of them passed.

"Perhaps, but if I have, I don't regret it. I want to go with you and hear what he has to say."

"You can't go with me to talk to him, and you know it. Besides, I'll probably just send a message for him to come see me."

"That will work for me too. I can meet you there," she answered excitedly. "I could wear my gentleman's clothing, and no one would ever be the wiser."

"I will know. Besides, I thought I told you to get rid of those clothes."

"I don't think so. I don't remember." Ophelia wrinkled her nose.

"Well, if I didn't, I should have."

"I wouldn't do that. I might need them again."

He closed the registry book with a thud, and in a voice that was almost a whisper he said, "No matter it was a *clever* disguise, if I hear of you wearing them again, I will personally come over, search this house until I find them, and burn them myself."

She gasped with pleasure at his boldness to say such a thing. Ransack her house, burn clothing? If he was trying to scare her, he was taking the wrong approach. She was intoxicated by the soft-sounding passion she heard in his voice. What she did mattered to him.

Not wanting to back away from his nearness, she answered, "I knew dressing as a man would be quite objectionable to you, but destroying perfectly good clothing seems quite unnecessary. I appreciate you admitting it was a clever idea. I only wish you had come up with a *clever* idea to aid me."

His gaze stayed tightly on hers and his face came so close she feared their noses might end up touching before he stopped his slow descent toward her. "Is that a challenge to out-clever you, Miss Stowe?"

She didn't know how long he looked at her without moving, without blinking. She didn't even know if she was breathing but heard herself say, "Please be so kind to accept it as one."

He stroked his thumb across her cheek. "You look

good enough to kiss," he said. "And I think I'm going to do that for you."

"What?" she whispered in a hushed voice. How could him saying such a thing enchant her? A hot dizziness spun in her head at the thought. It was ridiculous that she wanted him to do just that. She couldn't understand why she was having such feelings for this man.

"Don't worry," he said huskily. "I promise you I'll do it in a manner that protects your virtue."

"I'm sorry to keep you waiting, Your Grace," Maman said quietly, walking into the room with the grace and poise she'd always conveyed.

Ophelia and the duke peeled away from each other into separate directions.

Her mother stopped, curtseyed, and smiled. "Welcome to our home, Your Grace."

The duke nodded, laying the registry book on the table beside him. "I heard you were at the ball last night, Mrs. Stowe. I'm sorry I didn't get the opportunity to speak to you before you left. I wanted to see you and offer my sympathy."

"Perhaps that was best. Conversations about such things are usually safest handled in a private setting such as this and with the minimum number of words spoken."

The duke gave her a reassuring smile and nodded his understanding.

"It's so kind of you to make the time to stop by and let us know."

"It's good to see you, Mrs. Stowe. I have fond memories of Winston and being in your home when I was a youth."

"So do I, Drake. Oh, my. I just called you by your first name. I do remember my manners and know not to do that. First names are all but forgotten once a gentleman becomes a duke."

He brushed off her concerns with a smile and light chuckle. "I give you permission to always use my first name. You called me Drake for more than a year. No need for you to change now."

"Your kindness is appreciated, but I will do what is right and call you Your Grace. It's just that it has been so many years since I've seen you and old habits are difficult to break. It's remarkable how you haven't changed." She smiled again. "You've grown quite taller, of course, but you are as handsome as ever. I realize I've still been imagining you as the slender boy who taught Winston how to run and jump over our fences rather than use the gate."

"Which I had accomplished numerous times without mishap." The duke chuckled. "But I believe that gleam in your eyes means, Mrs. Stowe, you are remembering the time the leg of my breeches got caught at the ankle on the post when I went over the fence but didn't clear it."

It was easy for Ophelia to imagine what happened as Roberta and the duke laughed. She envisioned him dangling upside down and calling for help. She tried to hide her snicker but knew she hadn't when the duke glanced at her.

She turned away, pretending to give her attention to the inkpot and quill on the secretary while rippling her fingers on her wounded elbow. The conk on her head was beginning to give her a headache too. Or maybe the way the duke made her feel when she was so close to him was the cause for that.

"My face landed on the dirt and my head on a rock," the duke reminded her mother.

"I remember it well. We were so worried about you for days. There was a big gash on your forehead, and we didn't think it would ever heal properly."

"The scar is still there."

"I see it is," her mother said. "Thankfully not as prominent as I remember."

Ophelia whirled to look, but the duke's hair had already fallen over his forehead again. A scar? She hadn't noticed one, but his hair was long in front and always swept to the right side of his forehead. She was curious and now wanted to see it. Was that why he wore his hair so long in front and swept to one side? She wanted to know, but that really wasn't the kind of thing she could ask a duke or anyone else.

The voices of her mother and the duke faded into the back of her mind. It was best not to doubt him when he said he would burn the clothing. In fact, it was probably a good idea not to doubt the duke concerning anything. He seemed quite fervent about most everything he said. But not in an infuriating way. Most of the time it was more as if he was trying to make her understand what he thought was best for her. Maybe he was right about that, but it didn't matter. She had to do what was right for her brother.

In the meantime, she would forget about the interaction she had with the appealing man concerning the chest, if possible, and the near kiss that probably would have happened if her mother hadn't chosen that moment to come into the room. Ophelia needed to concentrate on the two things she learned from the duke coming over today: Mrs. Turner's recollection of the crest was accurate to a degree and encouraging, and the duke was related to a man who'd signed the church's registry. Both were her first good leads in her efforts to find the chalice since coming to London.

For the first time, she felt as if she was making progress and it wouldn't be long before she would close in on the thief.

CHAPTER 8

MAN'S PRACTICAL GUIDE TO APPREHENDING A THIEF
SIR BENTLY ASHTON ULLINGSWICK

Assess motives with discretion.

Through the window at White's, Hurst could see dense fog had settled over the cold, damp afternoon. No one would know spring was more than six weeks old. Hurst had arrived at the club early to meet his friends and had garnered one of the coveted tables near the fireplace. He liked the warmth, but Rick would complain that it was too damned hot to sit that close to the fire. Hurst would smile, and they'd both shrug it off.

Later, when he returned home, he'd send a message off to his cousin and ask that he come see him. Hurst didn't think for a moment that his cousin had anything to do with the missing chalice, but he was more than a little curious about what William was doing in the area of Wickenhamden and at Winston's church.

Feeling unsettled after his visit with Mrs. and Miss Stowe, Hurst looked around the room. He liked the quietness of the famed club. Distinguished gentlemen sat talking in hushed tones while sipping a coffee, brandy, or their favorite afternoon drink. Occasionally there would be loud laughter from someone, or an acquaintance might stop by and say hello, but mostly the members left one another alone if they didn't have a pre-appointed time to meet. Respect for privacy was of utmost importance to most everyone who entered.

Knowing his afternoon drinking habits, the server had brought Hurst a glass of claret almost as soon as his backside hit the chair seat, but he had yet to take a sip of the dark-red wine. He'd been too busy thinking about things he had no business thinking about as he stared into the crackling, popping fire. The past being one of them.

Hurst had often wondered what his father would say if he had lived long enough to see his son sitting in the most renowned club in all of England, and as a duke at that. Hell, what was he thinking? His father would have been the duke instead of Hurst if he'd been alive. It wasn't that Charles Kingsley couldn't have been a member of White's, but he'd never had the money. Not that his allowance and inheritance from his grandfather, one of the former Dukes of Hurstbourne, wasn't enough to sustain a membership. It was, and more. Or would have if his father hadn't wasted the generous amount bequeathed to him on livelier, less distinctive clubs and gambling hells that suited his habits better, and all the drink he could hold.

As the first son of a third son of a duke, Hurst's father had advantages but never learned how to use them to make his own way in life. He didn't have the discipline that would be required for military duty, or the control and temperament that would be needed for the service of a clergyman. Those were about the only two means of work a man of the ton could boast of having and expect to maintain even a smidgen of his status as a gentleman.

Hurst had considered the life of ministry for a while. Courtesy of the steadiness of Winston and his family's influence when they were boys. That was before his mother's sister paid for him to go to Eton and later to Oxford, and before he became close friends with Wyatt and Rick. There was a short time Hurst had acted as carelessly as his father, but it hadn't taken him long to realize that lifestyle wasn't for him. He wanted to be nothing like the man. He'd been reasonable, responsible, and respectable for too long to change into a reckless wastrel about Town.

His father had never learned to manage anything in his life. Not his allowance, nor the amount of his drink, gambling, or his temperament. So, Hurst had to learn how to manage them all—well, perhaps he hadn't learned not to raise his voice in a heated argument. Still, some of the lessons he learned were hard and he hated when thoughts of them came to mind.

There was another person he'd been thinking about the past couple of days. Miss Stowe was at the top of his short list of two. It didn't take much to remember her. And it was much more pleasurable than thinking about Charles Kingsley. If Hurst was awake, it was a sure bet she'd cross his mind every few minutes. She was inherently more and more compelling every time he saw her. He sensed an innocent vulnerability in her that matched a need inside him to protect her as if she were his very own. That had him fighting the feeling she was the lady for him.

She was rash, foolhardy, and wouldn't listen to his good, sound advice, and she irritated the hell out of him because of it. She was stubborn too. He wanted, expected, to marry a proper young lady. Not one who insisted upon going into people's houses to secretly search for a chalice.

Despite all that, he felt responsible for her. Maybe because he hadn't gone to see Winston but kept his plans to visit his aunt and the round of winter parties she'd planned for him to attend. Or because he hadn't followed through on his youthful promise to do whatever his friend might ask of him but instead took care of his lands. Possibly his feeling of being responsible for her was a combination of both and other things as well.

None of that usurped the fact that Miss Stowe was a danger to herself. Her courage was undeniable and admirable, but she still needed someone to look after her. Her mother would be the obvious choice, but she had the same feelings as her daughter in wanting to make sure Winston wasn't labeled a thief. All that was understandable to a degree. He didn't think either of them fully understood the ramifications of Miss Stowe's actions if she was caught pilfering through someone's belongings—no matter the reason. Love, loyalty, and a sense of right and wrong were driving them. Those were difficult things to fight.

Heat from the fire settled into his bones and reminded Hurst there was more to think about Miss Stowe. Touching her had been a nice reward for helping her wiggle out of that blasted chest. Thinking of it made him smile. He liked the way she'd felt beneath his hands. Her shoulders were slim but not bony. The muscles surrounding her rib cage were firm but not hard. He'd been tempted to slip his hand down to the curve of her waist, over the flare and roundness of her rump. But that wasn't his way.

Miss Stowe puzzled him. Everything about her told

him that with her he had met his match. That she was the one he was waiting for even though he kept rejecting the idea of it. He'd always expected to be knocked off his feet by a lady who looked and acted like the ones he'd met when he was visiting Aunt Sophie's house, the ones he danced with at parties and balls in London. All of them lovely, shapely, and demure. Not one of them would have ever dreamed of taking him to task over anything nor would they consider going after a thief.

But they didn't have Miss Stowe's intoxicating scent, sharp wit, or blue eyes. No, not just blue eyes—incredibly blue eyes that at times seemed to be peering into his mind and searching for his soul. The demure ladies his aunt introduced him to hadn't shown courage, determination, or strength to match wits with him. Not one of them had given him the desperate desire to pull her close to his chest and kiss the warmth of her neck. Not one of them had made him think that she was strong, intelligent, and brave enough to take care of herself even though it would be his responsibility to do it. Only Miss Stowe.

She had to be the one he was waiting for. Even with her boldness, her temperament, and her outlandish ideas of hiding behind men's clothing and sticking her head and shoulders into a chest.

Frustration over what he'd felt for her caused him to grit his teeth. He had to come to terms with the fact that her lips beneath his, and the weight of her breast—

"Good afternoon, Your Grace."

Hellfire.

Hurst straightened in the chair and cleared his mind of the enjoyable and purely masculine thoughts that were about to lead him to some heavenly daydreaming.

"Good day to you, Lord Gagingcliffe."

The man bowed. "Pardon my interruption, but I couldn't help but notice you were alone and wondered if you might enjoy some company."

"Gracious of you, but I'm waiting for someone. And I see they have just walked in the door."

"Perhaps another time. I wanted to talk to you about the Brass Deck Club."

That was odd. Gagingcliffe had to be a few years older than Hurst. "Are you interested in being a member?"

The baron laughed. "No, I'm afraid not. I know it's a younger men's club. I have a friend who is interested in joining. Mr. Wilbur Sawyer. I thought perhaps I could put in a good word for him."

"I know the name and he's been mentioned before. We do occasionally accept new members and are considering a couple at present. Certainly. We'll chat about him another time."

The baron walked away as Rick and Wyatt walked up.

"Looks as if you started drinking without us," Wyatt said as he pulled out a chair.

"Boredom set in waiting for the two of you to get here."

"Must have been something other than that." Rick glanced at the wine. "It looks as if you wanted to start early, but I can see your glass hasn't been touched."

"I was just about to doze off," he offered, knowing neither of them would believe that.

"If he hadn't been so hard to please and had married before he turned thirty, he wouldn't be so bored," Rick offered as if it were a fact.

Hurst looked at the two strapping men and snorted a laugh. They never minded giving him a hard time. He didn't mind either. Their friendships weren't predicated on tiptoeing around one another's feelings. They were more a brotherhood of friends who were more family to him than his own father had been.

His levelheadedness in most things was the characteristic that drew Wyatt and Rick to Hurst so long ago. He was just the kind of friend they needed to keep them out of more trouble than they usually got into. That was another thing his father taught him how to do.

"Both of you stop grumbling, sit down, and tell me why your messages were so insistent on meeting with me this afternoon. I've hardly seen either of you since you arrived in Town for the Season and suddenly, we must meet today. Is this about some of the new members of the Brass Deck? Gagingcliffe was just over wanting to talk to me about a fellow."

"There's that too. The club business can wait. I think you are the one who needs to tell us what's going on with you," Wyatt countered, pulling his chair up to the table.

"Since when is anything more important than our sporting club?" Hurst asked, smiled, and then added, "Other than your wives. Of course, that always goes without saying."

"True, but that's not the reason we needed to see you. You know new members always like to make their mark by trying to make new rules and bring in their own friends," Rick offered with an air of nonchalance.

"What do they have in mind this time?" Hurst asked. "They know everything has to pass by us before it can be voted on."

"They want to shorten the name to *the Deck*."

"Damnation," he whispered. "Why would they want to get rid of the word *Brass*? Don't they know what it means?"

Wyatt held up his hands to quiet Hurst. "We started the club, and we will handle it as we always do. Maybe we should plan an unofficial meeting and hear what they have to say."

"All right. Let's do it," Hurst agreed. "I'll have it at my house."

"Good. Now that we have that over with," Wyatt chimed in. "You looked well deep into your thoughts when we walked in. What's going on with you?"

He was and had been thinking about Miss Stowe since she came into his life and identified herself.

"Nothing," he answered without guilt. "Why?"

Wyatt shrugged. "We don't believe you. That's why. Fredericka doesn't let anything go on in her house that she doesn't know about," Wyatt continued. "So maybe there's something you want to share with us."

Hurst shrugged. "I don't know much about wives, but that sounds normal to me."

Wyatt chuckled good-naturedly. "What isn't normal is that she saw you eyeing a certain young lady last night, and then a few minutes later watched you follow her out of the ballroom."

That got Hurst's attention.

"Is she someone you met at one of your aunt Sophie's winter parties and forgot to let us know?"

Hurst brushed his hair away from his forehead. He studied the fact that his friends knew he'd met someone in secret and were now obviously eager to know all about her. Ever since they had married, Rick and Wyatt had always wanted to know about Hurst's quest to find the lady of his dreams. No matter what he said, he couldn't seem to make them realize he wasn't looking for her. He had always believed it would happen when it happened.

They had tried to give him help he hadn't wanted when they were in London last fall by inviting him to dinner after dinner at their homes and conveniently inviting eligible young ladies and their parents to join them. The trouble was that they were ladies he'd already met and knew were not the belle he wanted to marry.

Rick and Wyatt had known for a long time he wanted the lady who was right for him. And if he had found her, she wasn't who he'd been expecting.

"I didn't meet her at my aunt's house," was all he answered, not at all sure he wanted to tell his information-seeking friends anything about Miss Stowe, her reason for being in London, or her unusual search.

"Fredericka doesn't know where the two of you went to meet."

Just as well. Wyatt certainly wouldn't have liked the reason.

"You mean she didn't follow me to find out?" Hurst asked with a mock look of surprise.

Wyatt gave him a lopsided grin. "I told her she should have. Instead, she only kept watch on the doorway for your return. She knew the lady came back first, collected her nervous-as-a-cat mother, and they left almost immediately. You returned to the ballroom only minutes later, stayed only a short time, and left before speaking to either one of us."

Hurst blew out a disgruntled snort of disbelief. It was laughable that he was being observed while he watched Miss Stowe. "What's this?" he grumbled in mischievous amusement. "Am I being spied on in your house now?"

"Do you need to be?" Rick asked.

"What we really want to know is, are you in trouble that we don't know about?"

"No," Hurst stated, cocksure about that.

"Is someone trying to trap you in a parson's mousetrap?" Wyatt asked.

Frowning, Hurst gave another resounding, "No." A forced marriage was the last thing Miss Stowe had on her mind. Her mother didn't seem to have any leanings in that direction either. He would have picked up on that when he talked to her.

"You left before you'd even said hello, which is unusual for you," Wyatt said as the server quietly placed a glass of claret in front of each of his friends.

"Which we knew meant you didn't want to talk about her," Rick added.

That was an accurate assessment. "I'll have to remember how astute Fredericka is and be more diligent about who she is watching every time I pass under your doorway."

"We are curious," Wyatt admitted, picking up the conversation again.

"Since when can't a man have a rendezvous with a lady without anyone knowing about it or questioning him about it should they discover the secret meeting?"

"You can have all you want." Wyatt grinned. "We just want to know who she is."

Hurst chuckled. He was warming up to the idea that his friends were interested in who he was with. "She was in your house, at your party, Wyatt. Why ask me about her? Besides, I assumed you conveniently forgot to tell me you invited her."

"Hurst has a good point," Rick said, a wrinkle of concern forming between his eyes. "Why did you invite her to your house and not tell him?"

"How the hell do I know why she was invited? I don't know her," he grumbled, good humor vanishing from his face. "Unfortunately, I didn't see her. Fredericka only knew the young lady was new to Town. Mrs. Bristol asked if she could bring Mrs. Roberta Stowe and her daughter."

Hurst picked up his glass for the first time and took a drink. The wine went down easily and gave him time to take a much-needed deep breath when he realized they didn't remember the name Stowe.

"Who is she?" Rick asked impatiently.

"Winston's sister."

Wyatt and Rick locked eyes with each other.

Hurst knew what that meant. They didn't remember the name Winston from the hunting lodge. For a moment he wanted to be offended, but then he realized they had moved past the hunting trip, past the messenger who was so prepared he brought ink and quill with him so that Hurst could respond to the letter. Hurst had written the answer declining to offer marriage, and to Wyatt and Rick that was the end of it. The event was no more than a passing of ships in the night. They had no reason to remember. He understood.

"My friend who asked me to marry his sister when we were on our hunting trip."

Remembrance dawned on both his friends.

"The vicar's sister. The lady he asked you to marry," Wyatt said, rubbing the back of his neck thoughtfully.

"Yes. We talked about it and decided I had the option to consider it. The three of us did and I declined." And now Hurst wondered if he had made the right decision that night.

Had he gone to meet Miss Stowe and seen her for the first time dressed as a lady instead of a man, if he hadn't known about her schemes to find the sacrament, would he have known without the doubt churning inside him that she was the lady for him on first sight? Had all that happened tilted fate and clouded what he'd always felt to be true? He wouldn't know because he'd never gone to see his friend.

"And a vicar's daughter." Rick whistled through his teeth. "I'm remembering it now. He said she had a good soul."

"I think it was that she had a gentle soul," Wyatt corrected, but then added, "or maybe it was a gentle soul and good heart? Damnation, Hurst, we didn't remember her name, much less what her brother had said about her. Is she making her debut?"

In truth, Hurst's memory hadn't been much better until Miss Stowe showed up at his home. But he knew one thing: Winston didn't know his sister very well or he wasn't telling the truth in his letter. Miss Stowe wasn't anything like how her brother described her.

Rick drummed his fingers lightly on the table as all three men were silent while they each had a sip of their drink.

"Fredricka met her and said she was lovely, but she also said all the young ladies at the party were lovely so that is no clue whatsoever."

"They were," Hurst ventured to say. He'd met most of the ones making their debut, but Miss Stowe was the only one who had stayed on his mind.

"Did she come to Town hoping you might find an interest in her?"

"And did you?" Wyatt asked.

"Just cough up the details and tell us about her," Rick complained impatiently. "Don't make us pull it out of you question by question."

"She didn't come to Town looking for me. Someone else." For a moment he didn't know what else to say, but then he asked, "Do either of you know anyone who collects religious antiquities?"

They both sent curious looks his way.

"What does this have to do with Miss Stowe?" Rick asked inquisitively.

"She's looking for a particular person to ask about a specific item having to do with her brother's church."

"I know of some who venture into antiquities, yes, but religious?" Wyatt shrugged. "That would be unusual and no one that I know of."

"Me either," Rick responded. "Why does she need a particular person?"

Hurst saw no reason not to tell them what he knew about Miss Stowe's search for the chalice and the reasons for it. Leaving out, of course, that she dressed as a man to enter his home. No one should ever know that. Or the fact that the second time he saw her, she was actually searching Wyatt's book room to see if he might be the thief. Fredericka definitely wouldn't like that.

It was best to allow them to think he and Miss Stowe had met in the book room only to learn more about each other. If they wanted to believe it was more than a friendly visit, he would leave that up to them.

"Keep the information about the theft to yourselves," Hurst added. "If there really is a thief in London, he doesn't need to be forewarned that someone is looking for him."

Both men nodded understanding, making Hurst think he'd gotten out of that conversation easily enough until Rick surprised him with, "So what do you think about her?"

He thought too much about her too often, but wouldn't tell them that. In fact, there wasn't much he wanted to tell them concerning Miss Stowe. Each time he saw her, the pull was stronger that they were meant to be together.

Saying nothing wouldn't satisfy Wyatt and Rick so he offered, "She's even-tempered." *Sometimes.* "Strong-minded." *All the time.* "And definitely not a shrinking violet, which I'm sure you've already assumed since we met in secret at your house. I've always thought one of the things that made a lady beautiful was her attitude, and she has it in spades."

Wyatt studied him a little deeper than Hurst liked before remarking, "So she's nothing like the vicar portrayed in his letter."

Hurst smiled to himself. "That's safe to say."

"It sounds like we need to meet her." Rick picked up his glass and asked, "Will she be in London for the rest of the Season?"

Would she? Hell, yes. She might not believe it, but she didn't have a chance of finding that relic the way she was going about it. But damn if he didn't admire her for trying. And if only for her courageous effort alone, maybe he should try to help her in some way even though it went against his better judgment.

"I don't think she'll be leaving London anytime in the near future."

"Good. I'll talk to Edwina," Rick said. "We'll plan a dinner and make sure she's invited."

Suddenly Hurst had visions of Miss Stowe slipping away from the dinner party to secretly search Rick's book room as she had Wyatt's. He couldn't let that happen. Especially when he knew what she was searching for wasn't there.

"No," he said quickly. "That won't be necessary. I'm sure you will see her at a party soon and I'll introduce her.

If not, we'll plan something casual. Maybe we'll meet at Covent Garden or for a walk in Hyde."

Hurst picked up his drink again. Yes, he needed to do something to help Miss Stowe. And suddenly he knew exactly what he was going to do first.

CHAPTER 9

MAN'S PRACTICAL GUIDE TO APPREHENDING A THIEF
SIR BENTLY ASHTON ULLINGSWICK

Don't let the suspect know you're watching him.

Ophelia had attended several afternoon card games but never one as lavish as the Southperrys. The perfectly groomed grounds served as a backdrop for the vibrant spring flowers, shrubs, and trees. Guests entered by passing through a carved wooden arch that had been painted the same shade of blue as the sky and decorated with ivy. Urns filled with fragrant, colorful blooms bordered the stone-lined pathway that everyone took to their assigned tables.

Ladies were beautifully dressed in their finest visiting gowns of crepe, silk, or lightweight muslin. Their matching bonnets and hats were decorated with satin ribbons, netting, or a bit of organdy splashed around the band. Gentlemen cut dashing figures in their afternoon coats, white shirts, and neckcloths, with a palette of different colorful waistcoats.

Lord and Lady Southperry had managed to choose a beautiful day to hold their party. Cloudless skies and warm sunshine made a perfect canopy. The spacious garden was dotted with several white-linen-draped tables with two men and two ladies sitting at each, playing their choice of whist, cribbage, or speculation while quietly chatting. The chaperones and mothers who had escorted all the young ladies to the party had their own area of the lawn to pamper themselves while they watched and waited.

Ophelia stared at the cards in her gloved hands, but her mind was on the duke. She had wondered, worried even, that he might be at the party. Now that everyone was seated and the games had begun, she could rest easy and concentrate on what she had come to London to do without worrying about him looking over her shoulder. Or following her.

She saw the challenges of her quest being so much easier to meet if only she had his aid, but she could manage without him. Still, he probably knew Lord and Lady Southperry quite well and could easily slip into their book room unnoticed and peek at the bookshelves. But no, he couldn't be bothered. He had made up his mind and she had made up hers. Already, she had planned for the reason she would need to go inside the house in a few minutes and look for the precious sacrament herself.

For the short time Ophelia was in the vestibule removing her wrap, she'd purposefully chatted casually with the servant attending the ladies as they arrived and had found out exactly where the book room was. The house wasn't as large as the Duke of Wyatthaven's, so all should go well. She hoped to be in and out in a flash with only her being the wiser.

"Are you still thinking about your next play, Miss Stowe?" the rather handsome, but impatient Mr. Wilbur Sawyer asked.

"Don't worry about him, Miss Stowe," Lord Gagingcliffe offered immediately in her defense, while giving the younger man a disapproving stare. "Take your time and play your card when you're ready. There's no limit on how long we must wait."

Ophelia smiled at the older, good-natured gentleman. "Thank you, but I've made up my mind." She laid down the seven of spades and smiled pleasantly at the younger Mr. Sawyer. "I'm sorry it took me so long to decide, but the sun is so bright today, for a moment, I was having difficulty seeing the cards."

The beautiful olive-skinned Miss Georgina Bristol sat opposite Ophelia and had been monopolizing Mr. Sawyer's attention like a fledgling attending her first ball while almost completely ignoring the man her father wanted her to consider marrying.

"Are you feeling faint, Miss Stowe?"

"Not at all, my lord," Ophelia quickly responded to the baron, lifting her chin and breathing in deeply. "I'm quite splendid. After the cold, dreary days earlier in the week, I think the sunshine is refreshing and heavenly."

"But Lord Gagingcliffe is right, Miss Stowe," Georgina added with a concerned expression. "Some ladies, such as you, are fairer and more delicate when it comes to the sun. Most can't stay outside very long even when wearing a hat with a wide brim."

Ophelia rededicated herself to her hand and said, "So good of you to remind me. I shall bear that in mind and be sure to take a respite if needed. Now, I believe it's your turn, Mr. Sawyer."

"Forgive me, Miss Stowe, but I played while you were discussing the sun." He picked up his drink and gave Georgina a smile from behind his glass, which she returned.

It was easy to understand why Georgina would find

Mr. Sawyer more pleasing to look at than Lord Gagingcliffe. He cut a fine figure for a man and had a roguish appeal most any young lady would be drawn to. While the baron wasn't as young, handsome, or as strongly built, he was pleasant. And clearly both gentlemen had their eyes on Georgina.

"That is a striking signet ring you are wearing, Mr. Sawyer," Ophelia said pleasantly while waiting her turn again. "Has it been handed down through your family or was it made especially for you?"

He smiled as if pleased she noticed, and he took the time to admire the ring on his little finger too. "It has been passed down through our family for more than one hundred years now."

"Oh, my. That is a long time to have preserved something so small which can easily be misplaced or lost. Does anyone in your family enjoy collecting artifacts to add to your family's collection?"

He gave her a curious look. "Not that I know, but it really isn't something I'd be asking anyone about. Most everything in our family has been handed down for generations. Perhaps that makes all of them artifacts."

"Hmm." She smiled and turned to Lord Gagingcliffe. "How about your family, my lord? Any traditions of someone handing down various objects, such as rings, snuffboxes, figurines, or perhaps artifacts of some kind?"

The baron chuckled. "Like Mr. Sawyer's family, we have too many pieces that have been passed down through the years to even know. I can see where you, being a vicar's daughter, would be interested in such traditions."

"But we are not, Miss Stowe," Georgina said in an overly sweet voice and with a bored expression. "It's your turn."

"Oh, yes, you're right. It must be the sun keeping me off my game today. Thank you for reminding me."

Ophelia made her play and then looked at her cards again without really seeing them. She didn't like having to question the gentlemen about their family's habits of collecting or not collecting objects, but she had to. Perhaps along the way an innocently worded question would lead her to hearing about someone who indulged in religious relics.

Three games of cards and a glass of champagne later, the ringing of a bell sounded in the distance, the hostess' way of signaling they were to finish the hand they were playing and not start another. Mr. Sawyer teased Ophelia that she now had a time limit on how long she could hold her cards and wait to play her hand. She merely gave him an acceptable grin but was thankful when the second bell sounded and the gentlemen rose, said their goodbyes, and moved on to their next assigned table.

While the men were moving about, the servers came around with silver trays offering dainty confections, delicacies, and fresh glasses filled with champagne.

Georgina reached across the table and laid her gloved hand on top of Ophelia's and dreamily cradled her chin on her slender fingers. "Don't you think Mr. Sawyer is simply divine?"

"He is most handsome when he smiles." Ophelia paused and then finished by saying, "At you."

"I know." Georgina's breathy sigh embodied her besotted feelings for the young man. "I was so tempted to rub my foot up and down his leg."

Almost choking on the champagne she'd just sipped, Ophelia coughed. "I don't think that would have been a good idea."

"Why not?" Georgina asked innocently. "Perhaps you don't know, but I've heard it is a safe way for a young lady to let a gentleman know she's interested in him and would like for him to call on her."

"No, I haven't heard that before. Did your mother tell you about this approach?"

"Of course not. I would never mention this to my mother, nor would she to me."

"Then perhaps you shouldn't try. It seems a risky way to get a gentleman's attention. I would be afraid he might question the reason you were doing it and possibly think you wanted to see him for inappropriate purposes?"

"I suppose a man could think that. Katherine told me about this after you left the ball the other night. She heard—"

"Good afternoon, Miss Bristol, Miss Stowe."

Ophelia knew that voice. Glancing behind her in a rush, she saw the Duke of Hurstbourne joining them. His compelling presence caused her heart to lurch with apprehension. He wasn't present for the first round of games. She was sure.

Was he there to keep an eye on her whereabouts? She didn't know, but manners dictated that she and Georgina rise from their chairs and curtsey. But in their haste to do so, they bumped into each other, which made Georgina lose her footing. As if the stumble had been practiced between the two of them, the duke reached out and kept Georgina from falling. As he drew away from her friend his gaze met Ophelia's and held briefly. Then the heat of his palm lightly touched the back of her shoulder as if to make sure she was all right too. The twinkle in his eyes redirected every thought and feeling in her being.

The duke's unexpected arrival threw her out of sorts.

Focusing intently on his face, she barely listened to what he was saying until she heard the name of the man standing with him: Mr. William Halaway. And much to her delighted surprise, the duke and his cousin would be playing the next round of cards with them. Ophelia couldn't believe one of her suspects was at hand, ripe to answer any questions she had. She could barely manage to hold in her joy.

She could have thrown her arms around the duke's neck and kissed him. On the cheek. Or maybe the lips. Her stomach tightened at the thought, and she quickly brushed it aside.

He'd brought his cousin to the party and, somehow, managed to secure them both a seat at her table. Unable to rein in her broad smile, she pinned her gaze on the duke when she was once more seated on her chair, her mind in a scatter of thoughts.

Ophelia wanted some way to let the duke know how happy she was as they made themselves comfortable in their chairs, but that was impossible. Georgina picked up the conversation with gusto, unabashedly telling the duke what an honor it was that he had joined *her* for the next round. She couldn't have been showier if she'd been a prized songbird twittering her good fortune on a crowd in the park.

The duke remained attentive to her flirtation, and odd as it was, Ophelia couldn't help but wonder if Georgina was going to rub her foot up and down the duke's leg. And if she was brazen enough to do so, would he accept her invitation? Best Ophelia put thoughts about that out of her mind and center her attention on the other man at the table.

"Would you mind being the first player to shuffle

the deck for us, Your Grace?" Georgina asked in a voice as sweet as nectar, while she slid the whist deck toward the duke. Apparently, the sparks that had been flying between her and poor Mr. Sawyer were a distant memory.

"Not at all, Miss Bristol." The duke's features pulled into a disarming smile, sending Ophelia's pulse racing even if his smile was intended for another. She felt as if she were melting snow in the warm sun. With a tingling shiver, she composed herself to address the matter at hand. She owed him her gratitude but couldn't say that in front of the others..

She couldn't resist a glance at him, and, in a low whisper, she noted, "Very *clever* of you, Your Grace."

"The addition of my cousin?" he answered just as softly. "I thought so too. I knew you would approve."

The ease with which he picked up her implication delighted her. No doubt he could play any game with marked expertise. He gave her a light nod and a knowing grin as his fingers rippled through the cards.

Perplexed, Georgina asked, "What was clever?"

At first, Ophelia dismissed Georgina's question with a shrug and focused her full attention on the duke's hands. Though he shuffled the cards with the same technique most any man would, Ophelia took the opportunity to continue the impetuous word dance she and the duke found themselves in.

"The way His Grace is shuffling the deck is very clever."

"Yes, it is superb," she gushed.

Seeming unable to curb his wink, he boasted, "I do have a clever trick or two up my sleeve from time to time, Miss Stowe."

"I'm glad to hear it," she answered, and was pleased to say it. "I hope we get to see more than one."

"I've only just started, Miss Stowe." He chuckled and kept shuffling the cards.

"Did I understand His Grace to say you'll only be in London for the Season, Miss Stowe?"

Mr. Halaway's innocent question distracted Ophelia from her tête-à-tête with the duke, and she gave the man she really needed to talk to her attention. His hair was the color of dried winter wheat, and his small eyes were a bluish green. Weathered, yet genuine, his countenance offered pure sincerity.

From the book she'd read, she formed a mental picture of what a thief might look like, but Mr. Halaway certainly didn't appear the way she'd imagined. He looked more like one of the angelic men singing in the chorus at church. She wondered if she had wanted to pin guilt on someone so badly, she was jumping on the slightest of possibilitics.

"Staying in London?" she repeated part of his question. "That is what Maman is saying now. But one never knows. It's safe to say we don't have a certain date that we must leave. How about you, Mr. Halaway? Do you reside in Town all year or do you have a summer home?"

"I am mostly London-bound but do a bit of traveling from time to time to stay with family and friends."

"That sounds lovely," she said while forming her next question. "Any particular area you go?"

The duke cleared his throat with exaggeration, jerking her attention to him. The corners of his mouth deepened with annoyance. She took it to mean he wasn't happy with her questioning his cousin, but for what other reason would he have brought the man to her table?

"I do always enjoy myself when the duke invites me

for Christmastide at Hurstbourne. He's been kind enough to do that since he inherited the title."

"That is thoughtful of him."

Georgina, who had her limelight dimmed somewhat when the conversation included Mr. Halaway, vented an impatient sigh and started her own conversation with the duke.

The duke cleared his throat loudly, and Ophelia glanced at him. His brow wrinkled deeper as he started dealing the cards.

"Did I hear you were recently in Wickenhamden?" he asked his affable cousin.

"Yes," he answered and began picking up his cards.

Shifting to the edge of her seat, Ophelia leaned toward him. "Was that for warmer temperatures, a visit with friends, or something else, Mr. Halaway?"

The duke immediately gave her a look that told her he was the one who was to interrogate his cousin, but she wanted to ask questions too. Her tactic would have been more straightforward, to just come out and ask the man what he was doing in Wickenhamden since he lived in London, but knew she couldn't. That would tip her hand to what she was doing if he was indeed the thief.

"Neither, though both were welcomed," he answered with a friendly smile as he arranged his cards, seeming more interested in playing his hand than in the conversation.

Was that all he was going to say? She glanced at the duke, and he gave her an I-told-you-so shrug.

Before she could curtail her inquiry, she felt the words break free from her closed lips, "Do you, by chance, know of the Chatham's chalice that's held at one of the churches there?"

"Not clever, Miss Stowe. Reckless," the duke casually

leaned in her direction and whispered under his breath as he lined up the cards in his hand.

Ophelia could almost feel the heat of his vexed breath near her cheek as he'd mumbled the words.

But without hesitance, Mr. Halaway offered an easy-mannered reply. "Yes, it's on the main road through Wickenhamden."

"Did you by chance stop and see it?" she asked, deciding she wouldn't look at the duke. She had no doubt he would be scowling at her. She could live without that.

"We tried to and was told the vicar was ailing, so we'll have to return another time."

"What made you want to see it, Cousin?" The duke's mild query put Ophelia's racing pulse back in order.

Mr. Halaway scoffed with a chuckle. "Nothing. I didn't go for me. My father's sister, Aunt Maudine, wanted to see it. I didn't mind going along to keep her company. She's taken with historical objects and history. She said it's been seen by kings and queens through the years. That didn't mean much to me, but if she wanted to see it, I didn't mind going along. She's become more pious in the past couple of years."

If that story was true, it didn't sound as if the duke's cousin had anything to do with the theft. And according to Mrs. Turner, his aunt wasn't a potential suspect either. The maid was certain the person she saw was a man, but no reason Ophelia couldn't ask a few more questions.

"That's interesting, Mr. Halaway," Ophelia said as she shifted her cards in her hands. "Does she have friends who are also into historical artifacts?"

"There's a group of ladies, I think, who are into such things."

"Enough of this uninspiring talk of churches, kings,

and artifacts." Georgina's voice broke into the conversation with conviction. "It's making me quite flushed." She took up her fan and rapidly began cooling her ire. "Lord and Lady Farthingale are having a masked ball in a couple of weeks, and I'm very much looking forward to attending. I have decided to go as Greek Goddess Athena. I'm having a small golden apple made to wear on my shoulder."

Ophelia's gaze darted to Georgina. She was smiling sweetly, obviously quite pleased and lightly fanning herself with her widespread cards.

What could anyone say about that admission? The purpose of a masked ball was so no one would know who you were. Obviously, she wanted to make sure the duke knew who she was that night. And that made Ophelia wonder if her new friend was currently seducing the duke with her foot under the table. And then Ophelia wondered if perhaps Georgina had rubbed Mr. Sawyer's leg with her foot too?

"I'm sure you'll be enchanting to all the young bucks, Miss Bristol." The duke slowly turned to Ophelia. Merriment fixed in his gaze. "What about you, Miss Stowe? Perhaps you'd like to tell us what costume you will be wearing to the masquerade."

"I don't know if I'll be attending, Your Grace. However . . ." She paused and gave him a confident smile. "I've been told I have a very clever disguise."

Ophelia saw a brief sparkle of admiration flash in the duke's eyes and he chuckled attractively before paying his attention to the game. He could be so delightful when he wanted to be. And when he was, she enjoyed him immensely.

Well, perhaps she enjoyed him a little even when he was trying to tell her what she should and shouldn't do.

He was definitely a rascal of the highest order in either case.

She picked up her cards and proceeded to have a wonderful time.

Chapter 10

MAN'S PRACTICAL GUIDE TO APPREHENDING A THIEF
SIR BENTLY ASHTON ULLINGSWICK

Don't be afraid to make another plan.

Ophelia sat in a chair in their small garden and watched the sun crawling among the white clouds. Earlier in the day a fitful rain had heightened the scent of the flowers and shrubs with a damp, leafy fragrance. White trumpet flowers climbed high with their vines creating a spectacle of greenery. The area was more private than she would have liked. It would have been nice to see over their neighbors' neatly trimmed hedges, but they were too tall.

She closed her book. There was no use pretending she was reading. All she could do was think about yesterday's card party and her interaction with the duke and his cousin. As usual, the duke was maddening at times, delightfully funny at others, and, worst of all, he was very desirable all the time.

Ophelia would never forget how he looked at her when she met his gaze after he introduced his cousin. He seemed to take in every detail of her face as if wanting to enjoy how much he'd surprised her. And he had. It was completely unexpected and heady to learn he'd changed his mind and allowed her to listen to him question Mr. Halaway. Of course, he was surprised too. He hadn't expected her to help him do the questioning. Even as she remembered it now, her breaths deepened.

Leaning her head against the back of the chair, she smiled, looking up at the sky. It was somehow comforting and satisfying to just think about the duke. Whether she was recalling enjoyable times such as the card party, or regretful ones like the afternoon she'd slapped him. He was constantly on her mind. And she did regret slapping him. At the time she wasn't sure she thought he deserved it. Now she was certain he didn't. Her action wasn't just a knee-jerk reaction to the unavoidable accident of her getting stuck. She had come to think the real reason for her hasty and out of character response was that she'd thought about kissing him, and he knew it. Why should a man know a lady wanted a kiss from him? That wasn't something a vicar's daughter wanted a man or anyone to know.

In the grand scheme of things, she had done many things that weren't becoming to a vicar's daughter since she'd found the chalice missing that thinking about a kiss didn't sound so bad. She simply had to realize and accept that this was now her life. Her new life. And handle it.

Why the possibility of his lips pressed against hers would have even entered her mind after being trapped in the chest and embarrassed that she'd been seen she had no idea. Unless, maybe, it was because the duke's warm, strong hands had been on her back and shoulders helping free her. She couldn't stop remembering it. And . . . the duke should have just forgotten about being a gentleman, forgotten about being in her home without her maman or a chaperone present, and kissed her the way a true rake would have.

No matter how many times she told herself she had more important things to dwell on than the duke, she found herself thinking about him again. Thoughts of him simply gave her no peace.

Sighing, Ophelia shook her head and opened *Man's Practical Guide to Apprehending a Thief* again. She started skimming through the well-read pages as she had so many times before, hoping she would find a gem, a nugget, or something she'd missed along the way that might help her find the thief in a quicker way. The issue with the vicar could be solved any day now. She couldn't just sit around and do nothing.

Ophelia squeezed her eyes tightly for a moment, trying to shut out everything that worried her, but her first thought was why couldn't the maid have seen a scar on the thief's cheek, that he had a pronounced limp, or was missing an arm? Anything that would have made him easier to find.

The back door opened, and she looked up to see her mother walking down the steps with a shawl in her hands. It was so like her to worry that Ophelia might be feeling the chill, even with her velvet spencer to keep her warm. She laid the book aside and went to meet her.

"Thank you for knowing just what I needed," Ophelia said, taking the wrap as she noticed the worry furrowing her mother's brow.

"What is it, Maman?" Unease worked itself through Ophelia and a sense of dread seeped through her. With all her mother's concerns, she didn't need more burdens.

"This just came." She held on to a small note, the seal obviously broken. "I can't read it again." Distress had her fidgeting with the gold band she still wore.

Ophelia took the note from her mother's trembling fingers. "No need to. Let me see it for myself. Surely, it's not such dire—" But barely a sentence into the missive with its fancy penmanship marking the stationery of her mother's dearest friend in Wickenhamden, Ophelia's gaze lifted sharply to her mother's face.

"I can tell you what it says." Roberta spoke in a voice as fragile as a spider's silken thread. "The elders of the church have met and, as we expected, they contacted the bishop and asked that he send a new vicar as soon as it can be arranged. You know what that means?"

In a tone lower than a whisper, Ophelia said, "Inventory."

Maman nodded. "We must find the chalice, my girl. And soon."

She was right, but Ophelia couldn't let her mother fret over this more than she already had. While Roberta wasn't of an age to qualify her as an older woman, her health was not what it was in her younger years.

"We will find it, Maman. As you can see, I'm reading the book again." She pointed toward the book. "We've eliminated several gentlemen already. My list is getting smaller. You know we've made progress."

"Not enough. We haven't found one solid lead here. Maybe we should return home and examine every inch of the church and vicarage again. It is possible that we could have simply missed it because we were searching so hard. Maybe it fell behind a chest, shelving, or something else."

"No, we couldn't have." Ophelia shook her head. "You know how thoroughly we searched, Maman. We had servants moving every piece of furniture, every book, all the clothing, and everything else that was movable. You know Winston's devotion. He would never have taken the sacrament out of the church."

Maman looked down at her hands as if they would somehow inspire her. "We are not going fast enough."

"I know, but don't worry, Maman." Ophelia gave her

a quick buss on her cool cheek, a loving pat on her upper arm, and a smile of reassurance. "We've managed to get invitations to all the parties coming up that are being held at titled gentlemen's homes. We discreetly ask at parties if anyone knows of collectors. We've removed the gentlemen the duke knew from the crests I sketched."

"All that has yielded nothing."

"Not yet, but maybe tomorrow it will. But it is still progress when we eliminate someone. Given how long it took with the previous vicars the bishop sent, there will probably be meetings before a new vicar is approved for Wickenhamden and more time after that before he arrives."

"But he will move swiftly, my dear. The vicars' issues have gone on far longer than anyone expected."

"We will handle it, Maman," Ophelia said while attempting to steer her mother to a garden bench. "Come, let's sit down."

Roberta hesitated. "No, my dear. I will go inside and sit by the fire for a while. The warmth is comforting. Come with me. You'll catch yourself a fine chill out here with nothing on to cover your head."

"I'll stay out a little longer. The sun has been peeking from between the clouds. The intermittent sunshine is enough for now. Besides, I need to think about this." She squeezed the note in her hand.

"I don't want you to worry yourself sick."

"As if that would happen." Ophelia looked down at the note. "I'll join you soon."

"Very well, my dear. Do cover your head with the shawl."

"When I get cold I will. And have a cup of tea when you get inside!" Ophelia called to her mother as she walked away.

Alone, Ophelia returned to her chair but didn't sit

down. She read the note repeatedly before placing it on top of her book and the shawl beside it.

She stood a long while in quiet contemplation, coming to terms with the inevitable unless something changed for the better soon. Then she set off on tracing a thought-provoking path from one end of the short garden to the other and back again.

How she missed the wild open fields in Wickenhamden, with the wrens who flew from the brambles as she passed. What an innocent lamb she'd been to let the silliest things send her into nature for contemplation growing up and free to roam—if she didn't stray too far from the vicarage. As she grew older, she realized her best thinking had always been outdoors and walking.

Often, after her father died and Winston moved home and became the vicar, he would walk with her. They would go to the pond and throw pebbles into the water as they had when younger. She would play cards with him and then he would play charades with her. No matter what he was doing or how busy he was preparing his sermons or attending to his church duties, he always made time for her.

One of her fondest memories of her brother was the wintery day she caught him off guard and sprinkled his neck with the icy water. Luckily, he wasn't upset with her for too long, but he did chase her all the way back home. They both knew he could have caught up to her anytime he'd wanted.

She would have loved to go on a long walk alone in Hyde Park, but here in London such behavior was not just frowned upon; it was forbidden. Unless, of course, a young lady wanted to find herself ruined for life. Walking without a chaperone was a good way to do it. But the back garden, no matter how small, was safe.

Nonetheless, Society's strict rules aside, the most

straightforward way out of their current dilemma would be if the culprit who had stolen the chalice had an attack of shame and returned it. She wouldn't even want to seek retribution. Since that scenario proved very unlikely, she found herself traveling down the only road she had: investigating the matter herself and carrying on with her limited search. There were more houses and book rooms to get into before the sacrament was found missing, and only one of her to look through them.

Ophelia didn't want to fail her brother. The thought was so distressing she wanted to take to a sickbed the way her mother would do from time to time. But of course, that wouldn't help her or her brother or her mother.

She didn't want the duke to be right and that she was indeed on a fool's errand to even attempt to find the thief or the chalice. But how could she just do nothing even if she was destined to fail in the end?

She would plan to talk to Mrs. Turner again tomorrow morning while both were feeling rested and fresh. Maybe Ophelia could come up with a new question that would spark a detail the maid had missed on earlier questionings.

"Are you trying to walk a pathway into the budding grass, Miss Stowe?"

Startled from her pensive thoughts, Ophelia spun and saw the duke coming through the side gate, and he looked absolutely divine.

CHAPTER 11

MAN'S PRACTICAL GUIDE TO APPREHENDING A THIEF
SIR BENTLY ASHTON ULLINGSWICK

Take in the suspect and befriend him.

He shut the gate while she tried to calm her quickened heartbeat and walked toward him.

"Hello, Ophelia," he offered as he strode along the tall hedge line toward her.

She abruptly paused. His intimate greeting using her name caused a purely feminine reaction in her that seemed out of place, all things considered.

Although somewhat unnerved by his sudden presence, she asked curiously, "Why are you coming through the side gate and not the front door?"

His mouth curved into a slow smile. "Before I got out of the carriage, I saw you from the window walking back here and thought to come straight to where you were and bypass the servants."

"And Maman?" she questioned.

"For now, if possible. We have the most interesting conversations when we are alone."

Ophelia couldn't argue with that. Her breaths evened out as she met him at the corner of the house. "You are certainly forward to do that, but once again, you've managed to come at an awkward time. Maman isn't well and I'm afraid I'm not in a very good humor. It would be best if you paid a visit on another day."

His features softened. "I'm sorry to hear about your mother. Nothing serious, I hope, and I'm surprised to hear of your ill humor. I thought getting the opportunity to question my cousin without constraint yesterday would have put you in a very fine way."

"It did yesterday," she offered, trying to disengage her gaze from his. "Though I take exception to you saying 'without constraint.' You grimaced at every question. However, I do thank you."

"I take it you didn't find what you were looking for in the Southperrys' book room, or from Mr. Halaway."

She sucked in a deep breath. "How did you know I—you were following me again?" she asked through clenched teeth. It seemed an impossible thing to do, but he could raise her indignation and the fluttering in her chest at the same time.

The duke twitched his shoulders in such a charming way she felt the desire to do likewise and lifted her chin too.

"It was more like watching you," he admitted.

"You were so caught up by adoring young ladies and their mamas when I left the garden, I thought for sure I had managed to leave and return without your notice."

His gaze swept down her face and then back up to her eyes. "I always notice you, Ophelia."

His words warmed her all the way down to her toes. She noticed again he used her given name rather than properly addressing her. For reasons she didn't want to explore, she found it comforting that he was watching her. Her trepidation waned and her interest as to why he came over grew.

"So, what did you find in your search?" A sparkle of teasing flashed in his eyes. "More books?"

"Of course." Ophelia sighed. "And a shelf that had some exquisite snuff and memory boxes on it. There were some miniature portraits in some lovely frames but, regrettably, no historical or religious vessels of any kind."

"And what about my cousin?" He casually folded his arms across his wide chest. "After meeting him and hearing his story, did you settle in your mind that he couldn't possibly be the suspect you are looking for?"

"I admit there is a good probability he is not the one who has the chalice."

"And his aunt Maudine?" the duke prompted her. "Is she a suspect now? Or someone from her ladies' group?"

Ophelia looked past the handsome duke to the tall dark-green hedge rising over them and took her time answering. "Unless one of them has a weak nose and chin and wears a top hat, they are probably off my list of suspects as well."

Ophelia hadn't expected him to toss his head back and laugh. Nor could she have anticipated enjoying watching him. She liked the way the lines fanned out from the corners of his eyes, making him appear relaxed. He was so immensely attractive, she felt her mood changing and her spirits lifting. But then her gaze caught sight of the note her mother had received from home and the book on catching a thief that she was beginning to wonder if it was helpful at all. Their situation hadn't changed and time to save her brother's legacy was slipping by quickly as the hours and days passed.

"Why are you here?"

"To see you."

Though Ophelia tried not to read anything into his words, her stomach tightened at how intimate his words sounded. It felt as if butterflies fluttered in her chest as an errant wind fluttered a lock of hair that had found freedom from her chignon across her face. She brushed it away from her forehead and tucked it behind her ear. "I have things to do, Your Grace."

"Do they have anything to do with the letter?" He nodded toward the parchment with the broken seal.

"Everything I do has to do with that." She took a deep breath. "Why are you here?"

The duke shifted his stance and dropped his arms to his sides. "I've brought you something."

She peered around him but saw no evidence supporting his eager claim. Both hands were free, and she was sure he wasn't holding anything when he came through the gate.

Scoffing at his declaration, she quipped, "Where is it?"

"I couldn't be sure you were out here alone for my unplanned call, so I saw no reason to bring it into the garden for your mother or someone else to scrutinize or to examine my motives."

Curiosity loomed in Ophelia. In an even tone, she said, "You've piqued my interest and my frustration this afternoon, Your Grace. And now you are trying my patience. If you, indeed, came bearing a gift, where is your offering?"

Speaking in an amused tone, he answered, "I have none for the church, Ophelia. Other than begging its pardon for all my misdeeds of the past."

"Oh, for heaven's mercy, Your Grace. I find myself on the precipice of a headache caused by more worries than anyone should have to endure, and no patience left for your antics. And certainly, this is not the day for you to add to my distress by calling me Ophelia. What if Maman heard you or someone else?"

"What if she did? She wouldn't say a word. No one ever corrects a duke." He flashed a small, innocent grin. "It's a duke's prerogative to decide when it's time to be on familiar terms and give a person permission to relax." He brushed her concern aside so easily. "We are at that point now, Ophelia. I am Hurst."

Surprise glinted through her. She didn't think she would ever understand men who were not like her brother. He would never have been so familiar with a young lady. Not even one he'd known for years. But Ophelia was learning new rules. This one she could abide by. There were times she had no desire to be so formal with the duke.

He walked closer to her and gently said, "Say it."

She held her breath for a moment before answering, "Hurst."

"See how easy that was?" Before she became aware of his intent, the duke took her hand and began to walk. "Come with me. I left what I brought you beside the garden gate."

At his touch, shivers cascaded through her entire body and she realized she'd never held a man's hand unless he was helping her into or out of a carriage, and most of the time that was her brother and they had on gloves. Like hers, Hurst's hand was bare, but also snugly warm and full of strength. Yet so gentle sizzling tingles raced through her. She had to restrain herself from allowing her grip to match his.

She could hardly think, much less make her legs work properly and walk alongside him.

Gathering control of her senses, she looked over at him and declared, "This is highly improper, Your Grace."

"My name is Hurst. You must get used to using it, Ophelia."

"It will take time."

"I have plenty of that." He smiled. "Would you have come with me without asking me ten questions if I had simply requested you walk with me?"

"I can't speculate on that because I don't know what my options are, but you wouldn't have had reason to worry about Maman's scrutiny if you had a nosegay or another box of those delicious confections in your hands." She finished by giving him a tart expression, which caused him to smile.

"So, you indulged in the sweet treats I brought to your mother the other afternoon?"

"Of course, and Maman didn't have to insist."

He chuckled. "If I thought flowers and confections were all it would take to make you happy, I would have brought them today. But that's not what I have for you, Ophelia."

How could the sound of her name on his lips evoke the idea of kissing him? She brushed the anticipation of it away before it took root and got her in trouble once again.

Just before they reached the gate, there was a vine-covered archway. He let go of her hand and said, "Stop here. One moment."

He was barely outside the gate before stepping back inside and closing it behind him. They were sequestered in a narrow portion of the hedge and hidden from view of the house or street.

The duke held a musty-looking tome with gold lettering. At first, she was perplexed; then she held her breath as he held it out to her.

"You said you needed this. I hope it makes you happy."

In silence she read the title:

Debrett's Peerage and Baronetage.

Her lips parted in a silent breath of delight. She couldn't tear her gaze away from the book she'd longed to get her hands on.

Near speechless and trying to slow her heartbeat again, Ophelia found her voice as she took the large volume from him. "I am more than happy."

"I would have gotten it for you before now, but I was hoping to persuade you from your pursuit by not helping you."

Ophelia felt as if her heart were swelling as she held the book to her chest. The duke could play the hardened rake well, but he had a kind heart, and he'd just shown her the extent of that kindness.

Before she sought reason or rhyme why, and without thought or pause, she took a step closer to him. "I know this will make a difference in my search to clear my brother's name. I can't tell you how I desperately needed this encouragement today."

He looked in the direction of the small table where the letter from Maman's friend was located.

"Did you receive bad news today?" he queried.

"Disappointing," she answered, looking at him so intensely it pulled her field of vision away from all surroundings. "The bishop will be appointing a new vicar soon. He could arrive at Wickenhamden within a matter of days."

"I know that was unwelcomed news."

"Very." She inhaled so deeply her chest heaved as she hugged the book. "But this was good news. Thank you."

"Enough, Ophelia." He signaled his impatience and gently took the book from her hands and leaned it against the side of the house. "If you have more gratitude, deliver it in a physical manner." He stepped closer to her. "A handshake, a pat on my shoulder and a 'jolly good,' or even offer a kiss—on my cheek if necessary for your modesty—but no more words."

A kiss? Her heart started pounding.

"Just use the book well."

A hasty puff of air forced past her lips. "I will."

"I hope it is the magic you are looking for." Pointing a finger and a hot gaze at her, he warned, "And don't get caught."

By the way he looked at her, he knew she wasn't going to stop slipping into book rooms just because she had Debrett's volume. "I don't intend to."

Her breathing became shallow and fast. Perhaps she had lost all thought and good sense, blaming their absence on the gratefulness that he'd brought her the book she'd so desired. Whatever the reason, she found herself taking a tentative step closer to him.

The duke lowered his face to no more than a few inches above hers. The warmth from his body was so close she felt it and heard the uneven rhythm of his breathing and caught the clean scent of shaving soap. His eyes seemed to be memorizing her face.

Staring into his handsome green eyes, she considered her feelings of doubt about his desire for her, discarded them, and asked, "Do you want to kiss me?"

"What I want right now is nothing you should want." His voice was husky, sensual, intimate.

What he said was probably true, but she was fairly sure she wanted it anyway. The feel of his lips on hers, the strength of his arms around her, holding her close, and to taste the unbridled passion she'd read about in poetry. And she wanted it all from the irascible but captivating duke. The problem was, she didn't know how to let him know or whether he wanted to oblige.

"I want you to kiss me," he said huskily.

Her heart hammered foolishly. That didn't sound right. She thought it was always the man who kissed the lady, but perhaps it didn't matter. She didn't really know. She couldn't ever remember seeing her parents kiss, and her brother had never married. Not that she would have seen them kiss if he had a wife.

Confused by the trail of her own thoughts about something as intimate as a kiss, and the tightness in her chest, she couldn't do anything but admit the truth, "I don't know how."

He waited silently, keeping his penetrating gaze on hers.

For a moment, she wondered if she was brave enough to say what was on the tip of her tongue, but then the words left her mouth with confidence: "Will you show me?"

His breath hitched and a pleased smile spread seductively over his lips. "That's the best thing you've ever asked me to do for you, Ophelia," he rasped. "And that's exactly what I'm going to do."

The duke slid his hand to the back of her neck. It was deliciously and intensely intimate for him to be touching her in such a way, but she didn't want him to stop. He bent his head closer. Her eyes closed without prompting, and she felt his lips brush feather soft over hers with the merest amount of tender, languid pressure. His lips were cool and refreshing. In that timeless span of a short moment, all her insides tightened and tingled. She didn't know how he'd filled her with such intense pleasure just by a mere kiss.

He raised his head, and she lifted her lashes. The duke was smiling. Ophelia smiled too, wanting to savor and memorize having her first kiss.

"Do you think you know how to do it now?" he asked. "Or should I give you another kiss to make sure?"

The desirous feelings she'd had for him were suddenly flaming. Feeling flushed, Ophelia had no idea but wanted to try. She moistened her lips. "I can do it."

"Go ahead then," he answered, softly.

He remained still. Patient. Tentative, but curious, she reached up and lightly placed her lips on his.

"Perfect," he whispered into her mouth as his hands slid down her shoulders and back, circled her waist, and caught her solidly up against his chest. His arms held her as if he didn't intend to let her go.

There were times her brother had hugged her. Not often. He wasn't good at showing affection, but she never felt unloved because of it. And Winston's quick embraces had never felt like being in the duke's arms. His strength, the way he held her so firmly against him, was exhilarating. It was as if she sensed, somehow, she belonged to him, and he would never allow anyone to take her from him.

He pressed a short kiss to her lips, and then to each side of her mouth, and then several more. "I'm going to show you another way to kiss, Ophelia."

If there was more to learn, she wanted to know what

it was. Her first kisses had been so much more than she'd imagined, what more could there be?

The duke slanted his lips firmly over hers and moved back and forth. She braced her palms on his chest as he pressed her tightly against him.

A soft moan collected in her throat, and her lips relaxed and softened beneath his. Ophelia kissed him while he moved his hands up and down her back, gently in soft strokes that inadvertently tickled her sides as his thumbs moved against her rib cage.

Instinct took over and she followed his lead. Their kisses became harder, deeper, and longer. Without mindful effort, she lifted her arms and entwined them around his neck, clasping her hands together at his nape. She loved the feel of her fingers finding and then threading through his silky collar-length hair.

As if she'd done it many times before, she opened her mouth, and his tongue explored inside with light, caressing strokes, causing a tightening in her abdomen. This way of kissing, his lips moving seductively back and forth over hers while he held her tightly, sent pleasurable feelings swirling inside her. And though it might not be true because of her lack of knowledge, she sensed the duke was feeling everything she felt too.

His lips left hers and brushed along her jawline over to the shell of her ear, kissing the soft, sensitive skin behind it. She let out a moan, her skin prickling with tingles. She could have lost herself forever in such budding feelings, but to all things there is an end.

Too soon, the duke uttered a low sound and suddenly put an arm's length between them. A gulp of chilly spring air slowly cleared Ophelia's thoughts; her breathing started slowing down. It was the same for the duke as she watched his expanding chest slow and return to normal.

"I didn't intend to get so carried away," he offered.

The duke may have spoken like a gentleman, but he didn't present himself as one right now. His hair was ruffled out of place around his ears. Had she done that when she had her hands at his nape? His neckcloth was askew and his coat at an odd angle on his shoulder. Seemingly, the unwavering resolve he carried himself by had fled. Albeit temporarily, she was sure. Now she found she liked seeing him with his hair mussed out of place. If the wind were blowing in the opposite direction, she was sure she could have seen the scar he and her mother were talking about that day in the drawing room.

"Neither did I."

"I heard someone or something moving around in the neighbor's garden just beyond the hedge," he spoke softly.

Ophelia hadn't heard anything but their breath and sighs. "Perhaps a rabbit. No one lives next door. But I'm glad you heard it. I wouldn't want anyone to see us kissing. Or to even know we had."

Thank heavens the duke took control when she could not put propriety and privacy before passion. She had no doubt they had been kissing far longer than was respectable even for married people.

Maman had advised many times it was the lady's responsibility to keep a man in line concerning romantic pursuits. Clearly, Ophelia hadn't been able to. The experience had been too wonderful, and she wanted to continue enjoying everything she was feeling. She might never have another opportunity to be kissed again. There was no way of knowing. The duke was right. She could end up in prison or worse for searching book rooms of private homes.

It suddenly occurred to her that it might be appropriate to let the duke know how much she enjoyed the kisses. Her mother had taught her a thank-you was never out of line. And other things about decorum and proper behavior. But she'd never been taught the appropriate way to react after a passionate embrace with a man. That was probably because there wasn't supposed to be a long, passionate embrace between two unmarried people. But before she could decide what to say she noticed a serious expression on the duke's face.

Had she done something wrong? Had it been her fault they had kissed so long?

"I shouldn't have said what I did earlier, Ophelia. I don't know what I was thinking."

"I didn't mind," she answered, some of the afterglow of their embrace still with her. It would be a long time before she forgot this day, and, for a fleeting moment, she wondered if she would ever forget her first kiss. It was something worth remembering.

"I know it wasn't ladylike of me, and I shouldn't have been so eager, but I wanted to know what it was like to kiss and be kissed. I could have refused, but I didn't want to. I simply got carried away because of your—your—"

"My desire to kiss you too?" His voice was low and husky. "My passion for you? Because I wanted to touch you and hold you in my arms?"

"Because of your generous gift," she offered the correction, and didn't want to even think about the possibility what he said might be true. Had he really wanted to kiss her that badly? "You have no reason to apologize for your forward behavior."

He brushed a hand across his hair and then adjusted

his coat to correct his appearance. The threat of an attractive smile tweaked the corners of his mouth. Hers too.

"You have always been far braver than you should be, Ophelia, and I make no apology to you nor anyone else for our kisses. I don't regret a moment of it and don't want you to either." He paused as his expression turned serious. "One thing I can't do is allow you to continue to rummage through book rooms of homes."

All residual sensuous feelings dissipated in an instant. Drawing on all her deportment as well as determination, she fixed him with a rigid glare and said in a near whisper, "You are not my guardian. It is not up to you to allow or disallow anything concerning me. You can't stop me."

"But I am helping you in ways that will not get you in trouble," he argued. He quickly brushed the tail of his coat aside and propped his hands on his slim hips. "My help is what you have wanted from the moment you walked into my life. I went to *great* trouble to bring my cousin to the party so you could hear what he had to say about the chalice and be assured of his innocence."

A breeze freed the strand of hair from behind her ear and scattered it across her face, but she managed to stare back at him without flinching or blinking and say, "I know. I'm grateful."

He threw up his hands as if he didn't understand her simple answer and pointed toward the book resting against the side of the house. "I bought the book for you."

"I'm glad for all your help so far, but what I need you to do is start looking on bookshelves for me."

"I've told you it's wrong to search through anyone's belongings. Do you want us both to get thrown into Newgate?"

"We are both too clever to have that happen."

"It's not right, Ophelia. Neither your brother nor your

father would approve, and I'm not going to change my mind and approve of it either. I'm assisting you in other ways to keep you out of trouble."

"I understand, but I believe the sacrament is gathering dust on a titled man's bookshelf. We can share responsibilities. You help the way you can, and I will help my way. Together, maybe it will be found before it's too late."

His mouth narrowed and he gave a short snort of laughter. "I've told you it's preposterous, wrong, and will get you nowhere but in a pot of hot water. I've asked Wyatt and Rick, who have been dukes much longer than I have, about this, and neither of them knows of such a man among the peerage."

She swallowed hard. "It's all I can do right now."

The duke's brow rose in disapproval and his jaw tightened. "No, you can stop," he said on a hissing breath.

"And do nothing?" she exclaimed. "No, sir. That is what I cannot do."

"I know how much this means to you, but you can't sacrifice your character for it. I told you when we first met, I can pay for the chalice to be replaced. What you are doing is madness. I've told you invading someone's privacy isn't something that should ever be done to anyone. I know you've heard the saying that two wrongs won't make anything right, Ophelia. Take my word for it, that's true."

"No, whoever said that is wrong."

Despite her intentions to remain unaffected by his words, her heartbeat faltered. Her throat thickened. It did bother her that she was going against everything she'd been brought up to believe and how to behave. She wouldn't have chosen to steal anything from anyone. Not even a thief.

"Have you ever done anything wrong, Your Grace?"

He was prudently silent for a moment and didn't meet her eyes but finally admitted, "Of course I have."

"Wrong things for a good reason?"

"More times than you have for sure." He blew out a deep breath of impatience. "And every time I have, I've later wished I hadn't."

Ophelia wondered if something deeper than he was saying was going on inside him. Was it only that he had a strict code of honor, and maybe his own code about what was right and what was wrong for himself? Was there more to the faraway look that appeared in his eyes than just what she was doing and what he was saying? She sensed there was. Maybe he was thinking about something he'd done wrong in the past.

It wasn't that she hadn't reflected on what she was doing. There had been plenty of that. She didn't want to do bad things that she knew were wrong. Things that would have had her brother and father extremely disappointed in her. She felt guilty for being so willful, and one day she'd have to forgive herself for searching the homes.

But that wouldn't be today or tomorrow. For now, she had to continue with her plan.

"I will be watching you like a hawk after his prey tomorrow night at Lord Swillingwill's house, so don't try to get out of my sight," he said with a warning in his tone.

"And I will be watching you. I started this search without you, and I can finish it without you. I certainly won't force you to help me with anything."

"Force?" he questioned the word with a grunt as the word stuck in his craw. "You couldn't force me to do anything I don't want to do, Ophelia."

"You are right, Your Grace. If I could have forced you, I would have already done it by now."

He smiled at her sassy retort. "All right, enough of the madness you have created in my life. You want my help? Fine." He sucked in a deep breath as an expression of fierce concentration settled on his face. "Marry me."

CHAPTER 12

MAN'S PRACTICAL GUIDE TO APPREHENDING A THIEF
SIR BENTLY ASHTON ULLINGSWICK

Avoid danger at all costs.

Hurst caught himself, as well as Ophelia, off guard. They were both speechless, staring at each other in astonishment.

He hadn't planned to say, "*Marry me.*" Hadn't even thought about the possibility of proposing to her today or any day, but the moment the words left his mouth unbidden, he knew he meant them. They felt right. She felt right for him. He'd known it the first night they'd met, the way he was attracted to her even though he shouldn't have been. The way he was still attracted to her even though he shouldn't be. However, from the expression on her face, he wasn't sure she was as convinced as him that they were meant to be together and should marry.

He pushed aside his instinct to pull her close, smell the scent of her fresh-washed hair, nuzzle the warmth at the curve of her neck, and kiss the slight swell of breasts showing so pillowy soft from above the neckline of her velvet spencer. She wouldn't be convinced they should marry because of enticing kisses and sweet words. Nor because he'd felt she was the one for him almost the moment he saw her. Ophelia needed a reason and a plan.

When he'd held her in his arms and kissed her, damnation, he hadn't wanted to stop, hadn't wanted to let go of her. She was where she belonged. With him. Of all the women he'd been with or could have been with, he had no doubt she was the one lady for him.

Ophelia suddenly took a cautious step back and looked behind her and around the garden as if to make certain no one was listening or watching. "What did you say?"

"Marry me," he said again without any reservation. Hurst didn't mind repeating it. He felt as sure of it as he ever had about anything in his life. There was so much more than his desire for her. She was strong, loyal, and filled with more determination than a young lady should have. He admired her courageous spirit and certainly wanted his sons to have her attributes.

"We should go inside, and I'll make my offer official by asking your mother's permission for your hand in marriage."

"Wait." Her voice remained confident and steady. "You are talking too fast, Your Grace." She straightened her shoulders and moistened her lips. There was a determined set to her expression and validity in her eyes. "I know it's what the church believes, but I didn't think you would be catering to their strict views. Just because I allowed you to kiss me, and I kissed you in return, doesn't mean you have to ask me to marry you. No one will ever be the wiser about what just happened between us. Especially if we act normal and forget it happened ourselves."

Forget how she felt as if she belonged in his arms? Belonged to him as his wife? That would never happen.

Hurst smiled. Her response was so clear, rational, and charming he wanted to pull her and kiss her again. Her innocence and absence of guile or pretense were easy to add to the many things he enjoyed about her and made him want her all the more.

"You think I'm asking you to be my wife to keep there from being damage to your reputation?"

"Of course, but have no worries, Your Grace. Unlike some and even most people in the church and Society, I don't believe I am ruined for another man or for life. It was a kiss, not a—a union between us. That would be cause for concern that we couldn't possibly overcome, but I am not compromised. You don't have to be concerned about my reputation or my stability in handling this situation."

Situation?

She never ceased to amaze him. Her tenacious spirit had been evident from the moment he'd laid eyes on her, and he was still drawn to it like a beast to beauty.

"That's not why I want to marry you."

Ophelia gave him a quizzical look and folded her arms across her chest in a proud stance. "Please don't tell me that, at last, you have an attack of conscience and feel you must offer for my hand as a belated way of honoring your promise to my brother. You're too late for that."

It wasn't the first time she'd spoken to him in such an impertinent way. He had come to expect it and oddly looked forward to their spirited, spritely exchanges.

"Indeed, I am too late, and no, I don't feel I have to do anything to atone for that." But in hindsight, he wished he'd gone to see Winston instead of keeping his promise to his aunt and tending to the blights that had ravaged his lands when he returned to London. He had no doubt that the current relationship between him and Ophelia wouldn't be so complicated if he'd made different decisions. His eyes narrowed. "Maybe you are still upset with me because I didn't agree to marry you when your brother asked me to and feel you can't trust me?"

"Don't be ridiculous." She puffed a loud breath and glanced around the garden again as if needing time to gather her thoughts. "I didn't even know he was going to impose on you and ask. If I had known, I would have had him not do it and he wouldn't have. Winston would have never done anything I asked him not to. He considered it his place to care for me after Papa died, and he did. There were those who offered for my hand, but I wasn't interested. He never tried persuading me to settle on anyone even when there was a gentleman who would have helped our station in life."

So, she had other offers of marriage. That wasn't surprising. "So then, did Winston only decide to tell you he contacted me after I refused to offer?" That seemed a little cruel.

"No, of course not."

Her eyes seemed to bore directly into his, and for a moment he was sure he saw a glistening at the corners. "I'm sorry if asking about this upsets you."

Ophelia seemed to swallow hard again and took in a deep silent breath. "It never upsets me to talk about my brother. He was the kindest man I've ever known. He never told me anything about contacting you. I don't believe he ever would have. I found a copy of the letter he sent to you and your reply when we were searching among his things for the chalice. Otherwise, I wouldn't have ever known."

"I'm glad that's not the reason you often seem to find yourself dismayed with me."

"What unsettles me about you is that you were too busy with your own life and you let your good friend down and never went to see him when you knew he was ill."

"That is a regret I'll always carry with me, but it can't be undone."

"No, it can't." She nodded once and lifted her shoulders. "So, now that is settled and we have that business about marriage finished, I will bid you goodbye."

Settled? Finished?

Most ladies would have accepted his proposal immediately and other issues be damned. But not his beautiful, headstrong Ophelia.

And it was probably best for him not to try to explain to her what he was feeling about marrying her. That she had somehow been destined for him long before her brother wrote to him proposing marriage, or the first time he'd met her. It was difficult to understand and would be even harder for him to express the instinct that he knew to be true. He'd been waiting for her. No one else would do.

A more practical approach would be far better for her.

"My wanting to marry you has nothing to do with your brother at all. One of the reasons I didn't make it to see him was because I had plans to visit my aunt. She had arranged for me to meet three different ladies in hopes I'd agree to marry one of them. I'll be thirty-one in a matter of weeks. I need a wife and you're the one I want."

She blew out an audible breath. "I am a simple vicar's daughter. You are a duke."

"You are a member of Society by birth as am I," he argued. "And I can assure you that your father was better than mine."

"That aside, I know nothing about being a duchess."

His breath hitched. Did that mean she was receptive to the idea? "You don't need to. You can learn the same way I had to learn about being a duke. You didn't know anything about sneaking around in houses looking for a thief either, but you have done a very fine job learning how to do that."

She screwed up her face as if wondering if she should thank him for the compliment or rail against him for the slight. "I read a book that has been somewhat helpful."

How could he forget that? "Ophelia, what I am offering you is an arranged marriage of sorts."

That obviously piqued her interest. She looked at him closely to determine what he was trying to explain. "What kind of an arrangement?"

He grinned. "You mean other than a marriage of me conveniently saving you from Newgate?"

Ophelia pursed her lips and then frowned. "I'll have you know I haven't come close to getting caught."

"Except by me," he said with a hint of devilment in his tone and shining in his eyes. "So far. How long do you think your luck on that will last? I'm offering a marriage that will benefit you and me. I have been wanting to marry for a long time." She didn't need to know how long. "You will give me an heir to continue the title. I will do more to help you search for the chalice."

Her brows and lashes lifted in concern. "There were over a dozen young ladies at the Duke of Wyatthaven's ball and close to that number at the card party. Every one of them was almost begging to give you an heir."

"I know." He gave her another amused grin. "But I'm not asking them. I'm asking you."

A small flicker of emotion flashed in her blue eyes. "I don't know why I'm the one you want to marry when you're constantly annoyed with me and don't even like me."

He stepped closer to her as he slowly shook his head. "Oh, no, Ophelia. That is where you are wrong. I more than like you. I desire you and find myself constantly thinking about you and your enchantingly bold ways. There is a powerful attraction between us and has been from the first. Will you admit that?"

"Yes," she answered in an unhurried voice. "I'm not sure I understand it since we have a difficult time seeing eye to eye on something that is very important to me."

He wasn't sure he understood it either, but he had no doubt it was real. And right now, he couldn't help but have a pang of remorse that he'd rejected Winston's suggestion. If he'd accepted, Ophelia would already be his. He wondered if maybe Winston had somehow foreseen his sister and Hurst were meant to be together.

"Desiring each other is quite important in a marriage, Ophelia. After our kisses, I think it's quite clear we see eye to eye on that."

He watched her breathing kick up. So did his.

"In any case, I think you are being hasty, Your Grace. Marriage is sacred and for life. It shouldn't be taken lightly and certainly not simply just for the thrills of wanting a few kisses."

Only a few? Never.

She really didn't know what magic, wonder, and contentment awaited her in the marriage bed. That made thoughts of showing her even more exciting.

"I'm not taking anything lightly," he admitted honestly.

"Why don't you continue to help me as you have with your cousin and the book? I think, perhaps, you see marrying me as some sort of grand redemption because of your past misdeeds."

Ophelia was right. He was full of misdeeds. With a father like his there was no choice but to sometimes do the wrong thing. Hurst wasn't looking for any kind of liberation from them. Not concerning his father or even for the promise he'd made when he was a boy. There were many things Hurst would change in his past if he could, but he didn't think about them anymore.

"And what are you are seeking?" he asked her in return. "Revenge against me?" He softened his frown into a smile as he looked into her eyes and brushed the strand of hair that had been bothering her all afternoon behind her ear again. His fingertips trickled across her cheek as his gaze sailed down her face. "Because I am the beast you didn't expect and not the angel of rescue you wanted."

The tenderness in her eyes and expression let him know he was right, but it gave him no pleasure.

"Redemption and revenge are powerful motivators, and hard to settle in reality and in one's mind."

"Forget about both and say you will marry me, Ophelia. You will get the help you need to find the chalice and I'll get an heir with your strong attributes."

She clasped her hands together at her waistline and held them tightly together. A wrinkle appeared at the beautiful space between her eyes as she studied hard on what he said. "And will you allow me to continue in my pursuit my way?"

"Everything you are doing—except searching homes, of course."

"But that is where the vessel is."

"You don't know that."

"I feel it in here." She placed her hand on her chest.

"All right. Once you are my wife, I will look at your list and ask the gentlemen written there if we could possibly come and look at their book room because you want to renovate mine. That way you won't need to slip away and search on your own. You could help by asking the friends and the hosts of parties to give us tours of their homes or just the book rooms. But it will take time to get around to the peers you haven't already cleared from your list. While we wait, you must give me your word you will stop doing it on your own. You will be a duchess, Ophelia. I can't have you traipsing around other people's homes unescorted on a wild goose chase."

That stiffened her spine instantly and set her lips in a straight line. "You *can't* have me? You are not my guardian. You are not responsible for me."

"I will be after we marry," he insisted ardently. "I may not have agreed to what your brother asked of me, but he chose me to ask for your hand, not someone else. Did you see where he had written letters to any other gentlemen asking if they would agree to marry you?"

"No. Only you," she answered heatedly.

"Right," he confirmed, feeling his temper rising at the frustration of not getting the simple yes he desired from her. "Because he wanted me to take care of you and take responsibility for you. He must have had some inkling you'd be doing something to get yourself in trouble. Now, say you'll marry me."

"If I marry you, I will be obligated to abide by my vows to obey your wishes, will I not?"

He shrugged as the cool breeze rustled the budding tree limbs overhead. "That is the way of it. All wedding vows are to be honored."

"I've always believed that too. The wife listens to the husband, and he to her, but in the end, he is the one who has final decision over disagreements."

His gaze focused fully on hers, and in a more relaxed tone, he said, "I agree with that."

"And that's why I can't marry you."

Hurst stared at her with growing irritation. What the devil was this all about? Was she just being stubborn? Hurst let his gaze slowly peruse her lovely face. She wasn't just making idle talk, she was serious, and that was concerning. "I'm not asking anything of you that is impossible for you to do."

"As your wife, I would feel duty bound to honor my vows to you and follow your wishes and not deliberately disobey something you had forbidden me to do, so I will not make wedding vows I can't say I intend to keep."

"Of course you wouldn't." Frustration knotted in his stomach and the back of his neck. He shook his head again. "That's what wives do. Why would you have a problem keeping your vows to me? I'm giving you what you've wanted, Ophelia. My help. I'll hire a runner from Bow Street to start looking into the theft immediately. I'll hire men to look through every shop in London and elsewhere if necessary to see if it's been sold."

Interest flared in her eyes. "Will you hire one to sneak into the houses in the middle of the night through a window? Is that how he would get inside to look in the book rooms?"

"Of course not." He didn't like that possibility any better than what Ophelia had been doing. And damnation, he didn't like having to work so hard to get her to say yes. He was doing the best thing for her and for him. "I've told you it's wrong to invade the privacy of another person's home and start looking through their things and taking what you want."

"Did that happen to you?"

"What?" Hurst relaxed his stiffened body. Once again, he'd said too much to her. He couldn't let her drag him into a past he had no intention of talking about. "I don't know what is to be done until I talk to a runner. I'm sure there are many things he would do, including going to Wickenhamden to question some of the—"

"Wickenhamden?" she interrupted quickly.

Hurst forced himself to talk normally, though it was hard when she sounded outraged, but he was outraged too. He'd always known she was unreasonable when it came to what she was trying to accomplish.

Exasperated, he offered, "The usual place to start an investigation is at the scene of the crime."

"But he can't do that. Maman and I have gone to great lengths to keep this matter quiet. If someone travels there to ask questions about the chalice, it will raise suspicions and the vicar or someone else might go looking for it. That is the last thing I'd want a runner to do. I've told you no one knows it's missing, and we must keep it that way. Besides, I believe it's here in London. This is where we need to be looking."

Hurst rubbed the back of his neck again. It seemed everything he was saying was the wrong thing. He knew how important this was to her. "But the truth is you don't know where it is," he insisted. "Maybe the runner won't need to go to Wickenhamden. Maybe he knows what questions to ask without making anyone curious. You wanted my help, Ophelia. I'm trying to do that."

"Yes, help," she argued. "Not that you would take over and do everything the way you want instead of what I want."

"Your way isn't working," he insisted.

She gasped.

He realized how harsh his words sounded before he saw the depth of hurt in her eyes. Their color changed from bright to a dark stormy blue. Regret and anger at himself pierced him sharp as the tip of a blade. She knew she wasn't getting anywhere. It hadn't been necessary for him to say it out loud.

Ophelia's whole body seemed to lift in indignation. "I'm not doing this to gain some type of curious pleasure for myself but because I must. I will not promise to submit to your will concerning my quest, so therefore I cannot marry you, but I do thank you for the Debrett's book and your offer of marriage."

Without looking at him again, she reached down, picked up the book, and hurried around the corner of the house. Moments later, he heard the door shut.

For a second, he thought to follow her inside, but he caught himself and didn't. She needed time to think. So did he.

He hadn't won her over. Fine, but he wouldn't let her lofty rejection stand. A man was supposed to enjoy the hunt of pursuing the lady he wanted. He'd always understood that, but the truth was now that he'd decided he wanted Ophelia, he didn't want to wait. He had already hunted and found. All he had to do was capture her.

CHAPTER 13

MAN'S PRACTICAL GUIDE TO APPREHENDING A THIEF
SIR BENTLY ASHTON ULLINGSWICK

When one plan goes awry, make another.

Once inside, Ophelia shut the back door and leaned against it, shaking as she clutched the book about catching a thief, the book Hurst gave her, the shawl, and the note Maman's friend sent. Closing her eyes to catch her breath, the first thing she wanted to do was relive the precious moments in the duke's arms.

Her skin had pebbled with delicious, shivery bumps just thinking about Hurst's kisses skimmed all the way down to the hollow of her throat. The feeling was so extraordinary and like nothing she'd ever felt before. His touch, taste, and the sounds of his labored breathing were heady. She felt as if their bodies were melting into one. It was so thrilling she had no comparison to the experience.

For the first time in her life, she had known what it was like to desire a man and for him to desire her. It was exhilarating and she wanted to put it to memory for fear she'd never experience it again, though her body already ached for more.

There were too many things to think about all at once. Not only the ethereal feeling. The duke wanted her to marry him. Give him a son. That wasn't too much to ask of a lady. It was expected of her. Her problem was trusting Hurst that once they married, he wouldn't try to force her to stop looking for the chalice. It was a wife's duty to obey her husband and she wasn't sure she could do that. Right now, she couldn't put anything above making sure Winston's legacy wasn't tainted. A new vicar could be on his way to Wickenhamden by tomorrow or the next day. So yes, she would look in Lord Swillingwill's house and every other house she could get inside.

The duke was right; they were attracted to each other. How could she not be torn about her adamant decision? Was refusing the duke the right thing to do, or was she being foolish? There was passion between them that the kiss confirmed. It had been difficult to say no, but there couldn't be any other answer for her.

What was wrong with Hurst? Why did he think it was so wrong to simply look around someone's book room? Especially when you weren't trying to steal anything. Well, only if there was something there that had already been stolen and all you wanted to do was return it to the rightful owner. It wasn't like she wanted to go into someone's bedchamber and look through their personal belongings. Just a room of books. Mostly books. Why did he think that was so horrible?

She'd never pretended to understand Hurst. And this idea of marrying him made it doubly so. Like most young ladies, she'd always believed she'd marry one day, but not a duke. A desirous and handsome one at that. At times, she felt shaky and somewhat out of control when she was talking to him. The feelings he evoked were always immediate, demanding, and confusing.

Ophelia closed her eyes tightly and huffed. Why were things like that even entering her mind? Kisses, marriage, and the duke. Her feelings or wants didn't matter. Only what was right for Winston and her mother. Her brother didn't deserve to be labeled a thief, and her mother didn't deserve to bear the shame of it for the rest of her life.

Hurst agreed that once she married, she was duly bound to submit to her husband's will, and she wasn't prepared to do that. Though she didn't know what to do about how he made her feel. The feelings were there inside her, whether he was with her or she was alone.

A smile briefly touched her lips. She liked hearing him say her name. Saying his. There were many things to recommend to him other than the desirous attraction connecting them. He was a good man who wanted her to do the proper things—even when she couldn't.

"Is that you, Ophelia?" her mother called from the drawing room.

"Yes, Maman." She'd had enough thinking about starry-eyed romantic notions. All they were good for was keeping her from her goal. Those thoughts and considerations could be dealt with later. There were more important things to do now. "I'll be right there."

She headed toward the dining room to put the books on the table and almost ran into the footman coming out.

"Begging your pardon, miss." He stepped aside to allow her entry.

"Here, Mr. Mallord, take these for me," she said, barely slowing down as she stuffed the books and shawl into his arms, but making sure to hold on to the letter from her mother's friend in Wickenhamden. "Place them on the dining table. Light all the lamps bright and push the draperies aside wide. Find Mrs. Turner and ask her to come to the dining room. I'll join her there shortly. I'll also need paper, ink, and quill."

"Yes, miss."

Ophelia rushed into the drawing room but stopped short when she saw her mother sitting in a chair by the window holding a cup and saucer.

"I'm glad you came inside," she said without looking at her daughter. "I think rain is on the way again."

"I do too." Ophelia hadn't noticed the sky had darkened and the wind had kicked up while she was with the duke. When he was around, her attention was only on him. "Are you feeling better now that you've had a little rest and warmth from the fire?"

"Oh, yes. I'm fine."

Roberta smiled, but she didn't look or sound fine. Her voice had a slight tremble, and her face seemed pale and drawn. Ophelia decided she would go to an apothecary tomorrow to see about purchasing a tonic to invigorate her mother's health.

"This letter from your friend—would you like for me to put it with the others for you?"

"Would you, dearest? I don't need to read it again. I'll never forget what it says but I think will wait until morning to answer and thank her for continuing to keep us updated."

Ophelia walked over to the secretary, opened the drawer she'd put the sketches in, took them out, and then tucked the letter away in its appropriate place. "Yes, it's kind of her to take the time."

Her mother whispered a tired laugh. "It is, but she loves the gossip of it all, and you know that. But I don't mind. It helps us, and you are trying so hard, I know you are going be successful before a new vicar arrives."

Ophelia's heart squeezed. Yes, she believed that too. She had to, but she knew time was slipping by quickly. Was a runner from Bow Street the answer or would he, as she'd suspected, only stir up questions about what Ophelia had been able to keep hidden so far?

Trying to encourage herself, she answered, "We do have more help now, Maman."

"Do we?" She rose and placed her cup on a nearby table. "What is it you've done that I don't know about?"

"The Duke of Hurstbourne stopped by."

She gave Ophelia a curious look. "When and why didn't you tell me? How did I miss him?"

"Because it was just now when I was outside. He only stayed a moment—or two," she fibbed with guilt shooting daggers into her chest for the untruth. "That is, he didn't stay very long," she amended, and hoped the correction was enough to assuage her guilt. "He saw me in the garden and decided to join me there rather than come inside."

"Why would he do that?" she asked with a bit of a huff.

"Because he does what he wants, Maman." At least that was the truth. "He likes to pick and choose which rules he follows."

"Yes, I suppose that's allowed, now that he is a duke." She looked down at the sketches Ophelia was holding. "You've looked at those a hundred times, dear. They are not going to change, and they haven't helped us, even though you did beautiful work in your renderings."

Ophelia smiled a little sadly. Suddenly torn about her decision not to marry the duke. Was it possible his way was best? "No, they haven't, but on the other hand." She paused and took a deep breath. "Thanks to the duke, I now have the book we've needed to compare these crests to names."

Roberta's eyes brightened. "*Debrett's Peerage and Baronetage*? He brought it to you?"

"Yes, Maman." Her heart warmed just thinking about the duke's kindness, even if it went against his will to help her. "So, I think you can forgive him for not taking the time to come inside to say a proper hello to you."

"Indeed, I can. This is such wonderful news. I always knew he was a fine boy, and now it appears he is a finer man, even if his father wasn't."

Her mother's comment sparked Ophelia's interest. Hurst had mentioned his father wasn't good with finances or the amount of drink he consumed and just today he referenced the sentiment again that his father wasn't a good man. Wanting to know more about him, she asked, "What do you know about his papa, Maman?"

"Nothing really." She pulled a lace-trimmed handkerchief from the cuff of her sleeve and lightly touched her forehead. "I never met him. I don't think your father did either."

"But you heard something?" Ophelia asked, wishing she'd been old enough to remember Hurst.

Her mother gave her a placating smile as she had so often when Ophelia was growing up. "Only that his father often left him with relatives for months at a time and longer. I'm not sure what the problem was, dear. I would never question anyone, and you know your father wouldn't either. Not even a child. And he would never betray a confidence should anyone place trust in him."

And neither would her mother. As was usually the

case, Ophelia was the only one in the family who wasn't above reproach.

"Oh," Roberta added. "I do remember Winston once saying that Drake had mentioned that he and his father didn't get along, so it hadn't mattered his father was weeks late in coming to get him."

If Ophelia wanted to know more about the duke, she was going to have to ask Hurst. She had always sensed an innate pride and integrity in him and admired that and was drawn to it. And while she loved talking about her family, Hurst was reluctant to talk about his.

"I have no idea if Drake—I mean the duke—ever spoke with your father about anything personal. I do know the duke's mother passed when he was a little boy and his father didn't seem to take much interest in him. He was living with one of his mother's relatives when we met him. But he was a fine young lad, with all the proper manners, so someone had taught him well."

"I agree." And then before Ophelia knew what she was going to say, she added, "He asked me to marry him."

Her mother's eyes and mouth went wide. "The duke?" Not waiting for an answer, Roberta rushed to Ophelia, almost knocking her over. "Is this the truth? Why didn't you tell me when you first came in?" She grabbed Ophelia and kissed both her cheeks twice. "It's terrible of you to keep such remarkable news from me while I prattle on about things of no consequence."

"No. It doesn't matter. I said no."

Her mother's hands stilled on Ophelia's shoulders as she studied her daughter's face with first curiosity, and then disbelief. "What do you mean? That can't be true." She continued smiling but not as broadly.

Ophelia nodded. "I can't marry him."

Taking her hands off her daughter's shoulders, Roberta clasped them together on her chest and took a step back. "Bother and balderdash. You can too. It appears I've let you make the decisions for the two of us far too long. This one, my dear, is foolish, and I won't let it stand. If he wants to marry you, it's because he believes you are the one woman who can make him a better man and help him enjoy life."

"It would be a marriage of convenience," she admitted. "He needs an heir for the title and in return he will help search for the thief."

"That's perfect! Why not say yes? If it's love you want, that will come if you allow it to blossom and flourish. We need him. You wanted his help when we came to London. Your refusal doesn't make sense. Something must be wrong with you." She put her palm to Ophelia's forehead.

"I am not sick, Maman."

"You have to be." Concern etched lines around her forehead, eyes, and mouth.

Ophelia slowly shook her head.

"Don't worry, dearest." Maman backed away and brushed her hands down the sides of her skirts. "It doesn't matter what you said. You were in shock. Totally understandable and acceptable for a lady when she receives a proposal. He should have never asked you first. He should have come to me. I'll go see him and tell him you didn't know what you were saying and that you now agree to marriage." She turned away. "I'll go right away before he has a chance to ask anyone else."

"I can't marry him because I couldn't remain true to my wedding vows."

"That's the most ridiculous thing I've ever heard you

say. Of course you can hold fast to your vows. You were raised to do so. You are not thinking clearly, Ophelia. We can't pass on an opportunity like this."

"If I marry him, I vow to obey him. He said he wanted me to stop looking for the Chatham's chalice and I couldn't do it."

"Why would he? You said he would help you find it."

"He says that now, but I don't know that I trust him to keep his word."

"Why would you say that, dearest?"

"For one, he never came to see Winston when he said he would. I just don't want to take the chance he will forbid me to look for the chalice the way I think is best."

Roberta went still except for her lashes, blinked slowly, and whispered, "But he knows if it isn't found Winston will be considered responsible because it went missing under his tenure."

"He's offered to just make restitution and make sure the authorities don't place blame on Winston."

A puzzled expression appeared on Roberta's face. "Perhaps he could do that, but what about the history of the chalice itself? That can't be restored by money or just another sacrament. And what about the members of the parish, the neighbors, and townspeople? Could he make sure they won't place guilt on Winston as well?"

"We both know he can't. That's why I can't turn complete control of this search over to him. I want his help but I'm also fearful."

Her mother folded her arms over her chest, turned away, and stared out the window.

Ophelia swallowed a lump that had clogged her throat. It hurt to see her mother so distressed.

"Maman, we knew this would be difficult when we started, but we had no choice but to try. Right?"

"Right," she answered softly without turning around. "He's probably a scoundrel in duke's clothing. Far better for my lamb to stay away from a wolf."

Her mother's words saddened her more. Roberta had said far too many nice things about Hurst for Ophelia to hear what she was saying now.

"We're not going to stop searching, Maman. I asked Mr. Mallord to get Mrs. Turner and to wait in the dining room so we can start going through the book. Do you want to join us for a little while?"

She turned and faced Ophelia, a solemn set to her pale lips and sorrowful eyes that seemed to look but not see. "Of course, I do. The sooner we find the family name that belongs to the crest, the sooner we can figure out which relative rides around in a fancy carriage and devise a way to get the chalice from him. We'll do it even if I must dress as a servant and sneak into the house and do it myself."

"Please, Maman. You know I would never let you do that," Ophelia said, smiling that her circumspect mother would even suggest such an option.

"We will do what we must, young lady. As you said, we started this and we will finish it."

"I'm sure having the book will help us." It hurt knowing she'd had to pull her mother into her scheme to find the thief, but she was rising to the occasion. "So, no reason for you to worry anymore about this. All right?"

"Oh, don't be ridiculous, my dear. I haven't been worrying." Though her mother's voice wasn't much stronger, her words and smile were. "My faith in you hasn't wavered."

Ophelia gripped the sketches tighter and inhaled a long deep breath, readying herself for the task at hand. "Neither has mine. Let's go look at that book and get started."

But as is so often the case, sometimes things don't turn out as easily as one thinks they will. Ophelia was smart enough to know this. However, knowing it and being aware of it as it was happening were altogether two different things. In retrospect, she should have done things very differently in her search through Debrett's book. Especially where it concerned Mrs. Turner.

The book had many pages and, though they started late in the afternoon, Ophelia was determined they would look at every one of them before the night was over. At the time, she didn't realize that her stamina and excitement were not at equal levels with Maman's and the maid's. Along the tedious way, Ophelia made copious notes but only on pages where the crests were similar to what Mrs. Turner remembered.

When Ophelia was finished with the laborious task, the number of possibilities was extensive, so she trimmed down the ones she had doubts about but had added just in case. And then trimmed again. The truth was that the process took much longer than expected.

Later, when Ophelia reflected on this, she realized going through the entire book and working until late in the night was too much for Mrs. Turner—and quite possibly herself too. Only after she'd brought the poor woman to tears and stuttering about how sorry she was had Ophelia realized she was not being sensible about the pressure she'd put on the maid. She probably never had been sensible about the reasonable outcome of her search. How could she be? The stakes of the possible outcomes were too high.

Well after midnight, more than two dozen possibilities remained. Reality hit her hard, and in the cold dark of the midnight hours, the shock of it was disheartening. Mrs. Turner simply hadn't seen enough of it, and Ophelia had been tempted to throw out the book, her sketches, and all the notes she'd made during the marathon search, with the morning's rubbish.

She was doing exactly what the duke had told her she would be doing. Looking for her hairpin in a stack of hay.

CHAPTER 14

MAN'S PRACTICAL GUIDE TO APPREHENDING A THIEF
SIR BENTLY ASHTON ULLINGSWICK

Look, repeat, look again for what's missing.

After an unexpected rolling tidal wave of events and emotions occurred the next day, by late afternoon Ophelia found herself standing in front of the duke's front door, shoring up her weakening courage while once again dressed as a *man.*

The early post had brought the shattering news from her mother's friend in Wickenhamden that the new vicar had been selected, he was healthy, and would arrive within the week. After Maman read the distressing news, her face had gone pale and drawn. Her voice inflected with a slight tremble, she mumbled that she would spend the rest of the day in her bedchamber and didn't want to be disturbed until a tray was sent up for supper.

It was at that action a couple of tears slid free from Ophelia's eyes before she could stop them. Only a week before the new vicar arrived hit Ophelia harshly with worry too. A sobering reality chilled her bones. For the first time, she truly felt as if she might fail in her quest to save her brother's unblemished life and her mother's health. She couldn't possibly have time to look in the book rooms of all the homes that were left on her list.

She had to do something drastic. And she knew only one person who could help. If she wasn't too late. She sent Mr. Mallord to deliver a note to the duke asking him to come see her. The footman reported back the duke wasn't home, but the butler had insisted he'd give the note to him as soon as he returned.

By early afternoon no answer from Hurst had arrived. Was it because she'd rejected him? He'd made it clear he wanted to marry and have a son. Maybe he had already asked another to be his bride. As much as that idea caused an emptiness in her chest, she had to put it aside. She had to swallow her pride and admit she needed the duke's help.

Ophelia went up to get her mother. She couldn't go to see the duke without a companion and Maman was the only viable option. They must go to the duke's house and wait for his return so they could speak to him in person. That idea hadn't worked either. Her mother had developed a blinding headache and had taken a tonic that put her to sleep. There was no getting her up and dressed. Ophelia had no one else to turn to. Time was running out and she needed the duke's support. And as much as she hated to admit it, his comfort too. Even if it meant incurring his ire.

Ignoring the gnawing fear in her stomach that wanted to turn her into a weak-kneed ninny, she reached up to make sure her top hat was straight and then clanked the horse door knocker twice, just as she had the last time she'd visited the duke. She remembered Gilbert, the formidable butler, but wondered if he would remember her. And would it be good or bad if he did? The man would certainly recognize her if the duke had told him after she left that first night, *Never let that man back in my house again.*

She had to put thoughts like that aside and not let fear thwart her. There were no other choices available.

While waiting, she looked around the prestigious neighborhood. There were more carriages waiting in front of the houses than she remembered from her last visit, but it had been later in the day. It stood to reason gentlemen such as the duke who lived in homes as fine as the ones within her sight would want their conveyances ready at the front of the house rather than having to wait for them to be brought around from the stables or mews.

Ophelia had rehearsed what she would say after the butler opened the door, but after she was greeted by the stalwart man with bushy eyebrows, he set her off course. His hairy right brow rose midway up his forehead, throwing her off-kilter as he took a step backward to draw in the full picture of her standing on the Duke of Hurstbourne's stoop. For a moment she didn't know if he was the butler or a gatekeeper.

Lifting her kohl-brushed chin, she lowered her voice and offered, "Mr. Warcliff to see the Duke of Hurstbourne." She feigned impatience for good measure and because she was actually shaking. Formal and spoken in octaves lower than her natural voice, she hoped her reply would set her back on track.

Not surprisingly, the butler gave her a peculiar stare. No wonder. The late afternoon sun heightened her brazen male costume, giving the rich colors of her waistcoat an audacious, dandified sheen.

The butler seemed out of sorts too. The skin at the corners of his small eyes wrinkled tightly when he asked, "Are you in the sporting club?"

From within the house, Ophelia could hear the undertones of male voices and elevated conversations, and she remembered the unusual number of carriages on the street. Her stomach knotted. The duke had guests. That could be the reason she hadn't received a reply from him. Though she tried to think of every conceivable reason, the possibility he might be having a party had never crossed her mind.

However, taking the opportunity where it landed, she instantly regrouped her intent. Formal and clipped once again, she returned, "Yes." She would worry about guilt for doing so later.

The butler's other brow arched to meet its predecessor. Ophelia remained stiff and worried. He doubted her; she could sense it. He was about to throw her out, even though she'd never made it inside. If her plan went awry, she'd have no choice but to accept defeat and try a different tactic.

The possibility of surrender softened her shoulders, but then, thinking quickly, she blinked herself back to order and said, "You might recall I was here not long ago to see the duke." If that didn't help her gain some ground against the butler's seeming stone wall, nothing would.

"I remember you," he finally said in a pleasant tone. "Some of the Brass Deck members are already here, and His Grace is already entertaining. Follow me."

The butler turned so abruptly and started marching away, concern at what she'd accomplished turned to instant panic, but she forced it down. Making a quick decision, she stepped inside and followed him. She had to stop second-guessing herself and what she was doing. Yes, no matter the disguise, the fibbing, she was doing the right thing.

She'd heard of the Brass Deck club. The group of gentlemen competed in tournaments playing cards, fencing, racing horses, playing cricket, and other manly pursuits to see which club was the best. And, of course, for men to put down their wager on the outcome of the games, which was probably more important than watching the skilled men play the matches.

Feeling her courage bump up a notch or two, Ophelia stomped behind the butler down the corridor toward the deep rumbling sound of male talking bracketed by laughter. Now that she was in Hurst's house once again her courage felt stronger. If there was a chance she could win him over to help her on her terms, even though she had at one time vowed she never would again, she had to try. Dressing as a man was a sure way to, at least, get him to talk to her. She hoped, anyway. He'd been rather adamant that she never don the clothing again, so he probably wouldn't miss another opportunity to tell her one more time how she should never wear it again. Now that she thought about it, that was another reason she wasn't sure she could trust him. He very much liked to tell her what to do.

The butler paused at the drawing room and stepped aside, allowing her to enter the room with a silent nod; he then disappeared. Somehow, she managed to take in the whole of the drawing room at a glance before immediately easing toward the shadowy wall. Surprisingly, the duke didn't seem to be present.

A low-burning fire, and the delicious aroma of baking pastry dough drifting in from somewhere in the house, gave warmth and a welcoming ambiance to the room. There were eight to ten men gathered. Each held a drink and chatted with someone. No loners like she was. That wasn't good.

Ophelia didn't want to be observed too closely while she was trying to find the duke. It looked as if every one of the men obviously knew at least one other person in the room. Except her. Most of them were of the same age and had a physique much like the duke: young, tall, and powerfully built. Sporting men for sure. Handsome too. With her far smaller size, she would stand out like a daisy among a bouquet of red roses if anyone by chance caught notice of her trying to unobtrusively hide in the folds of the heavy velvet draperies for any length of time.

Where was the duke? All she wanted to do was ask if his offer to marry her was still a possibility. That shouldn't take more than two minutes of his time. If she could find him.

From the corner of her eye, she saw movement in the doorway and quickly looked. It wasn't Hurst, but it might be trouble. What rotten luck. The man was Mr. Wilbur Sawyer, and he was looking around the room much in the same way she had upon entering, wondering who he was going to talk to. None of the chatty group seemed to notice him any more than they had noticed her. But then, as bad luck would have it, before she could glance away, he caught her looking at him. Obviously discerning she was the only one not talking to someone else, he headed her way.

"Merciful angels," she whispered under her breath. Was there any chance the man would recognize her? Or her voice? There had only been the width of a table between the two of them at the garden card party they'd attended. At the time, it seemed Mr. Sawyer was more interested in Miss Georgina Bristol. Ophelia wasn't intimidated by him and his arrogant ways, but she would be foolish not to be wary that he might recognize her and tell everyone who she was.

Her stomach tightened to the point of hurting, but she would do her best not to spend much time with him—just in case something about her tweaked a memory or two. She didn't have many choices until the duke appeared.

"Good afternoon," he said, stopping in front of her. "My apologies for introducing myself, but I feel I'm among friends. I am Wilbur Sawyer, one of the gentlemen selected to be vetted and considered for membership in the Brass Deck. Are you under consideration too?"

She already knew from the card party that the man wasn't shy and was barely tactful. "Thad Warcliff," she responded with a nod, and keeping her lids low over her blue eyes so they wouldn't convey her inner turmoil or feminine qualities. "Very recently under consideration."

"What is your expertise, Mr. Warcliff? Marksman? Fencing?"

"Both." The response left her lips before she could reconsider saying it. That comment certainly wasn't in her best interest, considering the situation she was in. All this did was muddy her already-churning thoughts.

What would she do if he started asking her questions about the sport of shooting? She didn't know anything about it. In fact, had never picked up a blunderbuss, a musket, or even a pistol. She had seldom even seen one that wasn't mounted on a wall as an ornament of decoration.

"How about you?" she asked, quickly following her ill-stated answer with a question of her own and assuming he was waiting for her to ask. "Are you a pugilist?"

Shaking his head, he responded, "Cricket and cards." He looked her up and down rather doubtfully but, thankfully, not too closely. "Will you be playing matches with us?"

"Quite sure I won't," she answered, and then gruffly cleared her throat. Even with the two and a half inches of heel on her boots, she was still quite small compared to the size of all the men in the room. She had no doubt Mr. Sawyer was thinking she'd be squashed like a grasshopper underfoot in the summer grass on the first play of the match. "Cards for sure."

She glanced around the room again, doing her best not to show just how nervous she was. Where could the duke be?

A burst of laughter from someone caught Sawyer's attention. Thank goodness he was too busy looking as if to see who else might be available to talk to than to pay too close attention to her. That bought her a little time to try to figure out what to do since the duke wasn't in the room.

Going in search of the missing host seemed the most logical thing for her to do, but that idea bothered her a little. The duke was very particular that looking around rooms in the privacy of someone's home without invitation, no matter how saintly the reason, was wrong. She had a very clear feeling he would be especially displeased to find her rambling around by herself in his house.

A server approached them carrying a tray of glasses with a little amber liquid poured into the bottom of them. Mr. Sawyer took one and, because all the other men held a drink, Ophelia felt compelled to take a glass too.

"To the Brass Deck," Mr. Sawyer said.

After toasting him, Ophelia took a generous sip of the drink. Not used to such a strong, burning concentration of manly vises, she downed too much with the first swallow and dove into an unplanned coughing spree. Trying to quell the strong and very real reaction in her throat, she quickly pressed her man's handkerchief over her mouth to stanch the spasms. She occasionally enjoyed a glass of claret with her mother in the evenings, and champagne when available at parties, but she'd never tried anything as stout as brandy.

She gasped and managed to say, "Terribly sorry, Mr.

Sawyer. Swallowed wrong. Excuse me, if you please." She turned away from him and allowed her chest to heave in a deep clearing breath while remaining as quiet as possible so she wouldn't attract the attention of the other men in the room. She didn't need any of them to come over to ask if she was all right.

One thing was clear: Continuing to stand in this room wasn't the best course of action for her. She was getting nowhere and had had enough of waiting around for the duke to show while she played the part of a man without much success. She had two choices: go looking on her own or seek help. That was easy. She would rather find the staunch butler and take her chances with him again. All he could do was say no when she asked him where the duke was and if he could take her to His Grace.

While stuffing her handkerchief back into her coat pocket, she had the oddest sensation that her world was suddenly tilting and immediately knew why. She sensed Hurst's presence in the room. It was as if she felt the heat of his eyes upon her. She remembered the sweet passion of their kisses in the chill of the afternoon and how his body had seemed to warm her all the way down to her soul.

Without thinking, she turned toward the doorway, and their gazes met and for an instant she thought their heartbeats had too. He stood in the entranceway and she looked straight into the vivid green eyes of the impeccably dressed duke. All the other men in the room seemed to fade away as if they had disappeared from the room.

Her spirits lifted and she started to smile until she saw Hurst striding toward her as if with a life-or-death mission on his mind. One he didn't intend to fail at accomplishing. Even so, his stern stare as he approached with a menacing glare reminded her how immensely attracted she was to him even when his annoyance with her was flowing like a fast-moving current through him. There was something about him that made her know she'd rather be with him than anyone else.

Her heartbeat raced with thunderous pounding in her ears. She could feel his senses were alive and on alert.

In the next instant, she shivered with growing anticipation and fear for what he might say or do. In front of all these men he could call her out on her disguise. What would she do then?

He glowered at her with his jaw tightly clenched. She could almost hear his deep inhaling breath whistle through his white teeth. The closer he came the more she wilted.

CHAPTER 15

MAN'S PRACTICAL GUIDE TO APPREHENDING A THIEF
SIR BENTLY ASHTON ULLINGSWICK

Trust your instincts.

"Mr. Warcliff." The duke's strong tenor marked his stiff greeting. With a hard gaze leveled directly on Ophelia, he bridled his reproach. "Very good of you to come. Still have that cough, do you? I'll take care of that for you. Follow me, and I'll send for a glass of water."

Ophelia did her best to keep in step with the duke's impatient stride down the corridor. Laying her hand on top of her glass so the dark-amber liquor wouldn't spill, she almost missed navigating the corner he turned, quite unsteady in her haste. The men's boots she wore fit just under the bend of her knee and required some adjustment training with the way they fit. But she'd mastered them. Or so she thought. She felt as if lead had been added to the soles as she walked.

Dashing down the passageway, she shortened the gap between them. Then the duke had the ill timing to stop in his tracks so suddenly that she plowed into his backside. Her drink splashed against her fingers in her near stumble, but she didn't tarry a fraction of a second. Taking an intentional step sideways, she quickly broke contact. But not fast enough. The warmth of a blush blanketed her from head to toe.

Out of breath and out of sorts, Ophelia stood there unable to move as their eyes met. There was no doubt he was seething. It showed in every feature on his face when he glanced back to look at her. All the while, she could hear the duke's slow and controlled breathing. She was helpless not to gaze into his face. This close to him, it was as if she didn't want to tear her attention away.

He lightly took her by the right shoulder and, steering her ahead of him, beneath his breath he whispered, "Ladies first. Enter the second door on the right."

Trying to maintain calm, Ophelia did as he bid without question and entered what had to be the music room. A pianoforte, a harp, and a violin posed on a dark wood stand claimed the surroundings. She walked over to the piano, stopped, and turned around to face him. Her stomach jumped and she realized that no matter that he was upset with her, as impossible as it seemed, she was happy to see him.

His green eyes squeezed tightly at the corners, and his mouth was set and drawn. But none of that took away from the dashing figure he cut, and the man she was immensely attracted to.

Advancing on her, the duke said, "You are certainly filled with surprises, Ophelia."

"I could say the same for you."

"Me?" he questioned.

"Asking me to marry you was quite a surprise."

"It shouldn't have been. We were aware of each other the moment our eyes met. Even then we knew there would be passion between us."

Passion, no. She didn't know what passion was until he kissed her. A connection, a bond, yes.

He shook his head and inhaled deeply as if trying to settle himself. When he looked back to her, he asked, "What in the land of the living are you doing in my house mingling with my sporting club as if you were one of them?"

"I had no choice but to—"

"No, Ophelia, you had choice," he insisted.

He gave her no opportunity to explain and continued. "If one of the men had figured out you were a lady, it would be all over London faster than you could change out of those clothes into a proper dress. And that would be only if they didn't chew you up and spit you out on the front lawn before you had the chance. A man's club is sacrosanct."

Oh, he was in a bad temper. And she couldn't tell him he had no right to be angry with her. But he didn't. He was the one who hadn't responded to her note. Setting her glass on a heavy wooden table near the piano, she made her defense. "I didn't know you had guests until the butler showed me inside. He assumed I was a member."

"You blame my butler?" he asked, astounded.

She started to answer but decided it was best to remain silent after she saw the scowl that formed and creased the duke's forehead.

"And you allowed him to do so with no fear of consequences?" Hurst continued.

No, no. She had plenty of fear. Ophelia couldn't very well admit that, so she continued to remain silent.

"I cannot believe you came back to my house dressed like this." He pointedly gave her a critical up-and-down glance.

His overwrought attitude lent strength to her courage. She refocused on the reason she'd come. "I needed to see you and I don't apologize for coming. Had you rather I come as a young lady to your door?"

"Why didn't you just send me a note?" As was his custom when he was upset, his voice hitched a little louder.

"I did send you a note this morning and *you* didn't answer."

"Did you happen to think I might be busy?"

"There is no need for you to sound and look angry," she accused.

"Do I?" He threw up his hands in frustration. "Maybe that's because I am. Of all the men in there, what were you doing talking to Mr. Sawyer? I saw you playing cards with him at the garden party. You know him, Ophelia. He could have recognized you by your blue eyes, your voice, or your perfume."

Perfume? Startled, she hadn't considered that. She'd never given a second thought about her morning toilette routine of adding fragrance to her chest and arms with bergamot. It had been engrained in her.

"It doesn't matter how Mr. Sawyer perceived me," she answered without much conviction. "He was too busy looking for someone more important to talk to than to study over the likes of me."

"You are damn lucky he was. And I told you to *never* put on those clothes again." Changing course, he growled, "No, damnation, I told you to *burn* them."

Ophelia gasped and reached for the glass of brandy from the table as if needing the alcohol as fortitude to sort through this shamble of a conversation. Aghast, she questioned, "Did you just swear in front of me?"

"You're damn right I did." He didn't even blink at swearing again. "If you are going to wear the clothing of a man, you might as well hear the vulgar language of a man."

"All right, fair enough," she stated, her own ire rising. "I will. And just to be clear, I think you told me *you* would burn them, but in any case, it's a good thing I didn't dispose of them because I needed them again."

Clenching his teeth, his jaw tightening, he seemed to swallow back another oath. "You don't need the disguise to get in to see me, Ophelia."

Taking on a defensive stance, she snapped back, "I can't come to your door alone dressed as a lady. Would it have been a better idea if I'd hidden myself in that chest and had it delivered to you wrapped with a bow?"

He held on to a glare as if flinching one iota, he'd come unhinged. "And be slapped again after I get you out a second time? No thank you."

That was too much, even from the duke, who had begun to know her more intimately than she'd ever perceived a man would. And likewise, she had learned things about him she treasured close to her heart. All that said, her sensibility had been besmirched, and she had no choice but to take him to task in some way.

"No true gentleman would bring that unfortunate event up to a lady."

"What's going on in here?" came a masculine voice behind her.

Ophelia twisted around toward the entryway. Two well-dressed men with easygoing strides entered the room and stopped just inside the room staring at them.

The gentleman with chestnut-colored hair narrowed his gaze onto the duke. "Hurst, what's this about?"

The other man locked his eyes on Ophelia, and she wanted to sink into the floor and disappear. It didn't dawn on her someone might have followed them and heard them arguing. A flush of heat swallowed her. *Hidden, chest, bow,* and *slapped* were not words she'd want anyone to hear from their conversation. Neither would the duke. *Merciful heavens!* The duke would never help her now.

Clearing his throat, the gentleman with the light-brown hair observed wisely to Hurst, "It sounds as if a storm has been brewing between you two a long time. Let's calm it for now, Hurst. You have some introductions to make. You can save the explaining for another time."

"And next time you decide to have a row, it would be best to close the door before you start." Which the other man immediately accomplished.

Sage advice, but Hurst ignored them, though the scowl remained on his face.

These men had obviously heard her and the duke arguing. For how long, she didn't know. She would assume by her voice they would know she was a lady, and the way they were looking at her left little doubt. It wasn't her intention for anyone to know, but what could she do now? The damage was done.

Intent to slow the hammering beats in her pulse, and without thinking how it would look, she picked up the glass, brought it to her lips, and swallowed two hearty gulps of the brandy as fast as she could. Which was the wrong thing to do. Immediately, wheezing and coughing plagued her again as she tried to catch her breath.

"Give me that liquor," Hurst ordered through clenched teeth. "It's the last thing you need."

Ophelia did as he asked, and the duke set the glass on the piano top with a thud. Facing their visitors, he relinquished the awkward moment by turning to the gentlemen and saying, "Your Graces, may I present Miss Ophelia Stowe. Ophelia, the Duke of Wyatthaven and the Duke of Stonerick."

More dukes? She did the only thing she knew to do.

"Your Graces," she said, and as properly and humbly as possible, she pulled on the side legs of her trousers and curtseyed.

"Miss Stowe," the Duke of Wyatthaven said, holding his smile in check. "Hurst has mentioned you to us, but we never envisioned a lady such as yourself."

She was sure of that. His kindness made her feel all the worse, knowing she had searched the man's home for the chalice.

The Duke of Stonerick grinned without restraint as he looked at Hurst. "You never told us how delightful she is in trousers and a wig." Formally addressing Ophelia, he said, "It's a pleasure to meet you."

Unable to bear the attention of six eyes staring at her a moment longer, she whispered, "Thank you, Your Graces. I'll take my leave now and let you get on with your club meeting."

"You will stay where you are," Hurst said with the precision of an arrow hitting the center of its mark. "You and I are not through." Turning his attention to his friends, he glowered. "As far as you two go, I don't believe an explanation is necessary. Miss Stowe and I are simply trying to come to an understanding about something. I'm sure we will have reached a conclusion before she leaves."

The dukes looked at each other. Ophelia didn't think they were going to acquiesce to Hurst's subtle hint they should be the ones to excuse themselves.

Finally, the Duke of Stonerick chuckled. "I recall the days when we had to muddle through trying to explain the unexplainable. It's impossible."

"Indeed," the Duke of Wyatthaven agreed with merriment in his eyes, as Hurst remained silent. "Now we are happily married to them."

Ophelia could only assume that they were talking

about their own wives while Hurst was dealing with the shenanigans of an unmarried young lady, regrettably dressed as if a man.

"Don't worry, Hurst. We will keep the club members settled until you join us. Take your time. No doubt you have a lot to get through." Then both nodded to her and took their leave, low-voiced chuckles echoing between them as the door shut behind them.

Alone with the duke in the sprawling room, Ophelia regretted coming. Her disguise had been a rushed and foolish choice. But desperate emotions had led to desperate decisions that demanded she do so. But now he would be forced to try to explain her, the way she was dressed, and what they had been talking about to his friends. That might be harder to do.

Running a hand through his blond hair, he gazed at her through hooded eyes. She watched his exasperated expression change to resignation. "Why was it you said you couldn't have just sent me a note?"

She appreciated the calmer, lower-spoken voice he used. "I did, but I didn't receive an answer."

"I don't always look at messages when I first come home. I was running late for the meeting. Couldn't you have at least waited half an hour before dressing in such a way and coming over?"

"That is not fair," she said, filled with indignation. "It was several hours."

"Perhaps my timing was off, but I would have come to you when I read your note."

"Do you mean that?"

Culpability softened her, and she had no more defense on which to plead her case. She had been reckless and turned away from delving too deeply into consequences.

Hurst moved close to her as he nodded. She could feel his breath caress her cheek, her nose, and her mouth. A cascade of shivers rained through her very core. She wanted to look away from him but couldn't.

In a tender voice, he said, "Of course, I mean it, Ophelia. I asked you to marry me. Why would you think I wouldn't come to you?"

His closeness made tingles zing across her skin, and she could hardly form her next words. "Because I rejected you."

"I didn't lose sleep over it."

His blunt response unsettled her. Worry festered in her mind, and she all but wrung her hands in hopelessness that he would now help her save her brother's legacy.

Maybe she was right when she'd thought earlier that he might have proposed to someone else already. The very idea left her chilled, but she asked. "Are you already betrothed to another now?"

He didn't readily answer, and the longer he went without speaking, the more her heart swelled to a squeezing ache in her chest.

"The woman I desire heats my blood, occupies my head morning, noon, and night. She's quite unique but too daring for her own good. She sets mc back on my heels, makes me want to throttle her and ravish her at the same time."

Sailing on a ship of despair, Ophelia knew she had come too late. It was none of her business, but she couldn't help blurting, "Who is she? Has she come out this Season? Georgina?"

"Miss Bristol? No, my beautiful, strongheaded Ophelia. She's you."

The rhythm of her heart rate accelerated. Did that mean there was still time for her to make amends? In light of all things in the past, he did just declare he carried a fondness for her as well as desire. Gathering every ounce of courage, she said, "Since you are not already betrothed to another, I would like to discuss the matter again."

His brows rose with interest and his handsome features relaxed into a twinge of a smile. "I take it Debrett's book didn't help as much as you'd expected it to."

She slowly shook her head with much chagrin. At least he wasn't exactly saying, *I told you so.*

"The volume is quite detailed with its information, but too late, I've realized that Mrs. Turner simply didn't see enough of the crest to remember clearly what was on it. And there were far too many possibilities. Perhaps I pushed her too quickly right from the moment she'd mentioned overhearing the suspect's conversation with Winston. She became too confused to adequately be of any help."

"That must have been difficult for you to accept."

She startled when Hurst brushed the backs of his fingers slowly down her cheek, but the shock was quickly replaced by warmth and comfort. His touch caused the breath in her throat to feel thick and heavy.

"You could have warned me how difficult it would be."

"I thought I did," he said quietly, and gave her another tweak of a smile. "More than once."

Growing more at ease about what she was doing, she gladly gave him one too. She'd had to admit to herself that the idea of marrying him had been cause for excitement from the time he'd mentioned it. Though she didn't know exactly what it was or what to do about it, she recognized there was something always simmering between the two of them. Pulling them together as strongly and present as the moon pulled the tides. It was there whether he was with her or if she were alone. Whether they were in good humor with each other or bad. It didn't seem to matter. She was always happy to see him. Thoughts of him were always with her.

Both of them huffed a little laugh before he said, "I guess some ladies would rather find out things for themselves than be told."

She appreciated his words and wanted to tell him, but there was something more important she had to say, and the whole of it wouldn't be easy. "I'm not here just because we couldn't clearly define a family name from the crests. That is not the worst of it. Maman received a letter from her friend today saying the new vicar will arrive within the week."

He gave a brief nod. "Time is short."

"Yes. I admit I haven't gotten very far on my own." Her stomach quaked at what she was about to say, but she had to get it out. "I would like to propose an arranged marriage to you."

His brow rose even higher than before, and his eyes studied hers. "That couldn't have been easy for you to say."

"It wasn't. Admitting you were wrong about something never is."

Nodding, Hurst asked, "What did you have in mind?"

Ophelia swallowed and said, "I will marry you and do my best to give you a son." Was she as breathless as she sounded?

"And in return?"

"I would want my mother to live wherever I do and for our servants to be welcomed into your household staff as well. They have been faithful to us for many years, and I don't want to turn them off."

"There's no reason you should. That is an easy request

to fill. I'll make sure everything is arranged with Gilbert, and he'll find a place for all of them."

"Thank you, but there's more." She hesitated, not sure she could get the rest of her proposal out.

"Go on," he encouraged.

"I am willing to listen to you, but I don't want to be forbidden to do anything."

He folded his arms across his chest and shifted his stance. "'Anything' is asking a lot of a man, Ophelia."

"Specifically, I ask that you not hold me to the tradition of obeying you, as my husband, until after the issue with my brother and the chalice has been settled to my satisfaction."

His expression was somber. "A vow before God is still a vow, Miss Stowe."

She probably knew that better than most. Only a clergyman could have been to more services, teachings, and weddings than she had.

Suddenly she wished for another sip of the brandy to wet her dry throat. What she had in mind would be to go against something she'd been raised all her life to not only respect but cherish; the holy bonds of matrimony were not to be tampered with or taken lightly. Nevertheless, she couldn't excuse the fact that she'd recently done a lot of things she never would have thought she was capable of doing.

"Only if the vow is taken in the right spirit." She paused and moistened her lips to swallow down the raging feelings of guilt boiling inside her. "But just as a man can allow his wife to retain control of her monies and property if he so chooses, I assume you can release me from the vow to obey you. Perhaps the vicar can mumble the words softly under his breath or have a fit of coughing as he says them."

He seemed to study carefully on that before saying, "You are asking a lot of me, Ophelia."

"We are asking a lot of each other."

"You are saying if I release you from the vow as my wife of you serving, obeying, cherishing, or any similar words to me as your husband, you will marry me?"

CHAPTER 16

MAN'S PRACTICAL GUIDE TO APPREHENDING A THIEF
SIR BENTLY ASHTON ULLINGSWICK

A pleasant distraction may cause a thief to surrender.

Hurst walked out his back door and looked out over the well-tended garden. He thought he was supposed to be nervous on his wedding day and have a spot or two of brandy to get him through the pageantry of it all. Surprisingly, he wasn't the least anxious and he hadn't had a drop to drink. He was eager to wed Ophelia and begin his life with her. Truth be told, he would have married her the day she came to his house as Mr. Warcliff if there hadn't been a waiting period on getting the special license to wed.

He'd wanted sons and daughters and the opportunity to be the kind of father his father never was. It had taken him time to admit to himself she was the one for him and he'd almost let her slip through his hands, but fate stepped in and sent her to his door.

After she'd rejected his first proposal, if she hadn't come to him, he would have been back to her door again and again until she said yes. She was passionate and curious about life and what happened in the marriage bed. There had been no doubt about that when he'd held her in his arms and kissed her. Her response was everything a man could expect from a lady's first experience with sensual feelings. The excitement between them had been fervent and earnest. He couldn't wait to be alone with her.

Sunshine glared brightly in his eyes. The blue sky appeared to be popping white cotton ball clouds across the expanse. The tepid air felt more like midsummer heat than mid-spring chill. Birds chirped, bees buzzed around, and a couple of butterflies fluttered nearby, sipping from the blooms on the extra pots of flowers brought into the garden for the wedding. From the far end of the lawn a pianist, cellist, and violinist played softly.

The few guests he'd invited had assembled and were chatting. As if they'd been watching for him, Wyatt and Rick excused themselves from their wives and headed his way. Hurst had no doubt what they wanted to talk about before his bride arrived. In truth, he had no problem indulging them a little.

"You've been avoiding us," Wyatt said as he stopped and propped a foot on the bottom step where Hurst stood.

"Is it any wonder?" he replied with a bit of humor in his voice.

Rick snorted a laugh. "Not at all. I would have been avoiding you too if I had been caught in your position. That was a hell of a sparring match you and Miss Stowe were putting on when last we saw you."

"With good reason," Hurst didn't mind saying.

"No doubt about that, but I want to know," Rick said with a quirk of his head, "did you win or lose?"

Hurst grinned. "As for the argument between the two of us, it's anyone's guess, but I won her hand and that's what I wanted."

"After all these years you have looked for the right lady, are you sure she's the one you've been waiting for?"

Wyatt asked, all teasing and amusement gone from his tone and features.

"Completely," he answered with no wavering. "After all she and I have been through since we met, I can't wait to make her mine."

"Did you know she was the one for you the first time you saw her as you always suspected you would?" Wyatt continued his probe.

"Yes, and no," he admitted honestly as he caught Rick's mother, the Dowager Duchess of Stonerick, smiling at him. He gave her a nod.

"And that doesn't bring up any doubts that she might not be the one for you?"

Hurst inhaled a deep breath and looked at the colorful flower-and-vine-covered arbor he had erected. He knew and understood why his friends were tackling him with questions. By no means would he tell them everything, but perhaps they deserved a few more details given their long-held friendship.

Looking from one to the other, he acknowledged without qualm, "She was dressed the way you two saw her the first time we met. The situation we found ourselves in at that time didn't lend itself to be one of thinking along the lines of romance, marriage, or even fate."

"And are you all right with that? And her dressing as a man?" Rick asked.

"No," Hurst said with a shake of his head. "I'll explain it all one day. Today's not the time."

The friends looked at each other with what could have been mild concern. Wyatt was the first to speak. "I don't mind admitting that I'm dying of curiosity the reason she was dressed as a man when we saw her."

Rick rubbed the back of his neck. "And I find myself lying awake at night wondering what the devil she was doing in a chest tied with a bow and why she had cause to slap you when she came out of it."

The three men looked at one another and all started laughing. That would cause one to scratch his head looking for a reasonable answer to something that wasn't reasonable. Hurst wasn't going to try to explain that.

"Keep wondering and lying awake at night, my friends. I can't tell you everything I do or that has happened, but I have no doubts she is the lady for me."

"Then she has our blessings," Wyatt conceded.

Rick agreed with a smile, a nod, and a shrug.

On to more important things, Hurst asked, "Have either of you been able to find out any information about a man who collects religious vessels?"

"Sorry, Hurst. I haven't remembered to ask," Rick confessed.

"Really?" Hurst grumbled. "It didn't cross your mind not even once?"

"It doesn't matter," Wyatt was quick to answer with a single shake of his head and a dismissive wave of his hand. "We know most of the same people. I've discreetly inquired as you asked and haven't learned anything useful about such a man unless you want to accuse the prince himself. Everyone agrees he collects more rare, historical objects than anyone else in England or any other part of the world. Religious or otherwise. Should I try to get an audience with him?"

Hurst scoffed at Wyatt's remark as he heard the back door open. Turning, he saw Ophelia's mother step through the doorway. She moved quickly down the steps and onto the lawn to join the others standing near the decorated arbor. The music, chatter, and even the sounds of the garden went silent when Ophelia stepped out onto the stone landing.

His friends were forgotten as Hurst looked at his bride. His chest and stomach tightened at the sight of her. Wearing a simple ivory dress with a darker beige velvet spencer, she was stunning. She wore a small satin-covered hat with sheer netting that came down to rest slightly below her chin. In her hands she carried a small nosegay of delicate blue flowers.

Hurst jaunted up the steps to greet her. The veil was so sheer it was easy to see her startling blue eyes, the tempting shape of her inviting lips and smooth, delicate-looking complexion. She was so enticing he wanted to reach up and caress her cheek with his fingers. He wanted to kiss her now. In the bright sunlight with everyone watching, gaping at his audacity to do so before the vows were said.

Instead, he said huskily, "You are beautiful, Ophelia. No matter the day, the time, or the occasion."

She lowered her lashes for a slow blink and tilted her chin demurely high. Her shoulders lifted confidently. Neither could stop the prickle of sexual awareness that rushed through them.

"Thank you, Your Grace. You are most handsomely dressed for the occasion as well."

He wanted to take hold of her hands, squeeze them lightly, and reassure her, but with the flowers she clutched so tightly that was impossible and would shock some of the guests if he dared to touch her before they were pronounced man and wife.

"You've met Wyatt and Rick. After the ceremony you will meet their wives, Fredericka and Edwina, and Rick's mother, the Dowager Duchess of Stonerick. You will have to be on guard with her. She is a charmer, but all will adore you and your mother."

"I'll look forward to that." She smiled sweetly and looked at the few people gathered near the arbor. "I'm glad but surprised your two friends from the sporting club would ever want to see me again, let alone introduce me to their wives considering the situation as it was when they met me."

"They both appreciate a lady who knows her own mind and isn't afraid to go after what she wants no matter how she is dressed."

"That is encouraging." She hesitated as if she didn't know what to say, but she unexpectedly asked, "Did you speak to the vicar?"

A stab of annoyance nicked Hurst and surprisingly a little hurt too. Her feelings were honest, which he couldn't fault, but he didn't know why she doubted him. It was true, he never made it back to see her brother as he indicated in his letter, but other than that, he'd never given her reason to think she couldn't trust him to keep his word. That reminded him that his father had never kept his word to Hurst or anyone else. Time and again he promised no more gambling, drinking, or spending his allowance on frivolous baubles for his mistress, but he never stopped.

Hurst reminded himself he didn't like to think about his father anymore. Certainly not today.

With remembrance of his past buried again, Hurst continued to stare into Ophelia's eyes. He didn't know how to accept her lack of trust in him.

Why couldn't she just accept that he would keep his word as her husband? Did trust always have to be earned? Couldn't it be accepted on faith alone at first?

"Are you not willing to trust me on our wedding day?" he asked with concern.

"I worry. We don't have much time before—"

"Ophelia," he broke into her sentence and stopped her. "It's handled."

The simple truthful answer pierced him. Her goal was the most important thing in her life. He had always understood that from the first night they met.

"I've already arranged for you to tour two homes later this week under the guise that you will probably want to look into renovations on our current house in London and will be eager to get started."

She smiled and nodded once. "Thank you. I am eager."

He smiled at her too. "I'll get more invitations for you." He placed his hand on her arm and they walked down the steps and over to the arbor where the vicar stood and faced him.

The minister started with, "Dearly beloved, we are gathered here today in the sight of God . . ."

Shortly after the man started, movement out of the corner of his eye caught Hurst's attention. He turned his head slightly and looked at Ophelia. She was still and attentive. There it was again. He looked closer at her.

Hell, and damnation, there was a bee crawling around the underside of her veil! Near her ear. How did that get there? She hadn't even been in the garden very long.

What was he going to do? If he told her about it, she would probably panic and get stung. Possibly more than once. If he didn't tell her, it might fly onto her cheek. A natural reaction would be to brush it away. That would surely cause a sting because the bee had no way to get out. Neither of them could simply shoo it away.

How would she react to a sting? He usually had a red bump of swelling appear almost immediately and last for a couple of days. He imagined one on her beautiful cheek. And then he imagined several. No. Not if he could help it.

Only one thing to do. Hurst was going to have to slip his hand under her veil and see what he could do before the bee realized it was trapped and decided to fly. And he had to do it without alerting his beautiful bride.

The vicar cleared his throat and prompted, "You are supposed to say, 'I will,' Your Grace."

"I will," he answered hastily without taking his eyes off the bee.

He whispered, "Don't move."

He felt her go rigid and she cut her eyes over to him after obviously hearing something to be alarmed about in his voice.

"Is there a grass snake at my feet?"

"No. Be still."

From her profile he saw her eyes widen. "A spider on my shoulder? What is it?"

"Trust me," he whispered, trying to will her to listen to him for once in her life.

Assuming everyone's eyes were on the vicar, Hurst slowly eased his hand up, and gently slid his hand under the bottom of the veil.

Slowly and steadily, Hurst moved his hand beneath the fabric until, in a flash, he swept the bee into the palm of his hand and loosely closed his fingers around it. He swallowed a grunt. Damn, the sting pinged him good as the bee buzzed and frantically fluttered about as if enclosed in a glass jar. The vicar started coughing. Ophelia watched Hurst open his fist and the bee flew away. Gasps sounded around the guests as they witnessed what was happening.

The vicar mumbled apologies for coughing and the

disrupting of the insect, and continued with, "in sickness and in health; and forsaking all others keep thee only unto him, so long as ye both shall live?"

"I will," she answered.

"You need to take her hand in yours, Your Grace, and repeat after me."

Hurst stretched out his hand to her. They both saw the budding red welt in the center of his palm. She glanced back into his eyes and whispered, "I trust you, Your Grace."

He smiled and took hold of her hand.

After the ceremony, congratulations circulated among the guests while the staff served chilled champagne on silver trays. Hurst and Ophelia received good wishes and blessings for a long and fruitful marriage as everyone gathered around them at once. Thankfully no one commented on the muddled words of the vows but much was said about the bee.

Mere weeks ago, Hurst couldn't have imagined his wedding to a lady he'd rejected in a terse missive to an old friend. And yet here she was standing at his side, having absolved him of his lack of judgment in not coming to meet her or to see her brother. But truth be told, her forgiveness came at a price. She needed his help to do something he loathed to do. He knew all about houses being searched and looked through and things being taken away. Yet, he would honor her request until her pursuit ended.

Taking her arm and linking it through his, Hurst led them through the guests and made introductions where necessary as quickly as possible and moved on. Ophelia's mother seemed quite content, having engaged herself in conversation with Rick's mother in the shade of a tree.

Determination to be a gentleman on this day fell by the

wayside when, without preamble, Hurst steered Ophelia through a set of open double doors and into the house. And on the way, taking a glass of champagne from a tray. Sunshine slanted across the polished floor as if it were a pathway that led them to a quiet nook.

"Here, Ophelia." He pressed the glass into her gloved hand. "Have a sip."

Looking at him through lowered lashes, then directly into his eyes, she noted, "The last time I held a glass of liquor, you took it away from me. And with censure."

Under a soft chuckle, he admitted, "Yes, I did. But today is different. We are celebrating."

Hurst reveled in the mischievous smile she gifted him as she took a taste, then rubbed the underside of her nose with her gloved fingers before taking another then giving him the glass back. "If I am going to present myself worthy to bear the name Duchess and to bear your heir to the title, I best not indulge more until later in the evening."

Her innocent beauty took his breath. And his heart. With a furrow of his brows, he refused to recognize he may just have fallen in love with her, right here and now.

As he had her to himself, warmth heated his skin. He didn't want to escort her back to the reception just yet. He set the champagne aside. The quick kiss after he had attended to her veil, making sure he secured the delicate netting away from her face, wasn't nearly enough to satisfy his hunger for her. He was eager for more kisses, and there was a long afternoon of celebration ahead of them.

"Thank you for what you did during the ceremony." Her eyes shimmered with gratitude. "Had I known there was a bee inside my veil, I would have tried to flee its vengeful sting, and I'd be standing in front of you with my hat and my pride in shambles."

"I wouldn't allow an insect to sting my bride."

Her blue eyes swept across his face. "I'm glad you didn't damage its wings, and it was able to fly away."

The familiar tug of arousal tightened Hurst's lower body again. Her sensual mouth beckoned. He wanted to pick her up in his arms and twirl her around so she would know how happy he was that she was his. But he caught himself in time. She needed to be wooed, not rushed.

He smiled. "I'm sure the little insect lived to sting again."

Gently, he slid his hands around her waist and pulled her to him. She fit snugly and perfectly against him and gave no resistance to his maneuvers to get closer to her. A deep swell of anticipation melded into his mouth with a moan as the full swells of her breasts burned a satisfying imprint on his chest. Hurst drank in Ophelia's innocent smile.

"I will always stand in harm's way for you, Ophelia. You have my word." He then lowered his lips to hers.

Ophelia closed her eyes and parted her lips as he touched hers. They felt almost like silk, yet firm, full, and enticing. They yielded warmth. She allowed his tongue to slip inside her mouth and he probed the depths. Champagne and Ophelia quickly created a combustion of fiery heat inside him, and he wanted to take her away from everyone. With the simple kiss, he only meant to hold her tightly against him a moment or two and make it a brief satisfying embrace to hold him until they were alone in his chambers.

But sometimes things didn't go as planned. Slender hands came round his neck, and she clung to him. Unexpectedly, he knew she didn't want to resist him. Her arms wound further, and she pressed her body tightly to his, kissing him with fervor equal to his.

Her innocent move made his heart pound. It wasn't the

quick or prim kind of kiss a husband should give a bride of less than ten minutes. It was long, generous, and glorious. At times they managed short, gaspy breaths and others were long, contented sighs. He was on fire with wanting to be consumed by his wife.

Feeling her curves beneath his hands made him want to explore more than he knew they had time for and feelings that he wasn't sure she was ready to talk or even think about.

But their little interlude came to a halt far too soon with a recognizable male voice.

"Hurst, are you in here?"

The ill-timed call caused him to reluctantly break away from his bride with deliberate slowness. In a ragged breath, Hurst said, "Unfortunately, we are needed outside."

"And just in time, I think," she answered and reached up to straighten her veil.

Wyatt and Rick approached with their wives and Rick's mother by their sides as Hurst and Ophelia walked back onto the patio.

Wyatt addressed Ophelia directly with a nod and a smile. "Many happy years to you both."

"Hear, hear," Rick and the others signaled their approval with the lift of their glasses.

Pleasantries were exchanged for a few moments before Rick's mother looked at Ophelia and said, "Your Grace, I understand you are looking for a man who is attracted to religious artifacts."

Mrs. Stowe made an audible gasp, which she quickly recovered from by pulling her handkerchief out from under her sleeve and politely and gently coughed to cover her gasp.

Ophelia gave Hurst a startled look and he immediately

gave her a slight shake of his head. He knew nothing about this. Of course, he expected Wyatt and Rick to tell their wives about Ophelia's search, but telling his mother hadn't been expected.

"I mentioned it to the dowager," Edwina said quickly, looking at Ophelia with caution in her expression. "I hope I wasn't out of line in doing so. She knows so many people in Polite Society and is the epitome of discretion I assure you. I thought perhaps she might have heard of someone who might be of help to you. I hope I didn't speak out of turn."

"No, no. It's quite all right," Ophelia replied, giving her a forgiving smile. "If anyone can aid me in my search, we'd be delighted. Right, Maman?"

"Most definitely, my dear," she answered softly. "I find the weariness of our search burdens me more each day."

"That was my thought," Edwina explained.

"And if it's any comfort," Fredericka added with a genuine smile, "she sought my opinion, and I agreed. We both know what it's like to want something that seems out of reach or appears there is no answer for it. So, if you are going to be upset with Edwina, you'll have to include me."

"Oh, please understand I am happy for any help," Ophelia said with eagerness. "I thank you both for being interested enough to care. And you too, Duchess," she said to the dowager. "I find that my coffers of ideas are running low and my time to settle this affair is short. All assistance is appreciated."

Hurst was pleased with the way Ophelia settled Edwina's concern that she might have gone too far. And that she finally realized she needed help from wherever it came.

"Yes, of course." Rick's mother smiled with a bit of arrogance that always looked attractive on her and sounded like a sweet compliment no matter who she was talking to. “I want to oblige if I can. I’m a member of a group called the Insightful Ladies of London Society.”

“Your Grace,” Rick said in an annoyed tone to his mother. “You led me to believe you gave up that group after Edwina and I married.”

“Yes, I did for a while,” she answered innocently. “And I don’t attend their weekly meetings anymore, but I do like to keep in touch with them and see what they are up to and what they are reading. I still want to know about their discussions on various subjects. It’s—well, enlightening.” She lifted her brows as if to challenge him to say more.

Rightfully so, her son didn’t take the bait she threw out, but Edwina came to her mother-in-law’s aid anyway. “While I’ve never attended a meeting, I know they are a diverse group who study and read about superstitions, phenomena, the heavens, and many such subjects, so I’m not surprised that religious artifacts are one of them.”

“And it just so happens,” the dowager said with her light-blue eyes sparkling with confidence, and her voice as soft as a pluck of cotton, “one of the ladies in the group knows a gentleman who collects religious artifacts, though he doesn’t make it known to many.”

CHAPTER 17

MAN'S PRACTICAL GUIDE TO APPREHENDING A THIEF
SIR BENTLY ASHTON ULLINGSWICK

Don't lose your heart in the search.

Ophelia's stomach jumped with anxious trepidation and excitement as the last guest left and Hurst closed the front door. Her mother had retired to her room in the duke's house over an hour ago, claiming exhaustion. Which Ophelia knew to be true.

There was no longer anyone between her and the duke and their wedding night. There were plenty of jittery feelings inside and they weren't all about how the wedding night would proceed. Some were concerning the fact that the dowager duchess was going to find out more about the man who collected religious artifacts. The thought she might know by tomorrow who that man was and possibly if he was the thief only added to her stomach feeling as if it were tied in knots.

While all the busy preparations for the hastily planned wedding were being carried out, Ophelia realized she was actually looking forward to finding out the mysteries of the marriage bed. It wasn't something that was talked about in her house, and not something she would bother her mother with to add to her stress and worry. But from various readings through her educational studies, and the occasional forbidden conversations with newly married young ladies at the parish, she had an idea of what coupling was.

When Hurst turned to her, she immediately threw her arms around his neck, hugged him tightly, and kissed his smoothly shaved cheek three short times.

His hands circled her waist, almost spanning it from the tips of his middle fingers to his thumbs. "I'm glad you are so happy to finally be alone with me."

"Yes, I am." As she suddenly felt shy at her forward reaction, she let her arms slither down his chest and drop to her sides. "It was a lingering afternoon. I'm glad it's over, but the hug and kisses I just gave you were a way of saying thank you."

Merriment danced in his eyes, delighting her. His fingers spread out over her hips and tightened around her. "You don't have to thank me for marrying you."

She smiled softly at his teasing words. "I do. A thank-you is always in order when someone does something wonderfully nice, and you did that when you told Wyatt and Rick my plight. I thank them too for relaying the details of it to their wives, and then Edwina for thinking the dowager might know someone, and—"

Before Ophelia could gather her next breath, Hurst had nestled her up against his chest and was kissing her fully on the mouth, cutting off her words. She had no time to catch herself or resist. Moments later, she didn't want to. The kiss was unexpected and passionate from the first touch of their lips coming together. His demanding lips seared hers with urgency that momentarily confused her with his intensity.

There was no slow buildup of soothingly soft raindrop kisses and intimate caresses that slowly chipped away at her tensions and insecurities, as was the case the last time they embraced so intimately. Feeling as if a magical spell had been cast upon her, she fell right in line with his eagerness.

By instinct, she slipped her arms inside his coat and around his waist, holding him tightly to her before skimming her hands up his broad back to draw him closer. She wanted to feel his heart beating against his warm, firm, and muscular chest.

"I have been waiting all afternoon to hold and kiss you like this," he whispered into her mouth.

Ophelia didn't know what she said in response, or if she even tried to talk, but a deep-rooted moan of pleasure seemed to be what flowed past her lips in answer that she had been waiting as well. She only knew it was exhilarating to know of his deep desire.

The strong hardness of his kiss chiseled away at her innocence, concerning the depth of urgency two people could desire and share at the same time. His tongue swept into her mouth, searching and commanding. She joined the forceful passion of his embrace, allowing herself to feel and encourage all that he offered. His mouth, clinging to hers with such hunger, was a new experience and she wanted to embrace it all. Their breaths came together in ragged pants of eagerness that neither of them seemed to want to slow down.

He lifted his head and looked into her eyes. "No more talk of anything about your search for the thief, the chalice, or who might be able to help you tonight. Nothing can be done about any of your worries until tomorrow. There will be talk of you and me," he murmured against her skin as his lips left hers and kissed his way down the column of her throat to the neckline of her clothing and back up again. "Everything else will be for another time," he whispered.

With her locked tightly in his arms, his lips moving so sensually over hers, swirls of delicious heat spiraled through her. She wanted to bask in the sensations and think of nothing else but how wonderful her husband made her feel.

"None," she readily agreed.

He kissed her deeply, drawing the breath from her body as she shuddered in response. His tongue brushed and traced the fullness of her lower lip before he whispered, "I only want to hear your sighs and gasps and the way you moan when I—"

Sounds of masculine voices nearby broke them apart in an instant. A ragged gulp of air escaped past Ophelia's lips when the kiss ended so abruptly. Her heartbeat throbbed with the emptiness of pleasure left unfinished.

Hurst ran a hand through his hair a couple of times with a frustrated scoff. But then he looked at her and smiled. "I fear you might be dangerous to have in the house, my duchess. You make me forget there are others around when you are in my arms."

"I am becoming acquainted with that absentmindedness," she answered, straightening her velvet spencer properly on her shoulders after their flurry of madcap kissing that still had her wondering, even hoping there would be more of the thrilling passion he'd already shown her. If so, she was quite certain that she would enjoy marriage.

Mr. Mallord came around the corner, stopped, and bowed. "I'm sorry, Your Graces. Mr. Gilbert asked me to check the front door. I'll come back another time."

"Wait," Hurst said to the footman, studying his face. "I think I've seen you before. Do I know you?"

"He's Mr. Mallord," Ophelia spoke up. "The footman who came with us to London and is now in your employ."

"He looks familiar." He turned from Ophelia to Mr. Mallord. "Have we met before?"

"Yes, Your Grace." He looked at Ophelia as if seeking her help. "Months ago, I delivered a letter to you from the vicar and waited for a response."

"At the hunting lodge."

"Yes, Your Grace."

"I remember now." Hurst paused. "We're glad to have you here. That will be all, Mr. Mallord."

He nodded, turned, and walked away.

"He's a very thorough man."

"We've always thought that. He also worked for my father for a short time. It was very kind of you to take our staff so that we didn't have to turn them off."

"I was pleased to do it for you." Hurst picked up her hand and kissed it. "You go on up to your room and I'll join you shortly."

"All right," she agreed, still feeling as if she couldn't take in enough air. A little time to settle down and collect her thoughts would be good. She headed toward the stairs.

"Ophelia?" he called as her foot landed on the first step.

She stopped and turned back to him. "Yes?"

He gave her a twitch of a smile. "Dismiss your maid for the night. You won't need her."

That thought concerned and excited her as she climbed the stairs, made her way to her room, and did as he requested. She had always thought a lady's maid helped the bride get ready for the wedding night. Believing Hurst knew more about what was to take place, she didn't question him. It was possible for Ophelia to eventually work her way out of the half stays she was wearing without help. She could easily reach her back and untie the tightly held bow and work the laces loose so she could manage.

After her maid closed the door behind her, Ophelia looked around and wondered what she should do. A fire burned in the fireplace and the room was warm. Draperies had been drawn on both windows. On the tables that flanked the bed, lamps were lit but burning low. Another was on her dressing chest, giving the room plenty of comforting light. The white covers on the bed had been turned down and her best night rail had been laid out on top of them. All seemed inviting and tranquil.

The duke was coming to her room. That was good to know. She had wondered whether they would lie in her bed or his for their coming together. No one had told her. Her parents had only had one room to share. She hadn't known until arriving at the duke's house that morning and being shown to her room to dress for the wedding that she and the duke would have separate rooms with an adjoining door. She supposed she could get used to that.

If she was to ready herself for the night, she should get started. The first thing she did was remove her velvet spencer and leave on her sleeveless gown. After making herself comfortable on the stool in front of her dressing mirror, she removed her hat, fingering the netting as she laid it aside. Thinking about how quickly Hurst had taken care of the bee and what a disaster that could have been if he hadn't. Too, it couldn't have come at a more perfect time to cover the vicar's muddling of the vows. No one seemed to notice and the chaos that would have followed if she had started wildly swatting at a bee was averted.

More important than anything was that Hurst had

kept his word to her and that filled her with love for him. *Love?* Were her feelings love? Maybe they were.

With her hat off, she took the pins from her hair and was brushing the long length of it when the door between their bedrooms opened. Hurst walked in carrying two glasses of champagne and dressed only in his shirt and trousers. Even his feet were bare. In such a simple state of undress, it was easy to see his wide chest and shoulders, tapered waist, and muscular thighs in his formal trousers.

Ophelia had never seen a man so scantily attired, and the sight of him caused a shameless, primitive flame of desire to rush to her feminine core, curl, and blossom into an amazing feeling of yearning. It was close to madness that he could stimulate her just by the way he looked, and the way he was looking at her with such sensuality her skin pebbled with expectant shivers.

She placed her brush on the dresser, rose from the stool, and accepted the drink when he stopped in front of her.

"You look a little confused. Have you never seen a duke serve champagne before?"

"Certainly not one who wasn't properly dressed."

"Ah, I understand," he said with a nod. "That means you've probably never seen a man without a shirt."

"Never," she answered, her gaze sweeping down to the open V neckline of his shirt stopped just below the hollow of his throat. "Not even my father or brother. They never left their rooms until they were properly attired."

"That is not surprising. They probably never removed their coats and collars in front of you either. I must warn you that you will often see me without mine when we are in our chambers."

It worried her a little that the duke wasn't smiling

but seeming quite somber for the occasion of the night. "That will be all right. You look quite comfortable."

"There's something I want to say before we go any farther with the wedding night."

Ophelia's heart felt as if it jumped to her throat and her body went rigid. Had she done something wrong? When she was filled with all these beautiful feelings for him that were too deep to express with words. What was he going to say to her?

CHAPTER 18

MAN'S PRACTICAL GUIDE TO APPREHENDING A THIEF
SIR BENTLY ASHTON ULLINGSWICK

Take help wherever you find it.

"All right," she answered tentatively but knew she was fearful that something wasn't right.

"I want to propose a toast."

A toast?

That made the tightness in her chest ease a little. She nodded. A toast couldn't be too bad, could it? Perhaps even appropriate for just the two of them, even though there had been several from his friends throughout the afternoon.

"I want you to know that while I didn't agree to marry you when Winston approached me about the possibility, I am grateful fate later brought us together and I know that he had blessed our marriage long before it took place."

Ophelia's heart felt as if it melted into a puddle in his hands. The sentiment was so touching that for a moment she thought she might have tears glistening in her eyes.

"That is very kind of you to say and to remember Winston privately to me on this day. It means so much to me, and I believe that too. If he were here, he would be very happy. He wanted me to marry well, knowing if I was taken care of, so would our mother be."

"Her home is with us for as long as she wants," he assured her. They clinked their glasses, and each took a sip.

Hurst took a few steps away and leaned his back against the spiral bedpost. "I'm glad I can repay some of the kindness your mother showed to me when I was a boy. I've always felt she was protective of me."

Once again, Ophelia felt the need to know more about his childhood, but sensed this wasn't the right time to delve deeper into his past. Yet, she couldn't stop herself from saying, "I asked Maman to tell me about you, but she didn't tell me much except she was quite fond of you."

"As I am of her. There's no reason she couldn't tell you anything she might know about me. Winston and I did the usual boy things. We rode your father's horse and my uncle's all over the meadow and bogs. We fished in the pond and looked for frogs."

Ophelia laughed softly.

"I was always envious of your brother."

The faraway look in his eyes caused Ophelia's heart to squeeze. "If that is true, I'm sure Winston didn't know."

"Believe me. It is true. My father would leave me for months at the time and never once write and inquire about me while he was gone. And usually, he would be weeks late to return for me. Your father and mother were very protective of Winston. If we were going to leave the area around the vicarage, they wanted to know where we were going and they expected us to not change our plans without telling one of them. I didn't understand that kind of caring but I wanted it. My father never worried about where I went or if I came home. Winston said his father wanted to know in case he ever had to go looking for us, so he'd know in which direction to go."

It was difficult for Ophelia to imagine what it must have been like to not have the security of loving parents. Perhaps that is why Hurst had always seemed so protective of her. "It is comforting to know someone cares for you enough to worry. I suppose there were reasons your father was that way."

Hurst straightened. "And I suppose you are right. Tell me, are you feeling more relaxed now that everyone is gone, and we are alone?"

Accepting his signal that he'd said all he was going to about his past, she answered, "Yes, I think so." There was still the biggest part of the night to get through. She wasn't dreading it, but she did wonder how it would all come about that they would end up in the same bed together.

"I want you to be settled. Continue to drink the champagne."

She nodded and took another sip.

"Your hair is beautiful, Ophelia. I wondered how long it would be. I like the inviting way it spills around your shoulders and drapes down your back with waves and curls."

"Your hair is beautiful too," she replied in the same easy manner he'd spoken.

A chuckle rumbled in his chest.

"It's true," she said. "It feels like silk and the color is lovely. Especially when the sun sparkles off it."

Hurst's smile let her know he appreciated her compliment while his eyes narrowed with good humor. "You noticed that?"

"How could I not notice a sparkle? I find it very attractive the way you wear it low across your forehead." She glanced at his hair again. "Lamplight sparkles off it too. So yes, it's beautiful."

"I have never seen a man with beautiful hair, Ophelia. Or beautiful anything or that matter."

His mood and easy conversation relaxed her even more, while she enjoyed their inconsequential banter.

"That can't be true. Most of the gentlemen I saw at your sporting club meeting were beautiful specimens of men."

He grinned. "You were looking over the men in my club? And in my house?"

"I had no choice." She countered his teasing with an innocently playful smile, and then took another drink from her glass. "You will remember I was *looking* for *you* among them. I couldn't help but notice all were young and built very much like you through the chest and shoulders. All tall, and quite handsome too."

"Handsome?" he quipped with a frown. "It's a good thing I arrived when I did or you might have run away with one of them."

Ophelia sipped her champagne before saying, "I doubt that would have been a possibility with the way I was dressed, but I was afraid Mr. Sawyer was going to ask me a sporting question I couldn't possibly answer and realize I wasn't part of the club before I could find you."

"I will teach you anything you need to know about sports, and many other things as well," he added with a twinkle in his eyes. "But I think it best I keep you away from the members of my club before you start eyeing them again."

The sensuality in the way he looked at her with such intense desire made her want to kiss him for as long as she wanted. Still, she asked with a bit of seriousness to her tone, "You aren't really worried about me being attracted to one of the men, are you?"

"No." In one swallow he finished his drink and placed the glass on the table by the bed. With no warning, he pulled the tail of his shirt out of the waistband of his trousers, tugged it up over his head and tossed it onto the slipper chair in the corner.

Merciful heavens!

Ophelia gasped with pleasure at his boldness to bare his chest in front of her. Seeing him without a shirt caused a flutter in her stomach. She flushed. Golden light from the lamp made his skin appear a gorgeous shade of bronze. Her gaze raked over the wide span of his sculpted, rippled chest that looked as firm and prominent as the muscles in his arms. His skin appeared smooth, firm, and bulging with strength. There was no other way to put it. He was magnificent.

She couldn't help saying, "I didn't expect you'd be so, so—"

He smiled. "Tempting?"

That's exactly what she was thinking but remained quiet as she continued to be mesmerized by his perfect physique.

Hurst closed the short distance between them. Taking the glass from her hand, he placed it beside his before lightly brushing her cheek with the pads of his fingers. Staring deeply into her eyes, he asked, "Do I tempt you when I touch you, Ophelia?"

"Yes," she answered. "There is no mystery, no doubt. It is the simple truth."

"Good. A man wants to tempt his wife to touch him. As you tempt me to caress your beautiful skin."

Engulfed by the desire his words wrought, she ran her

open hand softly from one end of his chest to the other, feeling the rise and dips of the various muscles along the way. She then let her hand wander down his rippled abdomen to the band of his trousers, and then up and over his shoulders and arms. Each muscle jerked and tensed as she felt the contours.

Thrills like she could have never imagined swept through her. It had never occurred to her she might one day touch a man as she was touching Hurst. His skin felt as smooth as it looked. Her fingers splayed, fanning out to take as much of his strong upper arm into her palm as she could to feel its weight. The muscle was hard and warm like a freshly picked apple on a hot and sunny summer afternoon.

Staring directly into his eyes, she whispered in a hushed breath, "Never again say you are not beautiful, sir. You are, but there is one thing about you that I've been wanting to see."

His brows rose with interest. "Really?"

She nodded without reluctance.

Another teasing smile spread across his face. "Is this thing above my waist or below it?"

"You are being very naughty, Your Grace."

He chuckled softly. "You are the one being inquisitive about my body, my wife."

"Some of it for sure." She grinned. "When you came to pay your respect to Maman, I overheard the two of you talking about a scar on your forehead from an injury when you were a boy and jumping over their fence."

"So that is the part of me you haven't seen that has enraptured your curiosity? I have to say I'm more than a bit disappointed."

She loved his playfulness, and supposed it was proper now that they were married. "Can I see it?"

"The scar or the—"

"Don't say it," she said, putting her hands over her ears as she laughed. "Of course, the scar."

He circled her in his arms again. "Lift my hair and look at it all you want and then we will talk about the other part of me that you should be curious about."

Ophelia raised on her toes as she moved his hair aside. The scar ran about two inches and very close to his hairline. "That must have been quite a wound."

"As best I remember it hurt for weeks. Thanks to your mother and father for tending to it so quickly I had no infection, and it healed quickly."

"Is that why you've always worn your hair low on your forehead?"

"Probably and I've never had a reason to change it."

"I'm glad. Not because you can't see the scar, but because the way you wear it is very attractive."

His smile let her know he would acquiesce to her compliment once again. She was happy he wasn't worried about her eyeing any of the other members of his club. She was positive none of them could come close to the way she felt about Hurst. Certainly, none of them caused her breath to catch in her throat like her husband.

He put his hand to the back of her head and ran it down the length of her hair. Even in that small touch she felt gentle power in his hand.

Hurst reached over and kissed the side of her face near her ear and inhaled deeply. "You are the one who is very attractive and very enticing. I love to smell the sweet fragrance of your skin, your hair."

She loved hearing him say those things and feeling his lips on hers. Emotions deep and earnest swirled inside her. She only wanted to experience and enjoy them.

"Are you cold?" he asked.

She shook her head.

"Raise your arms," he said gruffly. "I want to hold you close to me without your dress between us," he murmured.

Ophelia obeyed without question. He took hold of the hem of her sleeveless silk gown, lifted it up and over her head, and sent it the way of the other clothing. The fine cotton chemise came off as quickly and was discarded as easily, leaving her standing in her lace-trimmed stays and drawers that ended just above her knees.

His lips slowly eased into a smile as his gaze swept over her. "You are the beautiful one, my darling wife."

He bent his head, closed his eyes, and kissed the pillowy rise of her breasts showing from beneath the lacy neckline of her white stays. The coolness of his lips on her warm skin was inviting. Luxuriant sensations stirred and mounted warmly inside her. Her breath grew short and fast. Ophelia kissed the warm space between his neck and shoulder and let her lips travel with short raindrop kisses to just beneath his jaw as if it was the most natural of things for her to do. She could tell it gave him breathtaking pleasure and her too.

Taking her into his arms, he kissed her slowly, delightfully, thrilling her. Her arms fell over his bare shoulders. Her hands caressed him as she returned his kisses, sweeping her tongue through his mouth as his fingers wove and tangled in the length of her hair while still holding her close to him.

She nestled against his chest as they settled into a mixture of slow, tender, and eager kisses that kept her softly panting. Hurst slid his hands up and down her spine until he found the laces of her stays. Quickly, he worked them loose, one after the other until the garment opened and fell at their feet. He hugged her close, hard chest to her soft bare breasts. Warm and strong, yet gentle. She could lose herself in the way he touched her, and the way his hands skimmed down her waist to the swell of her hips and down the sides of her thighs with tenderness.

He looked into her eyes. "You feel wonderful and as if you were made just for me."

A slight laugh passed her lips. "For some reason, I was just feeling the same—as if I were made for you."

"You were," he whispered, his lips pressing against hers once more. "That makes us both right."

"For a change," she answered in a hushed tone with a smile upon her lips.

"I want you, Ophelia. No other woman. Just you for the rest of my life."

"Just you for me too," she answered, kissing over his jawline down his strong neck and over the curve of his shoulder.

"You're not nervous, are you?" he asked as he cupped the back of her head in his hand.

"No." She fit her body closer to him. "Not anymore."

Keeping his gaze riveted on her eyes, he said huskily, "Long before the first time I kissed you, I recognized your sensuality. Ever since, I have longed to explore it with you, and I'm eager to bring it to life."

His words filled her with anticipation of what was to come, and she watched as his trousers and her drawers were easily disposed of. Hurst helped her to lie down and then he joined her, fitting himself facing her with her breasts pressed against his chest. There was no doubt he was aroused, and the wedding night had begun.

Taking his time while they kissed and kissed, Hurst caressed her breasts with gentle loving strokes, the flat area of her stomach and navel, over her hips and down the plane of her slender thighs. Ophelia didn't stop touching him either. Following his lead, she explored his body too.

Their lovemaking was frantic at times, but always tender and loving. There were moans, sighs, and gasps as he made her his. She wasn't prepared for the shock of pleasure that rippled and lingered, but there was no doubt that she had become his wife in word and deed. When it was over, she was sure she'd just experienced her first miracle. It had to be one. How else could coupling bring such gratification to two people at the same time? The intense moment was explosive and left them both catching their breath.

The pleasure and awe of their coming together as husband and wife was almost more than she could bear.

When it was over, Hurst rolled onto his back and placed his arm underneath his head. Ophelia curled beside him with her hand on his chest. They lay quiet, happy, and sated.

After a while, she lifted her head to look at him and asked softly, "Did you know how wonderful it would be?"

"For two people enjoying each other in bed?" he asked with a patient smile. "I had an inkling or two. About being married to you—" He reached down and kissed her bare shoulder before looking into her eyes. "I knew it would be wonderful, and it far exceeded what I'd imagined."

Ophelia smiled too. It felt intensely good to have his body against her. Sharing his heat, feeling his breathing from the rise and fall of his chest. "Will we share a bed often?"

He frowned and grumbled curiously, "Why would you suspect we wouldn't?"

"We have separate rooms."

His brows knitted closer as if he was thinking what he should answer. "It never dawned on me you might think of these chambers as mine and yours. It is ours. All of it."

"Oh," she answered.

"Separate rooms so I can get up in the mornings and dress without waking you. Whether we are in this bed or the one in the other room, have no worry, Ophelia. We will share it." He quirked his head and added with a slight grin, "Besides, that is how babies are made."

Dipping her head to kiss his collarbone, she nuzzled his skin and whispered earnestly, "I hope I give you a son."

"Look at me," he whispered as he lifted her chin with the tips of his fingers. "That will be if it's destined to be."

His voice was husky, persuasive, and his gaze was so penetrating she couldn't have looked away if she'd wanted to. Her head tilted back, and she looked deeply into his eyes. "Then so be it."

With the palm of his hand, he brushed her hair down the length of her spine, spreading his fingers wide so he could caress her tresses and her skin. "Along with all the other things you have on your mind tonight, and I know they are important to you. They are to me too but hear me. We will worry about them tomorrow when we can do something about them. Right now, I need to feel your heart beating next to mine. You make me want to forget about everything but you, and I want you to forget everything but me tonight."

She smiled and rose up over him. Her hair fell softly to the front of her shoulders and then pooled against his skin as she whispered against his lips, "I already have."

CHAPTER 19

MAN'S PRACTICAL GUIDE TO APPREHENDING A THIEF
SIR BENTLY ASHTON ULLINGSWICK

Hide in a conspicuous place so as to watch his every move.

Hurst knew when Ophelia had awakened, though neither of them made a sound. Maybe she thought he was still asleep and didn't want to disturb him. She slowly and carefully turned to her other side and away from him. That was all right. The way the sheet pulled away from her body gave him a good view of her lovely back and softly rounded shoulders he hadn't seen last night. She was beautifully shaped with the way the curve of her waist dipped in and the slight rise of her shapely hip.

How he felt about her was more than just realizing she filled something inside him that had felt empty most of his life, but no doubt that was a big part of his deep feelings for her. With her snuggled by his side last night, it was the best sleep he'd had in longer than he could remember. He'd found a peace that he didn't even know he was looking for. As he stared at her, heat surged through his veins, inflaming his need to feel her beneath him once again.

She was the most invigorating lady he'd ever known, showing him something different about herself every time they saw each other. He couldn't wait to learn more and fall more deeply in love with her each day that passed. *Love?* Yes, that is what his feelings for her were. Abiding love.

Hurst had been awake since the sun came up and had found its way straight into his eyes through the tiniest of slits where the draperies hadn't been tightly closed. He chalked it up to his good luck it happened. Had it not, he wouldn't have had time to consider his feelings for Ophelia and look at her without her being aware.

He'd studied every detail of her lovely face before she'd turned away. The pale complexion and the shape of her nose. The whisper of her dark, thick eyelashes as they occasionally fluttered in sleep. Though they were closed, she had the most beautiful eyes, the nicest skin, and smelled so good he wanted her near all the time.

Her tranquil face in sleep had reflected everything he loved about her. Courage and determination that had no boundary. Spirit and loyalty with limitless desire. He was lucky fate had brought them together after he'd rejected her brother's appeal to accept her as his wife.

Hurst couldn't believe how sure he was that he loved Ophelia with his whole being. A smile came to his face. She had been worth the wait, worth every moment of aggravation she gave him, and there had been plenty of that. And he had no doubts it would continue throughout their lives together. When she was passionate about something, she gave it her all.

Without shyness or restraint, she'd been eager to participate when he was showing her the delights enjoyed between a man and woman, husband and wife. She made him feel good beyond reason. Even now, he could hardly keep his hands off her while he waited for her to come fully awake. He didn't want to pounce on her the moment she'd awakened, but the possibility of doing just that made him smile again.

To their delight, he intended to focus and enjoy loving her again before the day started. Once they were downstairs, he'd have to shift his focus to keeping his promise and helping her find the chalice.

Hurst had already sent a runner from Bow Street to see what he could find out in Wickenhamden. Runners knew how to question people without raising suspicion, but he wasn't sure he could make Ophelia believe that so he would wait to see what, if anything, the man discovered before he mentioned it to her. He'd had drawings of the chalice made from his cousin's aunt Maudine's drawing of the cup. They were being shown to shopkeepers all over Town. Ophelia had thought that was futile, putting all her flowers in one basket—a titled man's bookshelf. She was so fixed on that; she seemed to push aside other ideas that might help. He also had a couple of men scouring the rumor mill in London's underworld to see if anyone had been trying to sell or buy religious objects recently. He intended to find that chalice even if he had to turn all of England upside down.

He didn't move but asked her, "What are you thinking about while staring at the wall?"

"That it's a very lovely wall," she said with a hint of amusement in her tone.

Hurst grunted. "I don't believe you."

She turned toward him smiling, propping herself up on one arm and holding the sheet in front of her breasts with the other.

"I didn't mean to wake you when I turned over."

"You didn't." Hurst reached out and brushed her lush hair to her back and caressed her shoulder. "I've been awake awhile. So, what were you thinking about while you were lying there so still?"

"That poets don't do the marriage bed justice when they write their romantic verse."

"Poets?" Hurst scoffed a laugh. "I could have told you that. I haven't read much poetry, and none in recent years, but I would have to agree with you. They like to believe they inspire, entertain, or lull unsuspecting souls into the throes of despair or unrequited love, and then they preen about it."

Her slightly arched brows furrowed easily, but beautifully, at his unhidden disdain. "Nevertheless, it is usually beautifully written. Most gentlemen do indulge in the art of the written word. Why don't you read poetry?"

"That's a long story best told by Fredericka. It has more to do with Wyatt than me or Rick, but we agree with his belief it's not necessary to learn to recite it."

"Did he do anything bad to a poet?"

"No. Wyatt is as honorable as men come. Only something he regretted not doing when he was a boy."

"And what about you? Are there things you regretted not doing when you were a boy?"

Hurst could see that Ophelia was genuinely interested in wanting to know more about him. But there were some things he simply didn't want her to know. "More things I regret doing for sure. Perhaps I should have been more understanding of my father's plight. Maybe he wanted a better life for us and tried to change his ways."

"That seems a kind way to look at a remembrance of your father."

Her comment struck something deep inside him that he wasn't ready to explore: forgiveness.

"For gentlemen or ladies, boys or girls, I do know that

it is always best to be honorable. I need to tell you something I should have told you before we married. When it first happened."

Her tone was serious and caused a shrug of worry to pass through him. "What's that?"

"I'm sorry I slapped you that day at my house."

Was that all that was bothering her? He didn't regret being so close to her that day, helping her, and touching her.

Hurst gave a curious expression and placed his fingers under her chin, tilting her head back. "When was that? I don't remember it."

She smiled at him. "You are deliberately not being truthful. There was no cause for it other than my own frustration with myself. I regret that I never properly apologized. I should have and wanted you to know."

With short kisses, he teased her lips lightly. Speaking in a ragged voice, he answered, "I am being truthful." Or maybe it was a justified fib. It really didn't matter. Why should she worry about that when he had enjoyed every moment of helping her wiggle out of the chest?

"Listen to me," he said while he continued to rain kisses on her face. "A gentleman always forgives and forgets when it comes to a lady—especially his lady wife."

She looked sweetly into his eyes. "Thank you for being so kind to me, Hurst. About everything."

He shrugged. "What else were you thinking about while you were looking at the lovely wall?"

"The chalice and where it could be is always on my mind, but I promised not to talk about that until morning."

A deep and masculine chuckle rose from his throat as he kissed the top of her nose. "It is morning, my darling."

She quickly looked around. "Oh. It would be dark in here if not for the lamps burning."

"We were busy last night, and I failed to get up to put them out as I should have. There is a slice of daylight right there." He pointed to the offending drapery that had awakened him.

Ophelia moved as if she planned to scramble off the bed, but he circled her in his arms.

"Wait, wait." Being in bed with her was too sweet to abandon so soon. "What are you doing?"

"I need to wash, dress, and get downstairs. We may already have a note from the dowager with an answer from her friend about who the man is that collects religious things."

Hurst glanced at the clock on the dressing table. "It is not past noonday. There hasn't been time for her to have an answer from anyone."

Ophelia moistened her lips and in a voice that was almost a whisper said, "But I want to be ready when we do hear from her."

"So do I." He pulled her closer and kissed her on the mouth, brushing her hair away from her cheek. "We will both be ready. But we must do this the dowager's way. If the man is a possible suspect, we don't want to scare him into hiding it."

"I know, but I'm anxious to hear from her."

"*We*, Ophelia. *We* are in this together. When we get belowstairs, if there is no answer, we'll go for a walk in the park to help pass the time."

She pursed her lips for a moment. "I really don't think we should leave the house today but wait here."

"And I heard there was going to be a fair in Hyde Park. I think you will enjoy the sights, and it will give you something to do while you wait."

"That sounds lovely on any day but today."

"You know we may not hear until tomorrow. Or the

next day. Her friend with the Insightful Ladies of London Society may not answer right away. A thousand different things could happen. Waiting around the house will be torture for you. We need to do something."

Hurst thought about telling Ophelia everything he was doing to search for the vessel but decided to wait. Right now, he wanted her thinking about him. "Come closer and let me hold you," he said gently. "Don't give me that look that means you don't agree with me." His eyes swept softly up and down her face.

She nestled into the crook of his neck, and he felt the fringe of her lashes batting against his skin. He stroked her back and the sides of her breasts while she cupped his nape, letting her fingers play in his hair. They lay snuggled together, relaxed and enjoying the languorous warmth and pleasure of being in each other's arms.

"There's something I've been wanting to tell you," he said, and then kissed the top of her head.

Curiosity settled on her delicate features as she skimmed her hand along his chest and shoulders. "What's that?"

"Look into my eyes," he said huskily. "I want you to see and know what I am saying is true."

She lifted her head and did as he'd asked.

He took his time, keeping his gaze on hers. "I love you, Ophelia, and I am so glad you are mine."

He felt her body tense and heard her inhaled raspy breath of air.

"Are you shocked?" he asked.

"Yes, but." She hesitated. "I think I love you too."

Hurst was quite sure his heart did somersaults in his chest. His first thought was to kiss her. Second was to ask why she only thought she loved him and didn't know for sure. But he didn't want to rush her. Hearing her say the words made him feel so damn good he could only ask, "What makes you think that?"

"I love being with you. I want to see you and be with you even when you frustrate me at most every turn. I never stay angry with you as I would like to at times. I forgive you quickly for raising your voice when you don't even know you are doing it. You make me smile and force me to think about what I'm doing even when I don't want to. And you made me feel things I didn't know we had been created to experience."

A deep rush of desire pushed through him. Hurst wanted to make love to her so badly right then he had to force himself not to lay her back on the bed and have his way with her while he pleasured them both.

But she kept talking when all he wanted to do was kiss her. "You made me start thinking about the possibility of my feelings for you when we talked about your sporting team."

His breath sucked in with a hiss and he leaned away from her, not believing she'd said what she said. Would she forever raise his ire and his desire? "What the hell— do they have to do with your feelings for me?" he asked with an expression that he felt sure was somewhere between a frown and a grin. "A bunch of strong, damn good-looking men."

"Yes. I was serious when I told you they were all handsome like you and with magnificent physical attributes to recommend them as do you."

One corner of his mouth quirked up. "I'm not likely to forget hearing you say that nor believing you meant it."

She placed her hand on his cheek and gave him a quirky smile. "But I realized none of them gave me the fluttering in my chest, the tightening in my stomach that you do. None of them stole my breath at the sight of them or made me think I wanted to be with them as I am with you right now. You are the only one that I have pined for. Do you think that could be what true love is?"

Her honesty made him swallow hard. He sensed she was filled with heat, hunger, and desire for him. And just like that, all he could think of was Ophelia. He had reached that place in his mind where nothing mattered but them being together. Everything else ceased to exist. Yes. She loved him and he wanted to feel and taste every inch of her sweet-smelling skin.

Hurst smiled. "Since you don't know for sure, let's see if we can find the answer between the two of us."

With one fluid motion, his lips came down on hers eagerly and impatiently as he rolled her onto her back and covered her body. Her hands hooked behind his head, a blast of white-hot arousal catching hold of his body. Hurst tasted and explored, running his tongue through her mouth before trailing kisses across her cheek to nuzzle the warm soft area around her ear. His hunger for her grew as he brushed his lips down her neck to her chest, her breasts, and back up again.

She swept her tongue through his mouth returning what he gave—a mutual pleasure that demanded more. It was beautiful being with her, teasing and satisfying her. Hurst didn't intend to stop making love to her until he'd dragged every bit of the breath from their lungs.

CHAPTER 20

MAN'S PRACTICAL GUIDE TO APPREHENDING A THIEF
SIR BENTLY ASHTON ULLINGSWICK

Search high and low, near and far.

The skies were gray but not threatening. Ophelia had prepared for her walk in the park with Hurst by donning a lightweight chemise, a long-sleeved white-sprigged walking dress, and a light-brown quilted spencer and matching pelisse. She wore a straw bonnet with a chocolate-colored ribbon tied into a perfect bow under her chin.

Hurst looked dapper dressed in a dark-blue coat and muted-blue waistcoat. The brass handle of a black umbrella was hooked over his wrist and his hat fit perfectly on top of his head. To her, he was the most handsome man in the world.

There were only a few other people on the streets as they walked the short distance before coming upon the entrance to Hyde Park, where there was a flurry of activity. Two other couples and a family with three children walked ahead of them and a bevy of people strolled behind them. The girl and two boys talked and squealed with youthful laughter as the parents quietly conversed with each other, seeming not to notice the youngsters' rambunctious actions as they skipped, tagged, and shouted to one another in fun. Ophelia liked the couple's ease and the children's abandonment.

The road leading into the park was backed up with traffic as people had stopped their carriages to chat with those leaving or others trying to pass those that had halted their horses. No one seemed to be in a hurry, including Ophelia. She was enjoying the time with her Hurst. Walking had always been one of her favorite pastimes. But at the back of her mind, she also had a need to finish the walk so they could return home. However, the duke was having none of the hurrying whenever she tried to pick up the pace. He insisted they stroll.

Truth to tell, she was honest when she told him finding the sacred church vessel was never far from her mind. Her brother had always been her best friend. She'd never rest easy without finding the chalice so there could never be a hint of scandal attached to his name. In her heart of hearts, she felt the man who took it was in London, and she prayed the Dowager Duchess of Stonerick would indeed somehow help her find the man she'd been looking for.

Distant sounds of lively music could be heard as they neared the area designated for the festival. It was no wonder the park was so full, having a May Day atmosphere and the sky slowly changing from gray to blue.

Some sections were thick with small trees and undergrowth while other areas of the terrain appeared wild and woodsy. The parcels that resembled open grassy lands reminded her of her home for so many years. Aside from the milk, vegetable, and other vendor carts that were pushed through the park every day, many people were milling about and intent on enjoying themselves. Some walking, others on horses or riding in various styles of carriages. It looked as if dozens were seated on blankets, enjoying refreshments and conversations.

"I don't want to lose you as we enter the crowds." Hurst extended his elbow to her and said, "Hold on to me."

She looked around. They were not near any crowds, but she didn't mind slipping her hand through the crook of his arm. It was warm and protective. "I was thinking about you," she offered as they walked.

"Me?" He gave her a quirky grin. "That gives me cause for concern. What was the reason? Did I do something right or wrong?"

"Neither really. I was thinking about me too."

Hurst tipped his hat to a couple they passed. The lady smiled at Ophelia, and she returned the silent greeting.

"That means you were thinking about us."

"All right," she admitted with a laugh. "Yes. Us. But mostly about you."

"I like hearing that I am in your thoughts, but am still waiting to hear whether I did something bad or good," he teased. "With you, I never know."

"I was remembering last night when we talked about how your childhood and mine were different. You've said before our fathers were nothing alike and handled life in their own ways."

The muscles in Hurst's arm tightened and he looked away from her. "That's not something I want to talk about today, Ophelia. The skies are clearing, the air is fresh, and I have you by my side. What more could I want?"

"It is I who wants more. I should know more about you now that I'm your wife. You are an only child, are you not?"

"Yes."

"Were you lonely at times?" she asked, paying no

mind to his remark that he didn't want to talk about his growing-up years.

"Not that I remember. I lived with various relatives from time to time as I did when I knew your family." He gave her a smile. "I'm sorry I didn't see much of you when I was there. You were usually wrapped in blankets and making strange noises."

Ophelia laughed. "I have never made strange sounds. That was baby talk."

"Oh, well, no wonder I didn't know what it was you were saying. I'd never been around a baby and still haven't."

"Not to worry. You will learn the language soon enough when we have one."

He placed his hand lovingly over hers that held on so tightly to the crook of his arm. "I can't wait."

"Neither can I," she answered, and was astounded at how true that really was. She wanted to have Hurst's baby. Soon. And a boy for him for the title. Maybe three boys. "So back to our discussion of you. Did you go off to school after you left Wickenhamden?"

"No. I went back to live with my father for a couple of years before that." He looked at her as if he were going to say something more but then turned his gaze back to the landscape again.

"Was it London where you lived with him or elsewhere?"

"London. I've made it clear I don't like talking about my father, or my childhood." Hurst gave her a low, throaty chuckle. "I lived with him from time to time before my schooling. After he died, my aunt Sophie took pity on me and arranged for my education."

"That was kind of her."

"And a good thing she did. I am grateful and look forward to you meeting her. At the time there was no chance I'd inherit the title, but through an unfortunate sickness that went through my uncle's family, the dukedom fell to me four years ago. Thanks to Aunt Sophie seeing I was properly educated, and my close friendships with Wyatt and Rick, who were already dukes and offered help, I was adequately prepared to assume the duties expected of me as head of the family."

"I don't know why you wouldn't want to talk about that and tell anyone the story. I find it's uplifting."

"Only that part is," he murmured, and nodded a greeting to a couple of gentlemen passing by them.

"Tell me more about your father."

Ophelia felt the muscles in his arm flex again. He was uncomfortable, but a lovely day in the park with warm sunshine and a pleasant breeze was the perfect time to talk about uncomfortable subjects.

"There isn't much to tell. His heritage was much like your father's. The younger son of a younger son who was taken care of by the titled uncle of the family. Where your father decided to go into the clergy to supplement his allowance to properly take care of his family, my father didn't. An adequate allowance from his uncle was an acceptable lifestyle for him. We could have had a good life. His problem was that he didn't use his allowance well. As I got older, we argued about that and many other things almost constantly. Does that satisfy you?"

"At least I know more than I did," she answered honestly.

"It's enough, Ophelia. Believe me."

As they made their way closer to the fair, the crowds

increased; the music and chatter grew louder. She could see the tents, stalls, and tables not far away.

"Come on," he said, taking longer strides. "I'll buy you a sweet cake to eat while we stroll. Later we'll head down the way to see the elephant."

"Do they have one here?"

A faint smile touched the corners of his mouth. "I heard mention there might be. I don't know for sure, but if they do, we'll see it."

Ophelia smiled too. "I'd like that."

The closer they came to where the fair and amusement area had been set up, the more festive the atmosphere seemed. It was the biggest fair Ophelia had ever been to. There were rows of tables lined side by side and covered in what looked like most anything a person would want to indulge in browsing or buying. Some tables were filled with trinkets while others had clothing, baskets, and fabrics on them. Booths housing puppets singing and dancing were mixed in with tables laden with cheese, bread, and various types of preserves.

Two men were walking along merrily as they each clapped two cymbals together. Ophelia didn't realize she shouldn't have smiled at them until she had already done it. Suddenly they were walking alongside her continuing with their banging the instruments together. She and Hurst laughed and ducked into the first tent they came to so they could get away from them. It was filled with herbs, seeds, and other plants. Happily, the cymbal men didn't follow them inside.

Farther down the park, the acrobats and tightrope walkers drew the largest crowds and she and Hurst stopped to watch for a while. Card tables had been placed on a grassy field where gentlemen and ladies were already playing chess, whist, or other card games. Croquet and horseshoes had been set up near the same area and people were lined up waiting for their turn to play.

Ophelia was enjoying herself immensely, taking time to stop and to look at a table of beautifully fashioned dolls while she and Hurst enjoyed a sugar-coated apricot tart and cup of spiced punch.

"I do enjoy being outside and going for long walks," she told Hurst while putting her gloves back on. "I've missed that since I've been in London. Maman hasn't been up to outings during the day, and I can't walk alone as I could in Wickenhamden."

"I'll see to it that we'll do more of this."

"I'd like that, and you were right. This is a pleasant diversion from the stress of just waiting around, pacing the drawing room floor." She laughed softly as they started walking toward the place that had been set aside for the animals. "It's been much better to pace at the fair."

"The countryside is beautiful at Hurstbourne. We'll go come summer. You'll enjoy walking there and riding." He glanced over at her. "Do you ride?"

"No, but whenever I've been near a horse I've felt a kinship of sort. I would love to learn."

"I'll teach you," he replied with a casual air. "I'm surprised Winston didn't teach you how."

"Don't think I didn't ask him. Neither he nor my parents thought it a proper thing for me to do, so I was denied the opportunity. However, one of my earliest clear memories of my brother was him teaching me to swim."

Hurst stopped and looked at her with a strange expression. "A girl? Did he?"

"Yes. You might not remember, but there was a deep pond not too far behind the vicarage where I grew up."

"I remember it well," he answered, looking for a

moment as if distant remembrances raced through his thoughts.

"Well, I couldn't have been more than three or four at most when I wandered down to the pond by myself one day, even though I had been told many times not to go near the water."

He lifted one corner of his mouth and grunted a laugh. "So, I see you had trouble obeying as soon as you got out of the nursery."

"Never mind about that," she said in a good-natured tone. "Luckily, Winston found me before I decided to dip my toes into the water that would have been over my head should I have fallen in. He was very upset with me. Perhaps the only time he ever was. Papa gave him permission to teach me to swim."

They started walking again. "Did Winston tell you he taught me to swim as well?"

"No," she said, delighted. "Thank you for telling me. I like hearing things about him I didn't know. He talked of how you two would often enjoy cooling off in the tepid water of the pond on hot summer days and on days when the water was so cold you both found slivers of ice in it."

Hurst chuckled. "That's true. There were occasions when our lips turned blue. Someday I'll have to share more of my remembrances of Winston with you."

"I would like that very much."

Only a few steps farther she caught sight of something glimmer out of the corner of her eye, and she turned to see a booth set up with dark-red draperies tied back with gold-colored tassels on either side. Shelving had been erected on a wall and there in front of her were several gold and silver wine goblets, one that looked exactly like Chatham's chalice.

For a moment she couldn't breathe or move.

"What is it?" he asked.

"That looks like the chalice."

"What?"

In the next instant Ophelia broke away from Hurst's arm and rushed toward the booth.

"Wait!" he called.

But Ophelia was running blindly. Reaching the booth before Hurst, she immediately leaned her whole body over the table and stretched to grab the cup off the shelf. Just before her hand closed around it, the shaft of Hurst's closed umbrella suddenly appeared like a gate in front of her, stopping her forward motion.

Shocked, she turned to Hurst. "I need to see it," she whispered frantically

"Let the man behind the counter get it for you," he said calmly, softly. "That's his job."

Ophelia looked over at the stout, red-bearded fellow who clearly didn't know what to make of a lady who was all but crawling over a table to get an item on his shelving.

"Yes, of course," she said, straightening her pelisse and forcing herself to smile at the confused man. "I would like to see it please if you would be so kind."

"Which one would you like to see?" the man asked.

She pointed to the chalice and realized her hands were trembling. When she took hold of it her spirits fell like a heavy rock; she knew immediately it wasn't the real cup. She had held the precious cup many times. This one wasn't heavy enough. Still, not wanting to believe the obvious, she quickly looked under the stand of the stem for the markings of the maker. There were none. It wasn't real gold. Her spirits, which had just soared so high, plummeted. Feeling lightheaded, she took several deep breaths.

Confident she was holding herself together and showing no signs of crumbling, she looked at Hurst and, somehow, found the willpower to say, "It's not the real one."

CHAPTER 21

MAN'S PRACTICAL GUIDE TO APPREHENDING A THIEF
SIR BENTLY ASHTON ULLINGSWICK

Don't worry as you speculate, write a list of plausible culprits.

By the time they'd made the quiet walk back to the house, half of the afternoon had passed. Ophelia appreciated that Hurst hadn't engaged her in idle talk. She knew all the things he would have said, including that historical sacraments were often copied with thin lightweight metals. Much in the same way prized pieces of jewelry were reproduced and made with colored glass stones rather than precious gems. She needn't hear him say it happened all the time. She knew it and it didn't matter to her. Her goal hadn't changed. She would leave no cup, no stone, no possibility unturned in her quest to find the chalice. She would not rest until she found it and returned it.

Ophelia walked through the front door, still marveling at the expansive Duke of Hurstbourne's foyer and all the elegant comforts surrounding her. She had gone from modest to richly elegant overnight. The feeling of nobility hadn't fully settled in as she stripped off her gloves and pelisse and placed them on a nearby chair.

While taking off her straw bonnet, she glanced at the silver tray that stayed on the side table at the entryway.

Its absence of notes, letters, and calling cards or anything else made her feel even more empty inside.

Suddenly the resolve she'd carried with her all the way home seemed to evaporate like warm breath on cold air—was she destined to fail, to resign herself to the fact that she couldn't save Winston's reputation? A different sadness seemed to settle over her as well. She wished Winston could have seen this house and have known his wish had come true. He had wanted her to live here as the duke's wife. More disappointment wove through her as she wished her brother could have known that she loved the duke, and he loved her.

Hurst ran a hand through his hair, momentarily distracting Ophelia from the jumble of thoughts mounting in her mind. She favored that quality about him, that at times it didn't matter if his hair wasn't in perfect order just because he was a man of wealth and title.

Unbidden, an image came to her mind of how Winston must have looked combing his hair in such a way after coming in from the fishing pond where he and Hurst swam and whiled away the daylight. When a boy, the mussy hair gave her brother a rapscallion kind of look, one that endeared him to her to this day. She never saw it that way the entire time he was the vicar. Not a hair was ever out of place.

From the corner of her eye, she saw Gilbert quietly coming into the vestibule, but he suddenly turned and walked away. Hurst must have given him the sign not to intrude. She was thankful for that courtesy as well, and silently commiserated with Hurst as he too made an obvious study of the empty silver tray.

There had been plenty of time for the dowager's friend to reply to her note, and for a note to have been sent to Hurst. Unless, of course, the friend was out for the day with family or appointments. Maybe out of town or just not sensing an urgency to answer. But it didn't matter why there was no message from the dowager; it remained, there was no answer from her. It was too frustrating to even think about.

After removing his hat and gloves and placing them aside, Hurst turned to Ophelia and gently took hold of her upper arms so she stood facing him. He placed a warm kiss on her forehead, letting his lips linger for a few seconds before whispering, "I'm sorry it wasn't the chalice."

"I know," she answered just as softly, allowing the weight of her weary head to lean against his lips. "It's just that time grows shorter by the hour. My hope was so high for a few seconds it was euphoric."

Hurst leaned away and gave her a teasing grin. "I don't want anything or anyone making you euphoric but me."

She huffed out an unsteady laugh and lifted her chin. By the look in his beautiful green eyes, he knew her heart was aching badly. Loving Hurst in peace, without the constant tension that was always on guard, was what she wanted, but she couldn't bear the thought of letting her mother and brother down.

"I don't have to tell you how I feel, Hurst. You know my hopes have been high since I came to London. Even before then. I knew I was going to find the sacrament in time and in a titled man's home. I felt it in my heart, and my whole being," she said earnestly.

"I know. It's very hard to give up on a powerful feeling that seems to rest in your soul. And you don't have to. We haven't heard the vicar has arrived. It might still be days before he does. And what if he has a disposition like the last one and can't or doesn't do the inventory for days? There is still time, Ophelia," he said encouragingly. "If the chalice is in London, it will be found."

"I think I am losing hope."

"No. I won't let you do that. I'll send Mr. Mallord to buy the reproduction chalice. It might come in handy to buy us some time. So let's not think about that right now."

"When should I if not now?"

"This evening," he assured her pleasantly. "You didn't sleep much last night. Why don't you go up to our chambers and lie down? I will stay here and watch for the message to arrive. I'll bring it up to you right away. I won't even take time to open and read it for myself first."

She smiled with weariness that settled on her shoulders. "I'm not tired or sleepy. I'm—"

"Disappointed? Worried? Frustrated?" he asked sympathetically.

"All that and much more," Ophelia admitted. "It just seems that every time I think I'm moving forward on finding the thief, I suddenly feel as if I've taken three steps backward instead."

"I want the person found as much as you do so you can focus on me and our life together."

She could hear the same harbor of feelings in his tone. He truly did embrace her disappointment as his, clearly worried for her and frustrated not to have this matter solved and literally placed back in the locked box where it belonged.

Bringing her protectively close to him, he wrapped his strong arms around her. She pressed her cheek against his warm, comforting chest.

"What if I go up and lie down with you?"

He kissed her temple and around her cheek and eye and then intimately on the mouth. Pleasurable tingles danced within her, but she couldn't give in to his tender kisses. "No," she whispered. "I'd rather wait belowstairs."

"I know for a fact that when you were in my arms last night you were not thinking about the chalice or the thief. The only thing you had on your mind was me, you and us together."

"I can't do that right now."

"I only want to hold you close like this. We don't have to talk, or kiss or caress. Just rest."

His suggestion brought a tease of laughter from her throat. "May I remind you, that anytime you say you just want to hold me close, nothing else, the 'nothing' becomes something that fully distracts me from whatever it was I was in a conundrum from."

Hurst merely curved a corner of his mouth in response. No words needed.

Ophelia was tempted to take him up on his respite, but just as she was forming her reply, her mother walked into the vestibule.

Exertion blushed a red stain on Maman's cheeks, and her breathless words came out in a rush. "Forgive me for interrupting. I don't mean to intrude."

Ophelia and Hurst stepped away from each other, not that she thought there was anything amiss about a husband and wife in a loving embrace, but her mother would not appreciate seeing it. If Maman was uncomfortable, she didn't display it. Ophelia could see her somber expression meant she had news of the utmost importance.

"You didn't intrude, Maman. Are you all right?"

"I was reading and thought I heard you come inside, but you never made it into the drawing room," she replied, looking neither of them in the eye. "I decided to see if you were indeed back from the fair." She pulled something from underneath her cuffed sleeve. "I wanted to give you this. It came while you were gone, and when I saw it on the letter tray, I picked it up for safekeeping. I didn't want anything to happen to it. It's from the Dowager Duchess of Stonerick."

Ophelia's breath quickened. "Why didn't you say so?" With haste, she reached for the letter, but her mother pulled it back.

"I'm sorry, dear. It's addressed to the duke."

"Yes. Of course," she answered, rubbing her hands together, realizing just how anxious she'd become. "I wasn't thinking properly."

Hurst took the parchment, broke open the seal, looked down, and almost instantly back up to Ophelia again.

"What does she say?"

"She just wrote the name Lord Gagingcliffe."

"The baron?" Ophelia asked, confusion working its way into her thoughts.

"There is no other lord by that name," Hurst replied, reviewing the note again.

"His name isn't in the registry. I'm sure of it."

"I don't remember seeing it either," Hurst said thoughtfully. "He must have used an alias."

"Or perhaps he somehow managed to slip by whoever was at the door and not sign the registry at all," Ophelia suggested. "If he is the thief, this is quite shocking. He doesn't seem to be a man who would take things that don't belong to him." Ophelia's forehead wrinkled in concern. "I played several hands of whist with him at the garden party. Hurst, Georgina's father wants her to marry the baron."

"I've known him for years, Ophelia. He's always been an upstanding man." The firmly set tone in Hurst's voice brooked no arguments. "He's a quiet, mild-mannered fellow who seems to be too scared of his shadow to do anything as risky as stealing a sacrament. I don't think he would take something from a church, and if he had, why would he play cards with you so easily when he knew your brother was the vicar at the church he stole from?"

A chill shook Ophelia.

"I met the man at the card party as well," Maman said. "I agree with both assessments of him. He was a pleasant person to talk to and I noted nothing out of the ordinary in his mannerisms or what he said."

"I didn't say anything to make him think we were suspicious," Ophelia added. "And remember no one knows it's missing. He has reason to feel safe saying anything he wants." Venting an exasperated huff, Ophelia pursed her lips before saying, "His name is the one the dowager wrote. I think it must be him."

"No, it doesn't." Hurst shook his head. "All we know is that the woman from the Insightful Ladies group divulged he collects religious objects."

"Objects?" In a strong statement, she restated his response. Ophelia knew Hurst was hedging in hopes to pacify her. "Religious *artifacts* is what she actually said."

Hurst continued to carry on the conversation by adding, "We have to realize we are hearing this from a lady who studies superstitions, believes the alignment of the stars predicts the future, and thinks a lady with red hair and green eyes like Edwina can read your mind."

"That's preposterous," Ophelia scoffed, an unpleasant taste of denial in her words.

"My point," Hurst insisted. "We don't know that we can trust her. We don't know what she believes, which includes why she thinks Lord Gagingcliffe collects—" Hurst paused. "Things, objects, or artifacts."

Defying him, Ophelia challenged her husband and stated, "Hurst, you're being obstinate for no good reason. She gave us a name and I'm going to confront the baron."

Throwing his hands up, he argued, "But *we* don't know yet if *we* can believe anything she says."

"I should excuse myself," Ophelia's mother said, wringing her hands. "I've caused you both distress. Dear me, if there is any way I can help, I'm willing to stay." Tears shimmered in her eyes. "This is as important to me as to you, Ophelia. If not more."

"I'm sorry, Maman. We don't know what any of us can do right now." A dull headache had been forming at the back of her neck since she'd lunged for the fake chalice. Nothing could be done at this exact moment because she didn't have a plan concerning how she could get into the baron's house to look at his bookshelves. Lowering her voice a little softer, she said, "I think I'm going to take Hurst's advice and go up to my chambers to think for a little while. You don't mind, do you, Maman?"

"Of course not." Her mother smiled and affectionately touched Ophelia's shoulder. "That's a good idea. I'm sure you'll figure out something we can do. You always do. I'll be in the drawing room if you need me."

"I'll join you, Ophelia, in our chambers," Hurst said curtly after her mother departed.

Ophelia didn't wait for him but started up the stairs, wondering how she was going to get into Lord Gagingcliffe's house. The duke's footsteps sounded behind her all the way, and until he scooted ahead of her and opened the door that led into his bedchamber. She stepped inside and turned to face him while he shut the door.

With just the two of them, the masculine room with its dark furnishings, heavily carved hearth, and the large bed with hunter's green bedding made Ophelia feel warm and protected for a few moments. She wished she had all this upheaval settled so she could enjoy the feeling longer. Forever, if possible.

Crossing over to his dressing chest, Hurst took the stopper out of a decanter and poured a dram of brandy into two glasses. He handed one to her.

"What's this?"

"Brandy."

Her brow rose suspiciously. "If you'll remember, I didn't have a good experience the last time I tried it."

"That's because you were trying to drink it like the seasoned sporting men you were conversing with that evening. Take small sips," he said patiently, and then proceeded to take a swallow like the seasoned sporting men he mentioned.

Ophelia followed his instructions and barely let the liquid touch her tongue. It went down much easier that way.

"Take another," he encouraged in a strained tone with his eyes pinched tightly. "It will help settle you as we finish the discussion we started with your mother."

"Gladly," she answered as tightly as he'd spoken, trying to slow her ragged breathing. "When I played cards with the baron at the party, I quizzed him and Mr. Sawyer about anyone in their family who might be a collector."

Concern edged his features. "I can't believe you did that."

"You sound as if you think there was something wrong with that. Did you think I was going to parties and balls just to enjoy myself? I was looking for anyone who could help me."

"I don't know how I'd forgotten, Ophelia." He nodded, sarcasm tainting his reply. "From the night we met, you never led me to believe you were in London for anything other than your mission."

"What I said to Mr. Sawyer and the baron made for easy conversation while trying to concentrate on the cards in my hand. I started it quite inconspicuously by mentioning the signet ring Mr. Sawyer was wearing. Both gentlemen said they didn't know of anyone in their families who collected things. This means Lord Gagingcliffe wasn't truthful. Perhaps Mr. Sawyer too. I have doubt about both being men of honor right now."

"It means nothing yet," he urged, stern resolve in his every word as he placed the empty glass on a table. "You could be condemning innocent men."

"I am not condemning," she answered pertly, taking umbrage at his words. "I'm considering possibilities that need to be considered. Let's go see him and find out what kind of man he is."

"And say what? 'Lord Gagingcliffe, since my wife is certain you have the chalice, will you give it back? Please,'" Hurst pretended to pose a question to the allegedly guilty man.

Ophelia's temper rose, but she managed to hold it inside. She landed her glass beside his. If this was what he had to say, she didn't want to settle down. "Stop mocking me."

"I wasn't criticizing you."

A rapid display of emotions crossed her face. "It sounded as if you were."

"Of course not," he insisted again. "It might have seemed to you, but I was being rational."

"Just because you say you are rational, Hurst, doesn't mean you always are. And I want to be successful. I know we couldn't be so brazen as to accuse him. We can go on the pretext of a business of some kind you want to discuss. While you distract him, I will do the searching."

"What are you saying? No." Hurst ground out the word as if he were crushing it under his boot. "I've told you I won't be a party to that kind of searching. There are other ways."

"You won't be doing anything you feel isn't right. Looking around a person's home isn't necessarily a terrible thing to do. Especially if they invite you to do so."

"Why are we having this discussion again, Ophelia?"

"Because people make their homes grand and filled with precious items just so guests will look at them and enjoy the bounty. In reality that is all I will be doing. To make you happy I will seek an invitation from the baron before I look around. It appears you want to dismiss this without even looking into it because you've known him so long."

"I'm not saying that," he insisted, his voice rising a little. "Let me think about this and I'll come up with a plan."

She gave him a level gaze. "Think about it? Make a plan? I already have a plan."

"You know the phrase 'Don't rush where angels wouldn't dare to tread,' Ophelia," Hurst cautioned.

A gasp passed her lips. "Are you calling me foolish?"

"Of course not." His back stiffened. "Don't put words I didn't say into my mouth."

"It sounded to me as if you did. It's true you only said part of the quote, but I know the beginning of it. You think I am being foolish to help a brother who helped raise me and loved me and my mother devotedly. You have always thought I was on a fool's errand."

The frown on his brow tightened. "I didn't mean it that way." He took a step toward her. "I said the part that was accurate concerning you. I don't want you to get your hopes up again. I don't want you to put yourself in danger again."

"Danger? I haven't been in any jeopardy."

"You aren't thinking clearly, Ophelia. You went over a table after a chalice that was a reproduction!"

"Don't yell at me," she answered with determination. "And it looked real."

"I'm not yelling," he defended, though lowering his tone considerably. "Replicas are supposed to look real. Everything you see concerning this stolen vessel looks real to you. The crests you sketched for Mrs. Turner, and the guilt you were willing to place on my cousin and every peer in London."

"There was no harm done to anyone, including me, at the fair."

"Only because I was able to catch up with you and stop you with my umbrella. Footpads abound at fairs and steal from the shopmongers and vendors almost at will. They keep themselves armed with a knife. That man could have assumed you were about to take something from him, pulled his blade out of instinct, and harmed you before I could get to you, and then I would have had to harm him."

She swallowed hard. "That is rather dramatic. You are the one talking madness now about such dire consequences."

"Know this now and forevermore, Ophelia." He spoke low. "You are my wife. I would never let anyone put their hands on you without retaliation. I will protect you above all else."

His words, and the passion with which he said them, chilled her, thrilled her, but not giving up, she said rashly, "I don't need protection to check out a man you say is a pillar of the community."

"I am on a mission to save you from yourself." Hurst's expression etched hard with lines of discontent. "I forbid you to go to his house."

His declarative words astounded her; her eyes filled with shock and her heart thudded in her ears. "You can't."

"I am your husband. When we married, I didn't take a vow giving up my rights as your husband."

"And I didn't give up mine. You said you would not forbid me to do anything until after the theft of the chalice was settled. You can't go back on your word."

"Listen to me, dam—" He bit off the last half of the word and swore under his breath instead, before saying, "Ophelia, I love you. I have from the moment I saw you even though I doubted my own feelings at the time. I love your courage, loyalty, and your determination. But at some point, you must give up your reckless ways."

"You want me to give up?" The thought sent chills over her again and made tears surprisingly spring to her eyes. She quickly blinked them away before one should happen to escape the corner of her eye. He knew how important this was to her.

"No. Not give up. Think. Plan. Let me help you my way. We can't accuse Gagingcliffe, Sawyer, or any other man. If any of them have it, we could tip them off and the chalice could be hidden so that it will never be found. We start with Gagingcliffe and will work together to see if he is the person we are looking for."

"If he has it, it's on a bookshelf and we will see it," she argued again.

"Do you think he's going to let you just walk into his house and see it?" His voice rose. "He knows you are the sister to the vicar he stole it from. Be reasonable about this."

"I am always reasonable," she countered, her voice raised too and her chest heaving.

"You came to my house dressed as a man twice. How are you always reasonable, Ophelia?"

"I had good, reasonable motives for doing it both times."

"Just do it my way this time." Hurst mumbled several curses under his breath and looked away.

He wouldn't be swayed, but neither would she. Perhaps the sip or two of brandy she had consumed was helping calm her after all. She suddenly felt calmer. "I believe you have said that to me before, Your Grace." She swallowed hard. "Don't ask it of me again. I believe you know that my answer is still the same. It is not in my nature. I wish you had known before we married that I cannot change my nature. You would have saved us both a lot of heartache."

Despair pushed from her aching lungs. Ophelia opened the door that joined their rooms and shut herself inside her chambers.

CHAPTER 22

MAN'S PRACTICAL GUIDE TO APPREHENDING A THIEF
SIR BENTLY ASHTON ULLINGSWICK

Make the suspect feel he can confide in you.

Hurst walked over to the table and downed the rest of Ophelia's brandy and poured himself another splash. The heat of the liquor swallowed so quickly sent a flush through him. He took off his coat and threw it with more force than necessary for it to land on the bed rather than the floor. But what the hell did it matter. He'd told Ophelia he wouldn't forbid her to search for the chalice and then he had. That was not his finest hour.

He knew it was close to the time the vicar would be arriving at the church. A missing sacrament would cause a rumble of concern. Perhaps a large donation would soothe the bishop's and new vicar's ruffled feathers. It would not soothe Ophelia's. But perhaps it would give them time to find the chalice.

He wasn't sure how long he stood in front of the window staring out while the sun hung lower in the sky with every passing minute. The strong drink helped ease the tension in the back of his neck and shoulders but failed to touch the ache in his chest.

Hurst didn't like arguing with Ophelia, or making her

feel as if he wasn't helping. And he certainly didn't like going back on his word.

Maybe he'd handled their conversation all wrong. No, hellfire, he had handled it wrong. Passionately was the only way he knew how to talk to her about her search to save her brother's legacy.

What was she going to do? Exactly what she'd indicated she would do and defy him? Probably. Perhaps she had legitimate reason to. He had acquiesced to her wishes and told her she didn't have to obey him. The surprising thing was he hadn't minded at the time. So no, he couldn't rightly forbid her to do anything. She was right. That had been the wrong thing for him to say in the heat of the moment or at any other time.

Of all the ladies in London, why did the most stubborn of them have to be the one destined for him to love and cherish? And he did with his whole being. He wouldn't make any excuses or apologies for that to anyone, including himself. She was all he could ask for in a wife. Exquisite, persuasive, and beautiful beyond any other woman he'd seen or imagined.

Hurst walked over to the slipper chair and plopped himself down while continuing to brood. In truth, he had to rationalize that she was much like him after he'd met her—feeling she might be the lady for him at times but believing she couldn't possibly be because she wasn't like the lady he'd always expected: demure, compliant, and obedient to his will. He couldn't count the number of charming ladies he'd met over the past ten years who were exactly like that, and with every one of them, he wanted to feel that spark of erotic sensation that told him she was to be his bride. But in his soul, he knew they weren't. Ophelia was.

She was meant to be his. Since he knew that, it was no

wonder he worried about her and that he was so passionate to make her consider another way might be better. Ophelia continued to take too many chances with her safety and reputation. She was not only a lady and a duchess, but was the love of his life. That made all the difference. Whether it was said clearly or mumbled, the word *obey* was in their marriage vows, and also *cherish* and *protect*.

Why wouldn't she just let him handle this theft the normal, practical way? By people who had actually done things like this before and knew how to do it with the most efficient means. He didn't know what he was going to do about her, because her will was as strong as his.

Raising his voice when he was angry wasn't the answer to anything either. He didn't mean to, and by the devil he might have been loud, but it wasn't yelling as she'd claimed. He knew the difference. He yelled at his sporting club's events. He'd yelled at his father. To her, he only talked loudly, but he was trying not to do that.

Maybe she only thought he was excessively loud because her brother and father had always been so damned calm and thoughtful about everything they said, even if they were furious with someone. The person would never know it by their tone or expression. It was their calling to know how to keep peace and live in harmony at all times. Hurst didn't understand it.

In life, there was nothing wrong with showing passion in your voice when it was called for. Not that it mattered to him, but Ophelia's voice had risen a time or two as well. Although he hadn't called her on it. And wouldn't. He didn't mind her emotions showing in her voice.

Someway he had to make her see that it meant he cared deeply for her, for what they were discussing. But admittedly, it was a habit he'd developed whenever he and his dad had rows. Habits could be broken, and he was going to break that one. For her. He would never be as discreet in tone as were those in her family. He didn't know anyone who was, other than the Stowes. Hurst wanted to be the kind of husband Ophelia wanted and deserved, but there was no way he could fail to show annoyance from time to time any more than he could remain expressionless when he was happy.

What was he going to do concerning her thoughts on the baron? Ophelia had mentioned her own nature. Hurst believed her. And it wasn't in his nature to suspect a titled man. Perhaps there were some peers who misused their duties to the title and mankind in general, but he didn't know any who didn't appear to do their best to be honorable at all times and in all things.

Whoever took the chalice had to have been someone who needed money or had a fetish for collecting religious objects. Hurst combed through his memories of the times he'd been with the baron. They had been at the same card tables a few times. He was an acceptable and honest player. As Hurst recalled, he was damn good at billiards. He always paid his gambling debts. Hurst couldn't remember anything that would make the man seem odd. In fact, if he wasn't mistaken, Lord Gagingcliffe once thought of being a clergyman himself. That didn't mean anything, though. Hurst had once thought about the possibility of the ministry too.

But what if Mrs. Turner was right and it was a titled man from London who had a collection of artifacts on his bookshelf? And what if the woman who was embedded into her beliefs of the superstitious realm of life was right about Gagingcliffe? What if Ophelia had been right not to give up on what she felt deeply in her heart was the only true way to go?

Hurst couldn't say he knew the baron well, but he

was good at reading a person. What would it hurt if he and Ophelia paid a visit to the man? It would make her happy. And hell yes, he wanted to make her happy. Hurst looked out the window and studied longer on the idea. The sun would be setting soon. That would make it past respectable visiting hours. But most people didn't mind what time a duke showed up at their door.

On their way over to the baron's house they could discuss the kinds of questions to ask him while there. If he seemed nervous, jittery, or tried to change the subject when talking about collecting things, religious subjects, that could possibly be a telltale sign. If necessary, Hurst would delve deeper into the baron's private life. For Ophelia, he would have the man's whole house torn apart piece by piece if necessary.

Hurst stood up, placed the unfinished drink back on the table, and grabbed his coat off the bed. There was nothing like assessing, or in this case reassessing, a situation to come up with a doable plan. His duty was to Ophelia, not the baron simply because he was a peer. She wanted to question the man, and they would.

He went to her adjoining door and knocked. "Ophelia." He knocked louder and called her name. He checked the handle. The door was unlocked, so he opened it and went inside. The room was empty.

Damnation! His heart raced. His first thought was that she had she gone to Lord Gagingcliffe's. Without him? Couldn't she have given him fifteen minutes to work through what needed to be done before she went chasing off on her own?

"Ophelia!" Hurst raced down the stairs and into the drawing room calling her name.

"Your Grace, what's wrong?" Mrs. Stowe asked from the settee where she was sitting as he rushed inside.

"Have you seen Ophelia?"

"Yes." She gazed at him with a concerned stare, closed the book she held, and placed it aside. "Ophelia came back down very shortly after the two of you went up. She said she was going for a walk."

A walk? He tensed. They had just walked to Hyde Park and back, and all around the fair too. It was more likely she'd gone to see the baron. Hurst would bet money on it.

His heartbeat thudded faster. "Did she have anything with her?" he asked. *Perhaps men's clothing and a wig.*

"Only a shawl that I saw and Mrs. Turner so she wouldn't be alone."

That she had someone with her was a relief. "Good."

"Please tell me if something is wrong, Your Grace. I might be able to help."

"No need for you to worry about anything, Mrs. Stowe. As soon as I find her, we'll talk and take care of everything."

Hurst turned to leave but quickly swung back when he caught a glimpse of the book beside her. Impatient, he asked, "Do you mind if I look at the book you were holding?"

"Of course not." She handed the copy of *Debrett's Peerage and Baronetage* to him. "I was looking through it again, hoping to find something we might have missed on the many other times we looked at it."

"I'm glad if it was helpful," he said absently, and quickly thumbed through the pages and found what he was looking for. With a few tweaks, the coat of arms for the baron's family would look somewhat like one of the crests Ophelia sketched.

A cold realization settled over Hurst. Mrs. Turner was right. Ophelia was right. Dowager Stonerick's superstitious friend was right. He laid the book on the settee beside Mrs. Stowe and saw the registry Ophelia had *borrowed* from the church. Memory flashed that he hadn't seen the baron's name in that book. Maybe he'd missed it because he'd been so caught up in finding his cousin's signature there.

He picked it up and slowly ran a finger down the names again, but the baron's name wasn't in the registry. If he was the titled man they were looking for, he must have used an alias, which was the right thing to do if he was planning on stealing something.

He returned the books to Mrs. Stowe. "Thank you. You have been most helpful tonight."

Mrs. Stowe gave him a wistful smile. "Have I?"

"I wouldn't say it if it wasn't true. You have helped me many times in life."

"That warms my heart, Your Grace. I want to be helpful, but Ophelia likes to do everything herself."

"I don't know how to reasonably explain this, but I knew that about her the first time we met, yet it seems I keep having to learn it over and over again."

"That makes perfect sense to me."

Hurst smiled and then headed toward the door calling, "Gilbert, I need my carriage immediately. And find the footman Mr. Mallord for me. Tell him I need him to come with me too!"

Only a few minutes later, Hurst was sitting in Lord Gagingcliffe's drawing room wondering where Ophelia was. She'd left home in plenty of time to make it to the baron's house before Hurst. He had halfway expected to find her dressed as a man chatting with the baron when he arrived, as she had been with Mr. Wilbur Sawyer at his sporting club meeting. Could it be that she had actually gone for a walk as she'd told her mother?

Lord Gagingcliffe's walls were adorned excessively

with paintings. Most were hung with limited space between the heavy frames, as if the baron wanted to be sure he'd impress anyone who crossed the threshold of his domain with his many exhibits of artworks.

At present, it was the Duke of Hurstbourne he was trying to impress.

While the baron poured two glasses of spirits, Hurst gave the drawing room a deliberate study. Through conversation he'd have to come up with a reason to be invited into the book room since that is the place Ophelia was certain the chalice would be.

The vastness of the collection bordered on obsessiveness. The men of nobility he knew boasted about increasing their landholdings, not procuring artwork. But there was no crime displaying a large painting or two in one's drawing room. Perhaps eclectic, but not normal. The man certainly had more than the average home or estate.

A small tabletop was used for a chess set and the fireplace's marble mantel exhibited a clock one would expect in a home of this stature.

Even so, the room piqued Hurst's interest. Was there a gold chalice in all this clutter somewhere? Was it in the book room or not here at all?

Ophelia wanted to believe the church's sacrament cup was in Lord Gagingcliffe's possession. But she had come to her wit's end with precious little time left and no other suspect. Pinning the crime on Gagingcliffe made for an easy mark for her. Even though her certainty came only from the dowager duchess' single name written on parchment.

The baron happily handed Hurst a crystal glass, the older man's face eager with prospect and wonder. "I'm honored to have you in my home, Your Grace. To what pleasure may I pray have you come to see me?"

Hurst's pre-planned fabrication came easily as the baron had set it up a few days ago when he'd stopped by Hurst's table at White's. "As you indicated not too long ago, Mr. Wilber Sawyer wants to join my sporting club, the Brass Deck. I remembered you know him well. Since we are getting ready to make our selections, I thought to ask your opinion of his suitability for fitting in with our group."

Flattery raised his brows as the baron replied, "I do know him from a card club where we are both members. I've always favored Sawyer as a good chap."

"I've thought so myself but given my limited knowledge it's prudent to hear all perspectives when possible."

The baron looked positively agog at the idea of helping Hurst. "I couldn't agree more. Once we have a man in a club, it's difficult to cut him if we conclude he isn't a good fit. It becomes a rather nasty business."

"True, Lord Gagingcliffe. Has there ever been a whiff of his being dishonorable at cards or anything else you might have heard?"

"He's above most at all things as far as I know."

"Good to hear," Hurst answered, distracted by a rather large painting of the Virgin Mary with a golden halo over her head. The serene smile on her lips held him still. It was almost as if she knew something. A secret she couldn't wait to share with someone if only they would listen.

The baron's prideful words cut into Hurst's thoughts. "She's majestic, isn't she?"

"The painting?" Hurst nodded. "Byzantine art?"

"Yes. A rare find she is. One of my favorite purchases. I bought her at an auction after having only seen a crudely painted copy of the original."

That could very well mean it came from the underworld where many private exchanges of money for art, horses, pleasures, and other things took place. Hurst didn't have an expert's eye for priceless art, but what hung on the wall certainly wasn't a replica.

Doing his best to sound genuine, Hurst questioned, "Where do you usually broker?"

"Penwicke House most of the time. They know what I like. Other places to be sure, but not often."

Hurst couldn't help but wonder if that was mostly religious art, even though there wasn't much sitting around the drawing room.

As calm as the vast morning sea, Hurst inflected a nonthreatening tone in his question: "Do you favor gold or silver when looking for objects rather than paintings?"

"I must confess, I do lean toward gold celestial objets d'art. I think there is great comfort in them. As if possessing them brings us closer to a higher power. Wouldn't you agree?"

Hurst had no opinion, so he nodded with vague noncommitment, antsy to be on his way, yet held captive by the man's esoteric discussion—mostly with himself. Gagingcliffe had not shown this side of himself over the card games and billiards they'd enjoyed at various clubs. Hurst felt that the man was just so thrilled he had come over that he couldn't help but do his best to impress him.

Taking a sip of wine, the baron admitted, "Most of the room's treasures have been handed down in our family for generations, so I've had many years to enjoy them."

The same as he'd told Ophelia. Hurst led the conversation in the direction he wanted. "We titled men all live with such items. Our homes are those of our predecessors and I would bet the rooms know more stories than the staff."

His voice lowering, he said, "My staff is well trained at eyes forward and ears back. They are there when I need them and not when I require privacy."

"As it should be." Hurst was not one to make small talk, but in this case it was necessary. Keeping the baron's trust was essential.

Their conversation continued as Hurst drained his glass, declined a second, and wondered where his wife was. Was she clever enough to have found a way inside and was now searching the house while he talked to the baron? Had she really gone for a walk as she told her mother? Had she gone somewhere else?

Gagingcliffe's sudden faraway look in his eyes caught Hurst by surprise. He confessed, "I fancied myself as a vicar, but I lacked the religious breeding." With a low chuckle, he confessed, "I have a profound respect for the teachings, but I like my vices too much. Art, cards, and women.

"I really should settle down and marry like you, which is why I am considering offering for Miss Bristol's hand."

"She's lovely."

"I think so. Do you know her father well?"

"Not well at all." And if Hurst had anything to say about it, he would make sure her father checked out the baron very well, should he approach the man for his daughter's hand.

The truth was that he just wanted all of this to be over no matter who the thief was. He wanted to go home and tell Ophelia she need not worry herself further. He had unintentionally hurt her by wrongly forbidding her to search for the chalice on her own. Now he wanted to be able to tell her the matters had been handled and resolved, the chalice being returned to its rightful place.

Distancing himself from those thoughts, he realized he'd missed some of the baron's prattling. His voice droned onward as he described various pieces and how they came into the family's estate.

Gagingcliffe continued, leaning into his chair as if he had no other captive audience scheduled for a visit today. The tedium of this verbal trip around the drawing room wore on Hurst's nerves, but he was careful not to let the baron know he found the entire conversation dull and distasteful.

"I've procured a few relics for my own private collection, most of which surround me in my book room. Do you have one yourself, Your Grace? A private collection?"

Hurst's ears perked up when he heard the words *book room* and *relics*. The very kind of room Ophelia had always believed was the new home of the chalice.

Contriving an answer, his mind was distracted with urgency to find a way to do a quick look through the shelving and be gone. "I'm not a collector unless you count waistcoat buttons. Every so often, mine have a habit of jumping ship from my clothing. Eventually my valet gathers them and has them sewn back on. But I meant to mention to you earlier that I had once thought of entering the clergy too."

"That is news to me." Steepling his fingertips over his breastbone, the baron hemmed and hawed, starting a sentence, then stopping to redirect his words to another thought as if he warred between being boastful or silent.

In the end, his pedigree of arrogance prevailed, and he formed his words deliberately as if he'd spoke them in a confessional. "Some of my most prized possessions are cleverly hidden in plain sight. The eye follows but where you look isn't what you see."

Keeping his pulse from jumping, Hurst projected deliberate firmness, showing no sign of relenting. "You've intrigued me. I must see this for myself."

With a shake of his head, the baron dismissed his request. "It's not possible today, Your Grace."

Hurst struggled to stay seated, but he couldn't run and search for all the hidden pieces of art in the book room with the baron pulling at the tail of his coat. Now he knew why Ophelia always thought snooping was the better plan. "Another time then," he said.

The baron's next words were enthusiastic as he spoke. "But while you're here, you must see this impressive piece I recently acquired—a bejeweled Anglican cross. Indulge me while I go upstairs to my bedchamber to retrieve it."

"Yes, if you insist." Hurst couldn't believe his good luck. The man was going to actually leave him alone in the house. Perhaps he thought a duke was above snooping. And until now, Hurst was.

Lord Gagingcliffe strode toward the doorway, then scampered off like an excited boy. There was no way Hurst was going to chase another man into his bedchamber where, if he indeed had the chalice, it might be. Instead, he stayed but for a short count, his mind considering all possibilities and thinking ahead to his next move.

Hurst couldn't wait long. Not when he had the opportunity, no matter how small a window to accomplish his quest or how distasteful it was for him to do. It was time for him to conquer his ghosts from the past and drive them out of his mind for good. No matter he vowed to never do such a thing. He swallowed it all and bolted out of the drawing room.

As he rounded the newel post, the front door knocker rapped with staccato beats. But Hurst pressed on, not listening for the butler's foot treads trailing into the vestibule to answer the caller.

The Duke of Hurstbourne had one mission in mind: get to the book room and search it fast.

He now found himself engaging in the criminal act he had forbidden his wife to do. That he swore to himself long ago he'd never do. Invading someone's privacy—taking something from them, even if it was for a good reason—was still wrong. But he loved Ophelia, and now believed her suspicions about Lord Gagingcliffe could be true. And he was damned determined to prove she was right.

CHAPTER 23

MAN'S PRACTICAL GUIDE TO APPREHENDING A THIEF
SIR BENTLY ASHTON ULLINGSWICK

If exposed, have a ready plan.

After returning from her brisk walk around the neighborhood, Ophelia was still anxious. Arguing with Hurst had gotten her nowhere. She wanted to find him and try reasoning with him once again about the urgent need to visit Lord Gagingcliffe. But she was too late. Maman told her he'd left the house in his carriage.

Ophelia had a strong hunch she knew where Hurst had gone. This time leaving the maid at home, she hired a carriage to take her to the baron's house. She knew her hunch was right and her husband was inside when she saw his black gleaming barouche with its sophisticated crest on the door parked in front of Lord Gagingcliffe's home. As she had suspected, Hurst had come without her. But why? She didn't know for sure what he'd planned to do, but she knew what he wasn't doing: checking the book room. Unless he'd managed to get the baron to invite him into it.

She had a sudden sinking feeling in her stomach as if something amiss was going on inside. Was Hurst there to warn the man, or had he decided to do a little digging on his own to see what he could find out? Either way, he should have waited for her.

Trying to settle her nerves, she had to keep to her own plan. She supposed she'd know the duke's strategy as soon as she got inside. Maybe Hurst being there would be to her advantage, she rationalized. If he was busy with Lord Gagingcliffe, it was all the better for her—as long as they were not in the book room.

Hoping she would be successful this time, Ophelia gathered her skirts and made purposeful strides up the short steps to use the knocker on the front door.

It seemed a long time before the butler swung it open, his face more than slightly puzzled to see an unaccompanied lady standing before him.

"I'm Miss Stowe to see the baron," she said, before she thought to say she was now the Duchess of Hurstbourne. But perhaps it was best he didn't know who she really was for now.

The butler's exterior didn't look nearly as polished as Gilbert's, and he seemed a little flustered by her. "He's not available. He already has a visitor."

"But you see I have information for him, and I know he will want to see me if you just tell him I'm here." She smiled sweetly, but exhaling an impatient breath of air.

Resigned, the butler said, "Your calling card, if you will, miss."

"I don't have one." Trying to keep annoyance out of her voice.

"I'm afraid I won't be able to speak to his lordship for you. Good night."

He went to close the door but Ophelia put out her hand and stopped him. "Never mind all that. It's dreadfully chilly out here and I'm without a cape. May I sit in the vestibule while you check with the baron?"

Ophelia brushed past him without giving him time to answer. Merciful saints and angels too, it would have been easier to sneak in rather than pass muster by the butler at the door and be gained entrance.

He stood tall and slim in front of her, barring her from a determined path toward a chair where guests would wait.

The butler stated, "I told you, Lord Gagingcliffe already has a visitor."

"I understand. I'll wait here in front of the door if you prefer I not sit down."

The butler seemed to be torn about his decision. While he was engaged with that, Ophelia noted the line of stairs on the right and opened doors of a drawing room. She heard no voices, notably not her husband's. Where were Hurst and the baron? Hopefully in the garden to take in the last of the bit of twilight.

The butler tugged on his sleeve cuffs, as if to right something that had not been out of order with his tidy livery, while mumbling something about it not being proper for a lady to show up at man's door without a companion.

Face flushed and a sheen of perspiration on his brow, he finally pointed to the chair and said, "Wait there. I'll be right back."

But his declarative order didn't matter to her. As soon as he was out of sight, she was out of the chair and peeking into the empty drawing room. There were two used wine glasses. She'd become accustomed to telling which way to go to look for the book room and took off. Half running down the corridor on tiptoe, hoping to make no sound. The situation wasn't funny, yet the preposterous way she had gone about this entire search now settled on her shoulders. She had to work quickly before the butler found her gone and came looking for her.

Plunging into this scenario could be her undoing, but she must. If the two men were in the book room, she would be doomed to make a choice. Neither option she had in mind would be good: confront them or hide until they were gone, and she could conduct her search when the house was quiet for the night.

In truth, she'd been reckless and hadn't been thinking clearly. Too focused on finding out if this man was the culprit, she'd taken chances she shouldn't have, especially now being married to a duke and the man she loved. She wouldn't have risked her reputation if the stakes hadn't been so high and failure so heartbreaking.

She came to two large doors, each on its own hinges so they could swing inward upon entering, but only one door was cracked open. Soundlessly, Ophelia peeked inside to see her husband moving about in the room, lifting pieces of art and looking behind them, moving over to the bookcase shelves, pulling books out as if seeking a hidden compartment behind. It seemed an unbelievable mirage. Her chest felt heavy. He was helping her! And in the one way he said he never would. Her heart thudded with love for him.

As she quietly entered the room, her breathless pants gave away her presence.

He turned sharply toward her, anger settling on Hurst's face as she knew it would. Even so, she was so happy to see him and wanted to rush into his arms and cover his face with kisses. Seeing him searching for her, her mother, and Winston's legacy put her on the verge of bursting into tears of relief and happiness. At that moment, she loved Hurst more than she could say.

Not so for Hurst. A harsh reprimand worked its ire

into Hurst's voice. "What are you doing here? I told you you're never to search a home alone."

Was that all he had to say? In a sweetened whisper, she reasoned, "I'm not alone. I'm with you." She could see his displeasure ease back a little. But she was certain he would argue the point more strongly at a later time.

In three strides he met her, pulling her close and away from the door. His handsome face loomed over hers, his eyes gleaming. "Ophelia, you vex me."

Ignoring his censure, she asked, "Have you found the chalice?"

"Of course not. I'd be out of here if I had. We could be discovered any moment. The baron will return and find I'm not in the drawing room and come looking for me. We must hurry. He mentioned that things could be cleverly hidden right before our eyes, and we aren't seeing it. And there are plenty of artifacts in here, but the chalice isn't on the bookshelves. Most of the tables and shelving are displaying all rarities. You start over there."

In one continuous swoop she glanced at everything. Late afternoon sunlight filtered through the room, dust motes danced off the heavy velvet draperies and anything else they touched. Ophelia went to a series of glass doors, very narrow and plain. She opened them.

Glancing her way, Hurst whispered, "What's in there?"

"Nothing," she answered, losing hope.

"I have a feeling in my gut that it's in this room," he whispered.

"What makes you think that?" she asked as she continued to look over a shelf filled with small figurines and delicate porcelain flowers.

"Because I believe in you. And you think it's here."

Ophelia's hopes soared as they both went back to searching. She gazed about, moving things and looking quickly. All to no avail. The paintings were dark and rich, a contrast to a large stained-glass panel that hung on a wall across from the window. A light prism reflecting colors far beyond those found in a rainbow eased its way across the wall as time ticked quickly onward.

Ophelia stood back. A gorgeous mosaic represented a man wearing a crown. She didn't recognize him as royalty, but he possessed a regal air. Ringed fingers held on to the hilt of a sword pointing down. The glass pieces were vibrant and colorful and didn't seem old, yet there was something odd about it.

"Hurst," she whispered. "Come look at this glasswork. How is it being illuminated?"

"There's a mirror on the other wall," he said, after looking it over. "Sunlight is being reflected to illuminate the stained glass. But it's more than that. The man in it is a likeness of Gagingcliffe wearing a king's crown."

"That's kind of eerie." She gave it a closer inspection. "I think you are right."

"The man is eccentric. The glass colors seem translucent in places, as if the wall behind it is hollow."

Looking left and right and then up, they saw that a series of pulleys had been anchored to the ceiling; the stained glass was suspended by them. "Ophelia, with just the right light shining through it, the sword's hilt disappears, and it looks as if the man is holding a chalice."

Gasping and unable to contain her excitement, Ophelia stared into the glass to see if she could see what Hurst had readily found.

His hands gripped the smooth sides of the heavy stained glass and she placed hers beside his. Slowly, they manipulated the chain to roll the pulleys and slide it open.

Ophelia's pulse sped up and her heart pounded as she

watched the mystery reveal itself. Indeed, the artwork served a dual purpose! The framed stained glass covered a vitrine or some kind of wall niche. Centered in the middle of the shelf sat a solitary object. One that took Ophelia's breath and chilled every inch of her body.

Chatham's chalice!

They had found it.

Hurst grabbed the sacrament and gave it to her. "Is it the real one?" he asked quickly.

In her heart she knew it was, and by its weight she was certain. Still, she looked beneath the base of the stem to verify the maker's mark. Her legs went weak with relief, and she steadied herself next to Hurst while smiling and blinking back tears of relief and joy. "It is."

His expression filled with urgent determination. "Good. I want you out of here now. Go home and get the registry book. I'll join you there and we'll leave for Wickenhamden. If the roads aren't boggy, we can have this safely back in the church before sunup."

"Yes." Her breaths were so labored with excitement she could hardly speak. She pointed to the vitrine behind him. "The bag that holds the chalice."

Reaching out quickly, he took the cloth and stuffed the fine silk into her hand. "Go to my carriage; Mallord is waiting inside."

"My footman?" she asked.

"I knew if there was trouble you'd trust him, and so do I. I assumed you were in the house and told him to wait until you came out; he was to take you home immediately. After you get home, tell him to bring the magistrate here. The authorities need to handle this." Hurst wound his arm around the small of her back, drawing her close with his face inches from hers. "Do you understand, Ophelia? Please do not disobey me on any of this. Go home straightaway. No stops. Hold on to that chalice."

"I'll do as you say and protect the chalice with my life, but I need to confront the baron for the wrong he did." Her heart pounded with outrage. "He would let my brother's name be sullied for all time because a relic caught his fancy."

Hurst gently but firmly took hold of her shoulders, intent on steering her out of the book room. "You can have your say to him later."

"Why wait? Let her have it now." Lord Gagingcliffe's voice came from the doorway.

Ophelia and Hurst turned and stared at him. His tone held no note of distress or concern as he stood in the book room's wide doorway looking beyond put out, his face tight as he saw Ophelia clasping the sacrament.

She could hardly hold her composure together.

To Hurst, he ventured with an uneven lift of his lips, "It took me a moment or two after I got into my chambers to realize you weren't here to call on me just for my opinion of Mr. Sawyer, or your seeming genuine interest in my treasures. You wanted something else from me. You were so clever to hide your true intentions behind such friendliness, and I accepted it without question."

Ophelia held the chalice with a firm grip. "How could you steal from a church? You are a criminal!"

With a shrug, Gagingcliffe noted, "And I turned you into one. You are trying to steal from me."

His slight stung Ophelia for its truth.

Hurst took a step forward, his eyes hooded and his mouth set in a hard line. "Watch what you say, my lord, or I will forget that you are ten years older and five inches shorter than I am. I would take great pleasure in pinning you to the floor and holding you there until the magistrate can get here."

"Quite right, Your Grace. There will be no need for such tactics, I assure you." He gave a bow. "I do apologize, Duchess. And commend you on your perfect performance when we played cards together. You never gave me one hint you thought the chalice was missing. I'll get the magistrate." He called for his butler.

"Why did you take it?" Ophelia eased closer to Hurst, his arm coming around her waist.

The baron shrugged. "Why wouldn't I take it when I had opportunity and the desire to possess it the moment the vicar agreed I could see it up close? He was already ill, so I went back a week later thinking to talk him into letting me hold it again, but the man was so ill he didn't even know I was there. The vicarage was quiet. No one about, so I had no problem slipping the keys from his belt and taking the chalice with me."

"That was an evil thing to do," Ophelia whispered so softly she didn't know if the baron heard. He kept right on talking.

"I admit thinking at first, I'd only make a copy for myself and return it, but once I put it in my vitrine, I simply couldn't part with it. Historically, I knew it was too valuable to be replaced, and I simply didn't want a reproduction. The thin hammered gold is done with a keen artist's eye; the rubies around the middle are small but flawless." With a willful shrug, he declared, "Who wouldn't want to have it?"

"An honest man." Ophelia tempered her boiling rage and disdain for a man she had considered a member of her small circle of acquaintances.

"I took it weeks ago. I hadn't heard anything about it

missing or having been stolen, so I thought no one knew it was gone."

"We deliberately kept it that way so we could search for it without the thief knowing."

The baron smirked. "I thought there was the possibility I was safe from ever being found out. Especially when I heard about all the troubles with first one and then another vicar getting sick so soon after arriving and then leaving. I figured the theft could be blamed on any one of them. I'm actually impressed you figured out it was me, Your Grace."

Suddenly his demeanor changed, and he took a few more steps inside the room. Rather than accommodating, he looked perturbed. As if bothered by this whole sordid affair.

Gagingcliffe called loudly for his butler again, who appeared so fast, one would think he'd been eavesdropping this entire time. The man stepped subserviently into the book room, looking almost frightened.

"Yes, my lord?"

"Send someone for the magistrate at once," he said indignantly. "The duke and duchess are trying to take something from my home, and I want to report them."

"You must be half-mad to think you can get away with this," Hurst said.

"I'll find a way. I always do. It will be easy to say I bought it from a stranger. Churches hate dealing with messy things such as robbery. They always want to settle things quietly and as easily as possible. They never want the parish members to know there's been any kind of trouble in the church." He turned to his butler and barked again. "Don't stand there; go for the magistrate. I want these two out of my house."

The baron's cavalier behavior had not been expected. His nerve filled Ophelia with contempt.

Movement outside the doorway made them all give their attention in that direction. Mr. Mallord entered the room with another man following closely behind him.

"That won't be necessary," the footman said. "The magistrate is already here. I hope you don't mind, Your Graces, but I took it upon myself to ask him to come."

"How?" Ophelia and Hurst said in unison.

"Like Mrs. Turner, I've known from the beginning that the duchess was looking for the chalice. I've been watching over her as much as possible to make sure she was always safe. I didn't know why you needed me to accompany you here, but I could tell it was urgent. And then when the duchess showed up and had trouble getting inside even though you were there, I sensed something was wrong, so I went for the magistrate."

"Good job, Mr. Mallord," Hurst said.

The footman nodded. "I like to be prepared."

CHAPTER 24

MAN'S PRACTICAL GUIDE TO APPREHENDING A THIEF
SIR BENTLY ASHTON ULLINGSWICK

Make the suspect think you know the truth.

Leaving the chalice and its silk covering in Hurst's capable hands, Ophelia pushed past him with a speed she didn't know she was capable of, bounded from the carriage the moment it stopped, and sprinted up the steps of their home, thinking only of one thing: getting the registry book she had "borrowed" from the church. Once she had it, she could mentally prepare herself to make the long, but fast as possible, ride to the church in Wickenhamden.

The thought was exhilarating. As she hurried into the drawing room calling to her mother, Ophelia's quick stride slowed, then stopped. Three stodgy men dressed somberly in black, except for the bright-white bands falling down like short, wide ribbons from the high necklines, stood in the room. Their demeanor left no leeway for anything other than sober displeasure. If not accusatory censure. Especially the big man with a trimmed beard who towered over her mother. There was no doubt he was the new vicar because she recognized the elders who stood on either side of him. All were giving Maman's good character an unnecessary dressing-down with their expressions, if not words that were said before Ophelia entered.

Fearful, Maman removed her handkerchief from under her cuff and dabbed her forehead. "Thank goodness you have returned, my dear. I wasn't doing a very good job answering the vicar's questions."

Understanding dawned within Ophelia, and her hopes for quick rectification of all that was amiss at the church plummeted. She was too late to put things back without anyone being wiser. The new vicar had arrived, inventoried the livings, and was looking for answers. Which, to be fair, was owed. But not with the malign treatment of her mother, who had done nothing wrong. That raised Ophelia's anger.

She walked over and held out her hand to aid her mother to her feet. "Maman, you look tired; please take your leave and I'll attend to this matter in short order, and there is nothing for you to concern yourself."

Maman rose to stand beside Ophelia. She linked her arm through her daughter's as if to give and receive support. "Anything more you have to say about my son must be with words of honor only. As I told you, he did not take anything from the church." Her posture inched taller, and she presented herself as a matron to be dealt with.

Ophelia couldn't have been more pleased with Roberta's demeanor and was about to speak up when Hurst blew in from the front door as if a storm brewed about him. His gaze quickly assessed the situation of his wife and her mother across from three stern-faced men.

"Good evening, gentlemen." Hurst took control of the room with his commanding presence. "No doubt you know I am Hurstbourne as you are in my home and standing in front of my wife, the duchess, and her mother. Step back, all of you."

Bows and properly murmured apologies and greetings followed as they traded glances with one another and then moved several feet away. Clearly, they were not used to being reprimanded, but that they had been made Ophelia feel very good.

Glaring at the men who he obviously suspected had come with ill will toward Ophelia and her mother, Hurst's eyes narrowed firmly on the man in the middle of the trio. "A married man can be a stubborn one, but a married duke with a wife who loves him in spite of his headstrong opinions is a rare one. I will declare as much in front of you as men of the cloth. I will swear no harm has been done to the church by this family."

The drop in his tone to one of sincerity and warmth brought a shiver to Ophelia. Her heart swelled with love for him as she stared in silent wonder at his admission. Looking into his eyes, she easily forgave all the earlier discord between them and gave him a loving smile. His deep voice continued to comfort her as he spoke in their defense.

"You were right, Duchess," Hurst said. "You believed the vicar would immediately blame anything he perceived might be wrong, out of place, or perhaps missing from the church on the former vicar and his good family."

While the men whispered among themselves, Hurst gently coaxed Ophelia with his eyes and a nod of understanding between them. She and her mother walked over to stand on either side of him. Ophelia slipped her hands behind her back and Hurst discreetly handed off the chalice to her and the silk sack that had protected it.

Ophelia felt such relief to hold it in her hands one last time. She remembered Hurst saying that Winston had blessed their marriage before it had happened. Now she was never surer that was true, and a warmth of peace settled over her as she looked at him with all the love she was feeling.

The objects were revealed to the vicar and elders while Hurst explained, "My wife and her mother realized this relic was missing and went to great lengths to find it so that it could be returned to the church." The cup gleamed in the glowing lamplight. "Here it is. Safe and in perfect condition.

"Where was it?" one of the elders asked.

The vicar's bushy brows rose with interest. "Who took it and who had it?" the vicar questioned.

"A man who is now with the authorities. We called in the magistrate, and he is currently talking to him. I'll have my footman take you to where they are. I'm sure you will want to have your say as to what you think needs to be done to the man and see that proper punishment is carried out."

"That was most gracious of you—" He looked at Ophelia. "And the duchess. The parish is pleased to accept your kindness in seeing the sacrament has been returned. We accept your offer for the footman to take us to wherever the authorities are."

Ophelia nodded her appreciation for his comments and was thinking it was all finally over when, out of the corner of her eye, she saw the registry book on the table near where her mother had occupied the settee. There was one more thing to do.

Crossing the room, she collected it and presented it and the pearl-decorated bag with spun silver and gold strings to one of the elders. She then gave the chalice to the robust bearded man who had the good grace to etch a semblance of an apology on his features as he accepted

Chatham's chalice. Each man took his turn to hold the vessel, no doubt wanting to make sure they held the real one.

After clearing his throat, he conceded, "I do believe we may have been too hasty with our assumptions when we arrived at the church and found the sacrament wasn't among the livings."

Hurst's brow rose skeptically. "*May have?* Sir, you owe the two ladies in my life an apology."

"Indeed, we do." The vicar bowed and the other two men followed him in acknowledgment and respect. "Our sincerest apologies are offered to you, Duchess, and to Mrs. Stowe."

While once again murmurs came from the two other men as well, their faces momentarily downcast, and just long enough for Maman to smile contentedly at Ophelia and for Ophelia to smile lovingly at Hurst.

CHAPTER 25

MAN'S PRACTICAL GUIDE TO APPREHENDING A THIEF
SIR BENTLY ASHTON ULLINGSWICK

You will know when you've caught him.

Ophelia paced in her bedchamber. It had been over an hour since the vicar and elders left. She'd hurriedly changed into her white sleeveless night rail and brushed out her hair, thinking Hurst would come into her room shortly as he had on their wedding night. But tonight, he hadn't. The more time that passed, the more worried she became that he didn't want to be with her.

They had both been quiet on the short but mad dash as they sped along the streets from Lord Gagingcliffe's house to theirs. She hadn't minded, understanding he was upset with her for going to the baron's house. But he had gone too, and before she had. Since all had worked out for the best concerning the chalice's return to the safety of the church and the magistrate's arrival to take charge of overseeing the baron's circumstances and what would happen to him, Ophelia was feeling better than she had in months. All she wanted was to be held in Hurst's arms.

And he hadn't come to her.

He had said such lovely things about her and Maman while the vicar was there. She'd hoped that meant he at least understood if he had not completely forgiven her and all was well between them again. But apparently there was mending left to do. Perhaps he was waiting for her to ask for his forgiveness, and she would if it wasn't too late.

Forcing down her fear of rejection and swallowing her pride, she bolstered her courage as best she could and picked up the box she had placed on the bed. When she got to the adjoining door, she wavered but quickly knocked before she could talk herself out of it.

Hurst opened the door looking splendid in his relaxed state of only trousers, open-necked shirt, bare feet, and tousled hair.

"May I come in?"

He stepped aside and she entered.

"This is for you." She extended the box toward him.

His expression turned curious. "What is it?"

"You'll have to open it to find out," she answered softly.

He took the box, lifted the lid, and stared down at the men's clothing she'd worn to his house.

Looking into her eyes with what she thought could be a hint of amusement, he said, "I don't think these will fit me."

She wanted to smile, but because he hadn't, she refrained. "Perhaps you'll allow me to give them away rather than have them burned."

"No man will wear these."

Ophelia's heart felt as if it plunged to her feet.

He bent his head and held the box near his nose as he breathed in deeply and loudly before raising his head and saying, "They smell of your perfume. You must have them washed first. Have your maid's brother give them to someone who needs them."

Relief sailed through her. "Thank you. I will."

"And tell her when he has finished his apprenticeship and is ready to open his own shop to come see me."

That was far more than she'd expected to hear, and her heart warmed even more toward him. "You will do that for him?"

"No." He placed the box on a table and turned back to her. "I will do it for you, Ophelia." He twitched a smile. "Besides, he does excellent work."

She swallowed down a lump of thankfulness for his kindness. She knew how he disliked her wearing the clothing, and though she would never be sorry for what she had done, she now no longer needed it.

"They will both be pleased. I expected you to ask me for the clothing before we married so you could burn it. Why didn't you?"

"I knew you'd give the clothing to me when you were ready to trust me with everything."

"I do trust you, Hurst," she answered earnestly, feeling the intimacy and honesty of their discussion. "I'm sorry I was so late in trusting you in all things."

He remained quiet, only looking at her, so she added, "I owe you such a debt of gratitude for everything you have done for me. My family."

"It is over now. All of it. I asked the magistrate to work out with the bishop how the church wants to deal with Gagingcliffe, but there must be punishment."

"I'm sure there will be well-deserved punishment, including his banishment from Society."

Hurst smiled. "I think I can see that's done if it will make you happy."

"Very happy," she whispered.

Hurst nodded. "So no more talk of that tonight, Ophelia." He put his hands on her upper arms and lightly caressed her. His warmth soothed her instantly.

"I feel we must. You have kept your part of our arrangement, but I haven't fulfilled mine. I expected you to come to my room so that I might continue my effort to give you a son."

His gaze swept sweetly up and down her face. "I was waiting for you to come to me."

That surprised her. "I didn't know."

"Didn't you want to come to me?" he asked quietly.

"Desperately," she whispered earnestly. "I thought you didn't want to be with me."

"I wanted to be with you desperately too, but I needed to think about some things first."

Ophelia tensed as worry crept over her again. "May I know what things?"

"I've been trying to decide if I should tell you or keep them locked away as I have these many years."

"I would like for you to share whatever it is with me. I want to be a part of all of your life: past, present, and future."

His low laugh eased some of her anxiety. He walked over and picked up his drink from a table. "Would you like to join me?"

She shook her head.

He took a swallow from his glass and placed it back on the table before facing her. "My father was a wretched man for most of my life until he died of lung fever in debtors' prison."

Merciful angels. She hadn't expected he'd say anything like that. "I'm sorry that happened to him and to you."

He shrugged. "I've done things I'm not proud of, Ophelia."

"So have I. You know most of mine."

"One of my earliest memories is when I was four or

five. My father came in with someone one night. They made a lot of noise and woke me. When it quietened, I walked out and saw him passed out on the sofa. A woman was standing over him searching the pockets in his coat. I'll never forget the grim satisfaction on her face when she folded his coin purse into her hand. That's when she looked up and saw me. Panic settled over her features, wondering what I was going to do. Rush her? Scream? Try to wake my father? I didn't do anything but quietly look at her until she left. I've always felt I should have done more to keep her from violating him by stealing from him."

His words had her heart hammering, but he seemed calm. Perhaps years of living with the memories had done that. Swallowing past a thick throat, she said, "You were just a little boy."

"Young and impressionable for sure." He shrugged. "She taught me something I needed to learn. It wasn't long before I was pilfering his pockets to hold back enough money so I could buy bread and cheese for us to eat and pay the lease."

Ophelia's chest tightened. "I'm sorry you had to do that."

"It never got easier, and my father never changed. His father was a younger son of a duke, so he was left with a bit of land, and horses, but he wasted it all on drink, gambling, and women. By the time I was older the debt collectors started coming around. More than once they searched our home, looking through and taking everything we had including some of my clothing, and my wooden soldiers and horses. I know what it's like to be on both ends of a violation of someone's privacy. Taking from my father and then having others take from me. Both ways felt wrong. When my father went to prison and my aunt sent me to school, I swore I'd never do that to anyone, and I hadn't until today."

Sorrow swept over her. "I didn't know that much about your past. I'm sorry you had to plunder Lord Gagingcliffe's book room today because of me."

Hurst closed the distance between them and caught her up to his chest. "Maybe I should have told you sooner, but there are reasons I didn't. I've tried to forget it, and I don't want your pity, Ophelia. I wanted you to know why I was always against what you were doing."

"Thank you for trusting me with this about your past. I understand why you felt that way." Ophelia slipped her arms around his neck.

"When my father went to debtors' prison, I felt I had failed him. That it was my fault I hadn't been able to hold back enough to pay his debts."

"But it wasn't your fault," she whispered softly, and hugged him close. "You were just a boy. I'm sorry some of my comments to you the first night we met were so harsh."

"You have never been harsh, my love. And if I ever sound that way to you just let me know. It will never be my intention."

"Thank you, but I don't think I will. I like seeing in your face and hearing in your voice what you are really thinking." She gave him a pert tilt of her chin but then quickly turned serious again. "With all your past, I can't believe you went to Lord Gagingcliffe's house and searched for the chalice. I now know how hard that must have been for you."

He shook his head. "It really wasn't. I couldn't let you lose. You always believed the chalice was in a titled man's home. I had to help you prove that was true. You once said you thought I was looking for redemption, but I never was. I was looking to finally forgive my father and myself. Today, I knew I had to stop fighting myself about whether what I did was right or wrong. I remember we talked about redemption and revenge being powerful motivators, but so is love. I did it because I love you."

Ophelia kissed his lips and then whispered, "I love you, Hurst. And, I know I don't have a lot of bad memories in my past to draw from and probably shouldn't be one to speak to it, but maybe you don't need to do anything about thoughts of the past other than embrace them for what they are when they come to you. A young boy learning how to be a fine man who knows how to care for people like me."

His gave her a curious look. "Like you? What does that mean?"

Ophelia placed her hands on his chest. She felt his heart beating beneath his linen shirt. "I haven't been the easiest of ladies you could have married."

"You had me from the moment you walked into my life. I love you, Ophelia." He chuckled softly. "I like that you came into my room looking for me tonight wearing your white gown with the ribbons untied." He kissed her neck, the hollow of her throat, and then nuzzled her ear.

She smiled and enjoyed every thrill his touch gave her. "Does that mean I should do it more often?"

He pulled her tighter to him. "Definitely."

Ophelia tugged on the tail of Hurst's shirt and pulled it from the waistband of his trousers. From there he took over and yanked it over his head.

"What's this?" he asked, tossing the garment aside. "Are you so eager for my kisses and attention tonight that you are ripping the clothes from my body?"

She ran her hand tantalizingly slowly down his rippled

ribs and up across his wide, muscular shoulders. "Is it all right if I am?"

"It's the way I always want you to be." He reached down and hooked his arm under her knees, lifted and carried her over to his bed. He slowly removed his trousers and stretched out onto the bed beside her as he pulled her close. "I love you, Ophelia," he whispered.

She saw the smoldering hunger for her in his eyes and she embraced it by whispering, "And I love you, my duke."

Their lips met and their bodies entwined.

EPILOGUE

MAN'S PRACTICAL GUIDE TO APPREHENDING A THIEF
SIR BENTLY ASHTON ULLINGSWICK

The real thief isn't usually your first suspect.

The midsummer sky was a beautiful dusky shade of blue, and the air so warm and velvety Ophelia hadn't bothered to bring a wrap or gloves to match her cap-sleeved, lightweight cotton dress. The open-topped landau rumbled, waddled, and bumped along the terrain of Hurstbourne Estate with no road, trail, or ruts to follow. She didn't even mind the tepid, breezeless air. Her short-brimmed straw hat and matching soft pink parasol protected her from the burning rays of the sun. But not even that heat could match the warmth that surrounded her when she sat close to Hurst.

They had left the manor house behind some time ago, and it was now out of sight as they headed up a gently rising grassy knoll. At the top of the rise, she saw a lush green valley below with a small pond off to one side and a large stand of forest trees on the other. Smaller sapling trees dotted the area near the water but not so many they obstructed the magnificent landscape of vistas and hardwoods in the distance.

"The view of your lands from here is stunning, Hurst."

"It all belongs to the title, my love. I am merely a caretaker of it for as long as I am duke."

"I know, but we could stop right here and enjoy our picnic and not go the rest of the way down. Not that I mind, but it's so wonderful and peaceful to look at. Should we park here and enjoy the beauty that surrounds us?" she asked, excited about the idea.

Hurst chuckled. "We will, but not today."

"All right," she answered, a little disappointed as he continued to handle the horses with ease down the slope toward the pond. "Is that where we're going to have our picnic?" she asked, pointing to a shady place near the water.

He turned to her and nodded as he put both leather ribbons in one hand and laid the other on her knee. She would never get tired of feeling the quickening sensations of his touch or being so close to Hurst with his body as warm as the sun that heated the back of her neck.

"My father and I didn't come to Hurstbourne often. He and his uncle didn't get along very well. But I remember coming to this place every time we were here."

"I can see why you would want to. It's a very tranquil setting. A quiet place to read or paint."

"Or kiss?" he said with an inviting smile.

"Yes, of course," she answered. "That too. And maybe even more than kisses."

"I believe I had that in mind."

"It feels very private and romantic here. Especially with the way the sunshine shimmers on top of the water. This was a lovely place for you to bring me on my first full day at Hurstbourne."

"I was hoping you would approve," he said, stopping the horses not far from the pond and under the shade of a group of small trees.

Hurst helped her down and reached into the back of the carriage, pulled out a blanket, and handed it to her. "You spread this while I get the hamper and fishing poles."

"Fishing poles?" She gave him a delighted smile. "I didn't see them."

"Maybe the blanket was on top of them."

She smiled again. "So you could surprise me?"

He bent his head and brushed his lips against hers in a soft, quick kiss. "The first of many while we are at the estate, I hope."

"I like surprises and will look forward to more. So tell me, where should I spread this? Over there under the shade of that tree?" She pointed in the direction.

"You look perfect to me—I mean the spot looks perfect, so yes, that will be fine."

Ophelia smoothed out the last wrinkle in the blanket as Hurst walked up with the poles and the basket.

While he made himself comfortable beside her and stretched out his legs, she took off her hat.

"Did I tell you Winston used to take me fishing when I was a little girl?"

"You told me your father gave him permission to teach you to swim, but I don't believe you mentioned fishing."

"I remember being furious when Maman said I was too old to go with him anymore, and that I must behave as a lady at all times."

His gaze slowly whispered down her face. "When you are with me you don't have to act as a lady at all times. It's permissible to just be yourself."

"Then perhaps we can go for a swim later." She reached over and kissed his cheek.

"That was another of my surprises." He answered her kiss with one to her, but it was on her lips and deeper and longer as they settled more comfortably onto the blanket.

"I haven't been swimming in many years. Do you think I will remember how?"

"Doesn't matter. I won't leave your side either way."

"I like your surprises, Hurst."

"Winston saved my life before teaching me to swim. Unlike you, I jumped right into the water, not realizing how deep it was or how little I knew about keeping myself afloat."

Her brows drew together in concern. "I'm glad he was there to help you. And he might have been the one who saved your life, but to him you were always his hero."

"Me?" He glanced out over the water. "No. I didn't do anything for him but teach him how to jump over a fence. He was the one who helped me to realize I didn't have to turn out like my father."

"You were his friend and gave him many happy memories. I know you moved on to others when you moved away, but Winston never did. He took his work for the church seriously and never allowed anything or anyone to distract him from it. I suppose we never know how we influence other people or what others see in us, but I think perhaps because he saw that you were a very fine lad, he knew you must be a good man."

Hurst caressed her cheek. "And I'm sure he has many good friends where he is now."

"I think so too." She smiled. "How did you know to bring me fishing if you didn't know I knew how to fish? Was teaching me going to be one of your surprises?"

"No," he answered. "The fishing is for me."

"Oh," she said quietly, allowing a curious expression to settle over her features.

"Do you remember telling me to embrace my past rather than trying to erase it from my memory?"

She nodded.

"That's what I am doing today. As I said, my father and I didn't come out to Hurstbourne often, but one of the first things we'd always do was grab the fishing poles and come here. We never caught a lot of fish or even a big one. We laughed, talked, and always had a good time. He didn't drink when we were here. His uncle didn't want him to, and I liked that. When we were here, I loved him the most and felt he loved me. That's a good memory and I wanted to share it with you." Hurst picked up her hand and kissed it.

"I'm so glad you did. I love sharing all of your life," she whispered.

"You helped me realize that watching debtors take everything we owned, a woman stealing from his pockets, and my own guilt of taking money to help us survive were never as bad as the good was good. Does that make sense?"

"Of course." She squeezed his hand in hers as she held it against her heart. "I'm glad you realize that now."

"So am I, my love."

"I have something for you." He reached into the basket and pulled out a small package of yellow silk held together with a black ribbon.

"What is this?"

"Another surprise. Something I wanted you to have."

She quickly untied the ribbon, and it fell away from the wrapping. There were three dainty handkerchiefs folded so that she could see a small bee had been embroidered in the corner of each one.

"These are lovely, Hurst. Thank you."

"I wanted you to have something to remind you of our wedding day, that you are mine, you can trust me, and I will always protect you."

"Yes. I believe that. I think I've always known it in my heart and the reason I came to London looking for you."

"But I wasn't what you expected."

A hushed chuckle passed her lips. "And I wasn't what you expected."

"We were both surprised," he agreed.

Ophelia nodded. "It may not have been clear when I first went to see you, but I trusted you with my deepest secret."

He leaned away from her and gave her a mock expression of disbelief. "You could have told me that at the time."

"I thought I did." She gave him a mock frown.

"I can't be expected to remember everything you said that night. It was very difficult for me, being attracted to a lady in men's clothing."

"I thought gentlemen liked for ladies to be mysterious at times."

"Not that mysterious, my darling, but I'm so glad you came to me." He slid his hand around her neck to cup her nape. "I didn't want to marry you until I loved you and I loved you the first time I saw you."

Ophelia hugged him. "You did not. You didn't even like me that first night. You railed at me and raised your voice to me."

"Did I?" he questioned with a twinkle in his eyes. "I don't remember."

"You know you did."

"I'm mending my ways. Besides, I stand by my belief that my true feelings were skewed only because you weren't properly dressed. It didn't keep me from being attracted to you and finally forcing myself to realize you were the one destined for me even though we were at odds with each other."

She looked deeply into his eyes. "I believe that too. I love you and don't want to ever live without you."

Hurst pulled her into his warm embrace and kissed her with his cool lips and caressed her with his warm hands. "You don't have to, my love."

Ophelia thrilled to his touch.

Dear Reader,

I hope you have enjoyed the last book in my Say I Do series, and that Hurst and Ophelia's story has touched your heart as it did mine. I am always eager to get to the last book in a series but a little sad too. After getting to know the three dukes in this collection, I don't want to give them up to go on to others but know I must.

It was so much fun to write about a missing artifact and the challenges of an ongoing search from a heroine who had no idea how to go about doing it and a hero who wouldn't agree to sanction her efforts and help her. My main focus was to keep the antics between Hurst and Ophelia light and humorous.

For the sake of my story, I have taken literary license for dramatic purposes concerning details about the proper handling, care, and safeguarding of the livings and sacraments of a church by a bishop, rector, vicar, or other owners. The word *obey* was used in some Christian wedding vows until around 1920. I also grayed the respected and acceptable mourning time for polite society so that it would fit into my story.

There are many interesting legends and actual events

of religious treasures of various kinds being saved all the way from biblical times, from Cromwell's forces, and from other periods throughout our history, which give relics, sacraments, and other items rarity and significance. Whether there is monetary value in the actual item without the history is at times up to interpretation.

If you missed the first book in this series, *Yours Truly, the Duke,* or the second, *Sincerely, the Duke,* you can order them from your favorite bookstore or e-retailer, and I hope that you will. Most of all, thank you for enjoying this series with me.

Hearing from readers is always a pleasure. You can email me at ameliagreyauthor@gmail.com, follow me on Facebook at facebook.com/AmeliaGreyBooks, Instagram at www.instagram.com/ameliagreyauthor, or visit my website at ameliagrey.com.

Happy reading!
Amelia Grey